Larimont and The Treasure of Jericho Mountain

Two Full Length Western Novels

Cameron Judd

WOLFPACK PUBLISHING

Larimont and The Treasure of Jericho Mountain: Two Full Length Western Novels
Paperback Edition
Copyright © 2022 (As Revised) Cameron Judd

Wolfpack Publishing
9850 S. Maryland Parkway, Suite A-5 #323
Las Vegas, Nevada 89183

wolfpackpublishing.com

This book is a work of fiction. Any references to historical events, real people or real places are used fictitiously. Other names, characters, places and events are products of the author's imagination, and any resemblance to actual events, places or persons, living or dead, is entirely coincidental.

All rights reserved. No part of this book may be reproduced by any means without the prior written consent of the publisher, other than brief quotes for reviews.

Paperback ISBN 978-1-63977-903-1
eBook ISBN 978-1-63977-902-4

Larimont and The Treasure of Jericho Mountain

LARIMONT

To Kate.

Part One
The Stampeders

PART ONE

THE STAMPEDES

Chapter 1

John Kenton wiped dust from the passenger car window and looked out across the Colorado landscape. There it was, the town of Larimont, looking no different than it had the last time he had seen it, with its weathered and grayish buildings standing with backs to the mountains and fronts facing a wide street of yellow dust. In the background of it all, the mountains loomed high and circled toward each other, joining to form a sort of vast open-ended ring all about the town, enclosing it in a slate-colored wall of stone and dirt, dotted with evergreens up its lower half, barren at the summits.

The same old town of his boyhood...but different now, because one who had always been here no longer was, and never would be again.

The train continued its wide arc toward the town, winding through the natural gateway that provided the only good entrance to the Larimont Valley. John glanced over to the other side of the train car and out the sooty window toward the road that ran roughly parallel to the tracks. A flatbed wagon rolled along, sending up a double cloud of dust behind the wheels. The wagon's driver lazily waved toward the train, greeting passengers he couldn't possibly see from that distance. John Kenton smiled. This was indeed Larimont, the Larimont he had known since childhood, the hometown he could never quite put behind him.

In the midst of all this humdrum, marvelously routine normality, it was very hard for John to really believe his father was dead, and that this homecoming would be the first at which his father would not be standing on the station platform to greet him. With the sun bright, and the wind stirring across the mountains, with Larimont's streets full of people going about the same daily routines they had done for fifteen years, how was a man supposed to realize that his father was dead and buried?

The station platform came into view, and John picked out the familiar form of Victoria Rivers standing among the handful of people upon it.

The train sent out a long and piercing wail, followed by a loud screeching as the noisy brakes engaged. John stood, picking up his carpetbag, and stepped down the aisle and out onto the platform. Victoria, a distinguished, dark-haired woman who retained both her beautiful face and impressive figure despite fifty or more years of living, approached him, her arms extended.

Seeing her made John happy, yet all the sadder at the same time. He wasn't used to seeing Victoria Rivers without his father at her side. The two had courted each other for years since John's mother had died, and there had been a lot of serious talk about marriage. Only a piece of paper and a wedding ring had separated Victoria from being John's stepmother.

"Hello, Victoria. It's good to see you."

"And it's good to see you, John." Victoria wrapped her arms around the slender young man and squeezed him hard.

"I'm so glad you could get away to spend some time here. And I'm sorry you couldn't get here in time for Bill's funeral." She smiled in a very sad way. "But on second thought, I guess it's just as well. That fool preacher did his best to make the service as sorrowful as possible. And I have to say, he did a pretty good job of it."

"How are you doing, Victoria?" John asked. He'd noted that she talked too fast and too furious, her words rushing out in a torrent—something she normally didn't do. He suspected she was trying not to cry.

For a moment a tear glistened in her eye. "I'm as well as I can be at a time like this. How about you?"

John shrugged. "The same." He looked around him. "But you know, even now it really is good to be home. It makes me feel a little better, somehow."

"I'm glad, John. And now, let's get you checked into the Donaho. A lot of folks got off that train, and they might just rush the place."

John walked with Victoria to her buggy, which was hitched and waiting beside the station house. He tossed his bag in the rear and helped her to the rider's side, then unhitched the horse and climbed up to the driver's seat. He took the reins in hand, clicked his tongue, and the buggy began rolling down the dusty road and deeper into town.

The grayness of the town, which had been so evident from the train, wasn't as obvious up close, particularly since the street ran by the fronts of the buildings, which were kept painted, unlike the rear sections visible from the train.

The grief that had weighed on John like a heavy cloak lifted a bit further as he looked around him. As he had on the train, he realized just how much he had missed his hometown. The picture of it had always been in the back of his mind, coming out into his consciousness only occasionally, usually at the times he was lonely.

Though he loved Larimont, John still had no regrets that he'd left it. He really had not had any other option. In youth he had desired more than anything else a career of putting things into words, and the only writing jobs available were with newspapers, of which Larimont had precisely none. So, at age twenty-one, discouraged with a dreary job at the local feed and saddle store and convinced that if he didn't leave then he never would, John had packed up, boarded the train, and headed away from Larimont, leaving behind his widower father, William Kenton, a man known all over Larimont as Bill.

Bill Kenton was a longtime clerk at the Larimont Bank and was in the eyes of the townsfolk as much a fixture at the institution as was the heavy oaken cage behind which he stood to do his work. John was sure that news of Bill Kenton's death must have stunned the whole town, just as it had stunned him. The idea of Bill Kenton being dead and gone was something that would take a long time to sink in.

As the buggy rolled along toward the Donaho Hotel at the far end of the street, John glanced over at Victoria Rivers's face. He could still see a faint look of sadness that showed most clearly in the mistiness of her eyes and the downturn of the corners of her mouth. As John looked at her, he felt a great wave of appreciation for the woman who had brightened his father's last years. It had kept Bill Kenton from growing old, and Victoria, too, John supposed. Even now, just days after her beloved's death, she seemed five years older than she had looked six months earlier, when John had last seen her.

Victoria Rivers had done a lot for his father. But not even she had been able to spare him from untimely death, not when his house burned like a furnace around him in the night and killed him before he could hope to get out.

"Victoria?"

"Yes?"

"I want to know all about my father's death. Everything. I know it isn't easy for you to talk about, but I feel I should know exactly what happened."

"Yes, you should, John. And you will—just as soon as we can be alone to talk about it. I'll tell you everything I can then."

"I can't quit thinking about it, Victoria. Such a horrible, absurd accident..."

"That's the rub, John. It wasn't an accident."

"What?"

"Your father's death was no accident. But let's not discuss it here, all right? We'll get you a room, and then we can talk there, where it's quiet, where no one will hear."

John, shaken, pulled the buggy to a stop in front of the Donaho and walked stiffly into the lobby with his bag in hand. He nodded a wordless greeting at the hotel clerk who checked him in, then climbed the stairs to his room at the west end of the third floor. Victoria was at his side, as silent as he. All the while his mind turned over what she had said, and the implications it held.

John thrust key into lock and walked into a cold room with the musty smell of a place where windows are seldom opened. He tossed his bag onto the bed and walked across the room, where he opened the dirty window that overlooked the balcony above the street. For long seconds he stared blankly out to the dusty street and the people and wagons moving along it, then he said:

"It was murder. Is that what you were trying to tell me out there?"

"Yes, John. I'm certain of it. I couldn't be more certain."

John slapped the windowsill with both palms, then wheeled to face Victoria.

"God in heaven, why? And who?"

"I don't know. The marshal is investigating, but he's keeping an unusually quiet front about it. He won't discuss it with me, won't even confirm to me that Bill was murdered. Not that I need his confirmation. I know his death was no accident."

John breathed deeply, forcing himself to calm down. "Victoria, I want to know who killed my father. And mostly I want to know why. I want to look whoever did it in the eye and ask why anyone could possibly have a reason to kill a man like Bill Kenton."

John sat heavily on the side of the bed, his hands clasped in front of him, elbows on his knees. He stared at the wall for a time, then looked up at Victoria, whose face had taken on a hard, stoic look that masked whatever emotions she felt.

"How do you know he was murdered, Victoria? Didn't he die in the fire?"

"No. He was dead before the fire ever reached him. You remember Malcolm Weatherford, the undertaker? He told me, in secret and against the orders of the marshal, that your father had been shot in the head. There were no signs of powder burns around the wound, so it wasn't a close shot. That rules out suicide. And from the looks of his throat, it appeared he had inhaled no smoke. He was dead before that fire started."

"How could Malcolm tell all this?"

"Your father's body was not completely destroyed, despite what the marshal said. Malcolm told me your father was on his bed while the fire burned, and a beam above him collapsed and protected his upper body and head from the fire. The rest of him was... No need to talk about it. Like fire is, it was horrible, Malcolm said."

"Does the marshal have suspects?"

Victoria smiled very strangely. "Sometimes I think he's going to arrest *me.*"

John was aghast. "You're not serious! How could he suspect you?"

"John, when it comes to killing a man like Bill Kenton,

how could you suspect *anyone* in this town? Who lived here who didn't absolutely adore the man? Everyone knew him, everyone had nothing but good to say about him. So I suppose I'm as good a suspect as anyone else. After all, lovers sometimes kill one another."

John stood, tense and nervous. "It's preposterous, Victoria. I don't even like hearing you talk about it. And if the marshal is wasting time suspecting you, then the true killer is getting away free and clear. I'm going to have a talk with him, and—"

"I don't recommend that, John. Marshal Roberts is a tight-lipped man about all this, and you know as well as I do how stubborn he is. He won't talk to you about it, I assure you. He has his own way of doing things and sticks with it."

"But I have to do *something!*"

Victoria's expression grew stern. "John, listen to me. This isn't the time to grow hotheaded. If you follow your feelings instead of your reason right now, you'll only find trouble. If you want to get involved, at least do it in a cool, rational way. That's how to discover who killed Bill, not screaming in the face of a marshal. Think about it. You know I'm right."

John looked down and saw his hands trembling. Embarrassed, he stuck them in his pockets. "Yes. You're right. I'm sorry I burst out like that."

"It's easily forgiven at a time like this." She straightened suddenly. "I'm leaving for now. I'm very tired, and I want to get some rest tonight. It's starting to grow dusky outside, and I'd best be on my way. You needn't bother to ask to drive me —I'd rather be alone tonight. And you should keep to yourself, too. You have a lot to digest and accept. Get some rest before you talk to anyone."

"Very well."

"Good night, John. I'll see you in the morning. And do try to rest tonight."

John watched Victoria walk down the hallway and descend the stairs. He walked back into his room and closed the door, casting himself down on his bed while dark, saddening thoughts flitted through his mind like restless bats in a cavern.

CHAPTER 2

By the time John Kenton had washed and dressed the next morning and headed down the stairs with a mind toward breakfast at the Rose Cafe down the street, Victoria Rivers was downstairs in the lobby awaiting him. Outside, hitched to the rear of her buggy, was a beautiful chestnut mare, already saddled.

"You'll be needing a horse to get around," she said. "Keep her as long as you're in town."

John expressed his thanks to Victoria and walked over to the animal, admiring the graceful curve of its powerful flanks and the strength of its sleek neck. Victoria couldn't have provided him with a better horse.

"Have you had breakfast yet?" John asked.

"Yes, but I could enjoy a good cup of coffee—if you're going to the cafe anyway."

"I am, and I'm buying. Consider it rent for the horse. By the way, does she have a name?"

"Kate. Katherine, really, but if folks heard you calling your horse 'Katherine' you'd be laughed out of town."

John grinned. "Kate will do fine."

He took Victoria's arm. Together they walked down to

the Rose Cafe, which had opened its doors about an hour before and was exuding a delicious aroma of fresh coffee and sizzling bacon.

John ordered a large meal, and Victoria ordered coffee, and as an afterthought, a fresh biscuit with molasses. Outside, the morning sun was beginning to warm the street, but the cafe, whose front doorway was shaded by a large cedar that grew alone right in the midst of the avenue, was cool and pleasantly dark.

Victoria's eyes took on a distant look as she sipped her coffee and stared out the open door into the street.

"You know, John, it's times like these that I can't convince myself Bill is gone. It's as if he should walk through the door at any moment, just like he always did. I wonder if I'll ever get over his death."

"I doubt you will. I discovered when my mother died that you never really get over a loss like that. You just get a little more used to it as time goes on. The pain is always there. You learn to ignore it and go on."

The breakfast ended quickly after that. The coming of morning had broken through John's gloom a little, but now the melancholy was returning, and the darkness of the cafe, which previously had seemed relaxing, was now stifling, filling him with the urge to get outside and into the open. Victoria left her coffee half finished, her biscuit three-fourths untouched. Sadness had overcome her, too.

The trip to the cemetery just beside the Presbyterian church came next. John had figured it would bother him, but when he looked at the fresh grave, he felt no great shift of his emotions. But the sight set him to thinking again of the fact that his father had been murdered, and that he needed to make sure that justice came to whoever had taken his father's life.

"John! John Kenton!"

John turned to see who called him and saw, approaching

at a half-walk, half-run, Lawrence Poteet, vice president of the Larimont Bank and a longtime associate of his father. Poteet, a stocky, red-faced man with round-lensed spectacles, slowed to a stop and extended his hand to John.

"Good to see you, John! Good to see you! But I'm so sorry it has to be in circumstances like this. Terrible, terrible, your father's death. He was a good friend, John, a good friend. And a fine father to you."

"Indeed. Thank you. How have you been, Mr. Poteet?"

Poteet took off his spectacles and began wiping them with a linen pocket handkerchief—a habit as much a part of him as his red face and small eyes. "I've been well enough myself, John. Of course, without your father, things have been difficult at the bank. He knew that place inside and out, and I never knew until he was gone just how much we relied on him. He'll be impossible to replace. I'm not sure the attempt will even be made."

"Hello, Lawrence," Victoria interjected.

The man's features turned even redder at Victoria's greeting, and John detected the hidden intent of her words. It was well known around Larimont that the old bachelor Lawrence Poteet had an eye for Victoria Rivers, but he was far too shy to ever make anything more than halting conversation with her. Whenever he tried he always turned a fiery red—"blossomed out," John had heard one snide observer once call the phenomenon—and talked in a voice that let everyone know his throat had gone as dry as Death Valley. Then out would come the handkerchief, wiping furiously at the glasses, and soon the conversation would end as the nervous banker became too edgy to continue it. Victoria Rivers knew exactly the effect she had on the stocky little man and was just mischievous enough to enjoy inflicting it.

"Well, hello, Victoria. Good to see you today."

"Why, thank you. Tell me, how is your poor old cat doing? I heard she was injured by a wagon."

"She passed away in suffering, sorry to say."
"Oh! How dreadful! Sad for you."
"Yes. Yes."
"Right. And how are people at the bank doing? Is Mr. Burrell well?"
"Fine. Yes. Indeed. Quite fine."

Victoria smiled warmly at Poteet, making his face turn even more of that famous blistering red. A following pause in the conversation was much enjoyed by John and Victoria, but Poteet was absolutely miserable, and suddenly found something fascinating about the tips of his shoes.

John couldn't watch the poor man suffer any more. Opening his mouth to break the silence, he found his words suddenly cut off by the noise of clattering hooves in the dirt as three riders raced around the corner of the dry goods store at the closest end of the street, heading out of town and into the Larimont Valley.

John glanced at Victoria and could tell by her expression that she had noted the same thing as he: The riders had been led by the county marshal, Drew Roberts, and they were moving in the general direction of the old William Kenton farm.

The old man had seen them coming before they were within a quarter mile of his shack, and even across that distance had sensed there was something out of the ordinary about the visit. He knew who it was—that buckskin horse of Drew Roberts's was an animal he knew well, having tended it many times in the livery.

He was drunk, as usual, and slightly embarrassed that in a few moments, others would be seeing him in that condition. He knew he was foolish to even care, since everyone in town expected him to be drunk most of the time anyway, but he had been raised in a good home, and it just wasn't proper for a man with a good raising to let folks see him drunk if he could help it. Even a town drunk has his pride.

Outside, the marshal and his deputies had dismounted, and were approaching the shack. And with a sudden, disconcerting burst of comprehension, the old man realized that they were approaching under cover, darting from rocks to trees to the well to the woodpile—and their guns were drawn.

Now he was really scared and confused. He had no idea why the marshal would be approaching his home like this. The palsy-like trembling of his hands increased. He had been nervous ever since Bill Kenton's home had burned a few days earlier, only minutes after he had been there—and now this! He wished he could run out some back way and into the woods behind the shack, but there was no back way. He would have to face Marshal Roberts and his deputies. No way out.

"Scruff! Come out of there! This is Drew Roberts!"

Scruff Smithers's left eye narrowed as it always did when he was thinking. His drunken brain, scared through and through, blocked his very reasonable impulse to walk out the door with his hands up and find out just what Roberts wanted of him. No, there was something odd going on here, and he wasn't going to do anything without thinking it through first.

Scruff edged over to a nearby cabinet, opened it, and produced from inside a rusty but loaded Remington revolver.

He stared at the rickety handgun as his heartbeat grew faster and faster. The county marshal, outside with armed deputies...what could this mean?

A joke. A joke! It had to be. Drew Roberts was his friend, after all, and a man known to pull the occasional jest. Scruff grinned. That was it! Old Drew was trying to scare him, for fun.

Well, two could dance at that party! Maybe he could turn that little joke around, maybe scare Drew and his boys a bit in return.

"Scruff! You heard me! Come on out peaceful and nothing will happen. I need to talk to you!"

Scruff, blinking to clear the fog from his bleary eyes, staggered toward the door, gripping his pistol. He pushed the door open, stepped onto the porch, and raised the gun.

"Howdy, Drew! Come to roust out old Bad-man Smithers at last, have you? By granny, you ain't going to take me alive, no sir!"

And before he knew what his trembling hands had done, the old Remington roared and spit orange flame, the recoil knocking the pistol up to pound hard against his own forehead, knocking him down.

He hadn't meant to fire, not yet, and he had intended to shoot high. He'd forgotten about the hair trigger on this old pistol.

He had to make sure Drew understood the shot had been accidental. The old man tried to rise, but he'd stunned himself and his movements were slow. He pushed himself up on his right side, looking out fearfully to where Drew Roberts had just come to his feet, his pistol raised before him. The look on Roberts's face, Smithers noticed, was anything but playful.

In one horrible moment the old drunk realized that this wasn't a joke at all. Never had been. He raised his hand to gesture for the marshal not to fire, realizing only as he did it that the Remington was still gripped in that same hand.

Drew Roberts's pistol roared, and Scruff Smithers's body was kicked upward and back as a .44 slug tore through his chest, shattering a rib, tearing through his lungs, and exiting through his back. The world went black. He was vaguely conscious of another shot being fired, and it was as if a mountain's weight had crashed down onto his skull. By the time his next breath passed over his lips, he was dead.

Drew Roberts let his .44 slip back into its holster. He stood staring at the still, bloody figure that lay half in, half out of the shack doorway, and slowly shook his head.

It was really too bad. He'd always liked old Scruff.

Chapter 3

The news traveled fast, making the rounds in Larimont seemingly moments after the town marshal and his two deputies arrived with Scruff Smithers's body draped over the back of his old mule. The body was wrapped in burlap sacks that had been dug up by the lawmen at Scruff's old shack, but they weren't sufficient to keep hidden the deep stain of blood on the limp corpse with its dangling arms. The marshal steadfastly refused to comment on what had happened; one of the deputies, though, a nervous, excitable greenhorn, let out a description of what had happened, and after that, telegraph lines couldn't have transmitted the story quicker.

Poor Bill Kenton hadn't died by accident at all, the story went—Scruff Smithers had gone to his home, robbed him, then killed him. Somebody—nobody knew just who—had gone secretly to the marshal and reported that Scruff had been seen riding away from the Kenton house just minutes before the fire started, and the marshal and his men beat a path to Scruff's old shed as soon as they heard the news. But Scruff refused to surrender, coming out firing instead, and the lawmen had been forced to kill him. And sure enough, there in Scruff's pocket they had found Bill Kenton's watch. Sufficient proof that Scruff Smithers had killed poor old Bill and then burned down the house to cover the evidence.

It was unbelievable—Scruff Smithers just didn't seem the type to kill anybody. He was worthless, sure—and a drunk—but the story took a lot of telling before it really began to be believed.

And before long, people who at first had sworn Scruff Smithers couldn't possibly be guilty were talking in serious, covertly excited tones about different things they had heard the old drunk say throughout the years—things that at the time had seemed perfectly harmless, if perhaps a bit incoherent—but which in light of what had happened now seemed pregnant with diabolical intentions.

And in the midst of a Larimont buzzing with the sordid, unbelievable, and therefore delicious news, John Kenton sat in Marshal Roberts's office with a stony expression and an adamantly skeptical attitude.

Roberts, as usual, had little to say about the matter.

"You've already heard the tale, I guess, John. Scruff killed your father. It wasn't an accident, not a bit of it. Scruff killed him, and then wouldn't surrender to us. Shot at us! We had to drop him. No choice."

John shook his head. "Mr. Roberts, you and me have both known Scruff Smithers for years. Do you really think that he could do what you're saying? You know good and well he was a friend of my father. Scruff said a lot of times that he could always count on Bill Kenton when the rest of the town let him down. My father was almost a caretaker to Scruff—and he was a friend to him. Scruff wouldn't kill him. I know that."

Roberts's brows lowered ever so slightly. "Couldn't it be that it was your father's friendship with Scruff that led to this? Just imagine that your father tried just this once to shove old Scruff out. Maybe just one time he got tired of trying to help out the old bum. That could have made Scruff mad...mad enough to kill. And if Scruff was innocent, John, then why did he shoot at us? Hmm?"

John grew slightly sullen. "I don't know. But I don't think Scruff killed my father. I *know* he didn't."

Roberts sighed. "Then I'd appreciate it if you would fill me in on who did it. Me being the marshal and all, I'd think you might want me to know." The marshal made no effort to hide the sarcasm in his voice.

John stood up, twisting his hat in his hands. He thrust his hand up into his thick shock of sandy hair and ran his fingers through it like a man thinking hard about something he can't quite get a grasp on. Then he shook his head.

"Marshal, I don't know who killed my father, or why. I just can't believe Scruff could do it." He paused, his eyes clearing. "Just who put you on his trail, anyway?"

Drew Roberts tightened his thin lips into a hard line. "I can't tell you that, John. Official business."

John sneered slightly. "Just like everything else you don't want folks to know about, huh? Just call it official and shut up about it, right?"

Roberts showed no reaction to John's bitterness. John knew he was being a bit testy, but things had happened so fast, and he was feeling so confused and bewildered by it all that he wasn't in the frame of mind to apologize. Roberts deserved some criticism, anyway, John figured. For a man on the public payroll, he was terribly closemouthed about things the public had a right to know.

"John, I've got work to do," the marshal said. "If there's nothing else, then why don't you just move on now? I think you'll realize that we have your father's killer after you've had time to get used to the notion. It seems to me it ought to make you happy."

"I don't see anything in all this business that could make

anybody happy, Marshal. But we all look at things in our own way. So long."

John plopped his hat down on his head and headed for the door. He threw open the heavy oak door just in time to almost be barreled over by a tall, stout man who seemed in a terrible rush to get inside. John was pushed back and thrown off balance, managing to stay on his feet only by hanging on to the doorknob.

"Watch it!" he snapped, pulling himself upright again. The man who had rushed past him turned a pale face toward him and said nothing—but recognition cut off the torrent of invectives John was about to heap on him.

It was Alexander Layne, a neighbor of Bill Kenton and a man John had grown up nearby since his birth. And he was staring at John as if he were a total stranger.

"Alexander?" John queried in a tentative tone.

The husky man turned his back on John quickly, pretending not to hear. Confused and strangely bothered, John ducked out the door and closed it behind him.

Strange, he thought to himself. But then, what wasn't strange anymore, with his father murdered and an old friend dead because—supposedly—he was the murderer?

When John told Victoria Rivers about Alexander Layne's strange behavior, she was as unable as he had been to give any good explanation for it.

"It's hard to imagine Alexander Layne not being friendly," she said. "Especially to an old friend like you...and at a time like this. Some folks are hard to figure—though I thought I knew Alexander better than that."

John's mind had already strayed back to Scruff Smithers.

"Victoria, do you believe that Scruff could have killed my father?"

Victoria's brows lifted, and she shook her head quietly.

"John...there's something about the whole thing that leaves me feeling like the mystery of Bill's death hasn't been solved yet. I've known Scruff for a long time, and though he was not an angel by any means, I'm convinced—at least I always have been—that he was harmless to everyone. Except himself."

"That's exactly how I feel, Victoria. Marshal Roberts may be ready to declare this case closed and let the whole thing slide, but I'm not. I've got to find out who really killed my father. My father's memory deserves that much."

"And maybe Scruff's memory, too," Victoria said. "Especially in light of this."

She reached over to a small end table beside her chair and pulled a letter out of the decorative oak box that normally served as a resting place for her spectacles.

"I got it today," she said. "It's from Sharon Bradley. Do you remember her?"

John knitted his brow. "Sharon Bradley...why, that's Scruff's sister's daughter, isn't it? The one who lived in Larimont until she was ten or so?"

"That's right. I've kept in touch with Sharon through the years, especially since her mother died. I did it partly out of friendship, partly because they wanted to always keep tabs on how Scruff was doing. They always called him Oliver—that's his real name...*was* his real name, you know. Sharon seems to have turned into quite a young lady. More and more through the last few months she's sounded concerned about her uncle, worrying about him, wishing she could get him away from Larimont, to someplace where he could get over his drinking. She was always worried about him...and now this." Victoria waved the letter.

"Get to the point, Victoria," John said.

"The point is that Sharon Bradley will be arriving in Larimont tomorrow about ten o'clock to meet her uncle

Scruff and try to talk him into coming home with her, back to St. Paul. She doesn't know he's dead—there's no way she could. She's probably three quarters of the way through her trip now."

John winced. "I don't look forward to seeing her find out what happened to her uncle. And especially when she hears that he's being called a murderer by the law."

"There's nothing we can do about it, John. She'll be getting off that train tomorrow, and she'll be in for a big shock."

John had a sudden thought. "Victoria—the odds are that she'll want to clear her uncle's name, if she cared for him like you say she did."

"I'm sure she will."

John walked over to the window and pulled back the lace curtain. Down the dirt road he could see the steeple of the church and the corner of the cemetery. For a long moment he was quiet.

"Victoria, the law isn't going to be looking any further for my father's killer. They think they've got him. We both know they haven't. My father was a good man, and he was killed. He deserves to have whatever vengeance he can, even after death, even if it has to come through his son finding his killer.

"And Scruff Smithers was a good man, too, in his way. He doesn't deserve to be called a killer. I owe it to him to clear this up, get him vindicated, though I know I can't bring him back.

"I've got to stay here until I can find out the truth. I've got to search out the killer and see him either dead or brought to justice."

Victoria nodded. "I understand. And I'll be at your side all the way. If you hadn't decided to do it, I would have taken the task on myself, alone. Somewhere, probably still in this town, there's a man who killed Bill Kenton in cold blood. I, for one, want to find him, and I'm glad to hear that you do too."

"And something tells me Sharon Bradley will have an interest in this as well," John said. "Maybe she'll be some help."

He turned back to the window. "But to me, this is almost a private thing. It's my search—the last thing I can ever do for my father."

It was almost sundown when John ran almost full-face into Alexander Layne outside the hardware store. As before, Layne appeared preoccupied, and seeing John standing before him seemed to almost frighten him.

"Hello, Alexander."

No answer but a nervous grunt.

"Is something bothering you? You didn't even say hello to me today."

Layne's eyes looked like those of a trapped animal. Abruptly he pushed past John, walking rapidly down the boardwalk.

"Alexander!"

The man turned, staring with a disturbed expression back at John.

"Was it you who told the marshal that you saw Scruff Smithers going out to my father's place the day he was killed?"

Alexander Layne's face went pale, and he turned and stalked away without a word.

Chapter 4

They buried Scruff Smithers the following morning, and folks came to the funeral to ogle the closed casket and hear the preacher expound about the wages of sin and the dangers of drink, about how Scruff Smithers had let himself become something less than human and how he had paid the price.

John sat on the back pew, feeling disgusted and knowing all the while that Scruff didn't deserve such a tirade. Probably the man who really killed his father was sitting in the sanctuary right now, feeling sure that his crime was going to be buried forever just as soon as they threw the dirt over Scruff's pine box.

John didn't go to the burial. It didn't seem important, somehow. Instead, he mounted up his horse and rode out to what remained of his father's house.

He found a hollow shell of a building that looked as if Sherman's army had marched through the middle of it. The rear walls were gone, as were most of the side walls, with only the front remaining in place, licked black with fire. The smell of smoldering wood ash still hung heavy on the farm, and the maple that had leaned over toward the front door was a blackened, dying relic of what it had been.

The house was like a thing dead; the farm was like a graveyard. John found himself growing increasingly depressed. He stood still for a long time at the front gate, staring blankly at the devastated remains of his boyhood home. Tears flowed down his cheeks for a full five minutes before he even realized he was crying.

He couldn't take it for long. He stayed at the farm for a little over an hour, then felt a strong desire to leave. He fetched Kate, who had wandered away toward a clump of thick clover east of the house, and began riding back toward town, resisting the impulse to turn and stare once more at the ghost of his past behind him.

As he rode, he thought about Alexander Layne. The man's behavior still bothered him, but he was increasingly sure he had hit on the reason for it when he had confronted him last night. It made sense, too. Alexander Layne's farm lay directly between Scruff's old shed and Bill Kenton's house, and Alexander Layne's front door and window looked right out toward the road. If anybody was likely to have seen Scruff riding away from the Kenton place, it would be Alexander Layne or one of his family.

Whether Scruff actually had been at the Kenton house before the fire was of little concern to John. He was sure that Scruff was innocent of his father's murder, and anyway, Scruff spent a lot of time at the Kenton house. As for the fact that Scruff had Bill Kenton's watch, John guessed that his father had given it to him, as he had given him many other little gifts through the years. Bill Kenton had always been a compassionate and generous man, especially with those who, like Scruff, were looked down on by most folks who considered themselves better.

John passed the Layne farm and resisted the temptation to stop and once again try to get something out of Alexander Layne. He saw no sign of life around the place. Probably Layne was out somewhere on his farm grounds. John rode on past the dirt road that led down to Layne's front door.

Up ahead he noticed a buggy rolling along. It was a fancy rig, shining and almost new, the kind that Larimont didn't see very often. Without making any attempt to catch up, he found himself gradually gaining on the slow-moving buggy, and before long he was alongside of it. He looked around and nodded at the driver. It was Frederick Burrell, president of the Larimont Bank, where his father had worked.

Burrell smiled at John, showing an even row of ivory teeth for an instant between his thin lips. Burrell was a tall man, not plump but slightly hefty and big boned. Ladies considered him handsome, John had heard, but he expected a good deal of the banker's attractiveness lay in the fact that he had more money than any other man in Larimont.

Burrell was a nice enough fellow, and he had always paid Bill Kenton a good salary. John remembered that when he was very young, Burrell gave him a shiny five-cent piece every time he went into the bank. So the young man couldn't really figure out why he disliked the banker so. He always had, just as he had always hated spinach.

Shouting over the rumbling and creaking of the buggy, which was being shaken about a good deal because of the rough road, Burrell told John to pull over for a talk. John complied, not really anxious to talk to Burrell, but feeling there was no polite way out of it.

"John, there's no words that can describe the sorrow I feel about your father's death, especially with it being such an untimely and tragic passing. We miss him terribly at the bank."

"Thank you, sir. I appreciate the sympathy."

"You've been out at the farm, John? I saw it myself only a

day ago—it was a painful thing to see. Of course, now that Scruff Smithers has paid the price for what he did, I guess—"

"Yes, sir," cut in John. He literally had to bite his lip to keep from bursting out at the tall banker. And he didn't want to hear any more talk against Scruff—not from Burrell, not from anybody.

"What brings you out this direction, Mr. Burrell?" John asked, trying to detour the conversation from the unpleasant direction it was taking.

"Visiting Alexander Layne and his wife," the banker said. "Or I should say, visiting Mrs. Layne. Alexander was out in the fields, and June and her mother were at the house. You know of Mrs. Layne's illness, don't you?"

"No," John answered. "I hadn't heard. What's wrong with her?"

"A bone problem, a stiffening of the joints," Burrell said. "She's bedridden and has been for about six months now."

John frowned. He had heard nothing of Myrtle Layne's illness, and he was sincerely disturbed. Myrtle Layne was a woman he had liked since childhood.

"I hate to hear that," he said. "Is she in pain?"

"Comes and goes," said Burrell. "Lately it comes more often than it goes, I'm afraid. I try to visit her often—Alexander has always been a good friend, you know."

" Yes, sir."

Burrell picked up the traces and smiled thinly at John again. "I must be on my way, John—a lot to do today. Would you like to ride along? We can hitch your horse behind."

"No, thanks. I think I'll stop in and see the Laynes. It's been a while since I saw Mrs. Layne, anyway—at least a couple of years. So long."

John turned and started back toward the Layne house, while Burrell yanked the traces and began slowly rolling toward Larimont once more.

John felt a bit uncomfortable when he hitched his horse

to the fence around Layne's yard. He knew that Alexander Layne for some reason didn't like to be near him now—his actions alone made that clear. But perhaps the Layne women would be different. And possibly he'd find out what was eating at Alexander.

June Layne answered John's knock. For a moment he was struck speechless, for the little brunette child that he had last seen maybe seven or eight years before had turned out to be a striking young woman.

Her eyes were wide and deeply brown, and her skin was fair and unblemished, though her cheeks were slightly sunburned. She had an honest, unpretentious look about her, and her figure was slim and very feminine. John couldn't help but notice that she had, as polite folks in Larimont put it, "filled out" very well.

"June? You remember me? I'm John Kenton."

"Yes... I remember you." June's voice evidenced no welcome. Her wide eyes had narrowed somewhat, cagily, and her expression was almost stern. Suddenly she didn't seem quite so pretty.

"I heard your mother is ill, June—I wanted to see her."

June shrugged and opened the door. It was the most reluctant welcome John had ever received.

John slipped off his hat and walked in. June closed the door and turned to wordlessly stare at John. Fingering his hat nervously, John asked how she had been.

"Fine."

An uncomfortable pause. "Good." John looked around. "Where is Mrs. Layne?"

"In the bedroom."

"May I see her?"

"Suit yourself."

John walked toward the bedroom, wondering if his reception from Myrtle Layne would be as cool as that her daughter had given him.

It wasn't. Myrtle Layne, her hair now gone almost completely white, greeted John warmly. Her fingers, John noted, were twisted and claw-like, and her frame appeared generally drawn. Her eyes showed that general weariness that marked a continual presence of pain.

"How are you feeling, Myrtle?" John asked. "I didn't know until today that you were sick. No one told me."

"Oh, I'm not really sick, John." She smiled. "Just getting old. That's what I tell myself, at least. Things could be a lot worse you know. How's Victoria?"

"Fine. She's just fine. I take it you haven't seen her in a while?"

"I can't get out myself, and with us living out and away from town, I don't get many visitors. Occasionally some will come out for a visit, but it's all too often people are too busy. Good old Lawrence Poteet is good about stopping by, and occasionally Frederick Burrell does as well, though I haven't seen him in a couple of weeks."

"But, Myrtle, I just saw—" He stopped short, confused.

"Yes?"

"I...just feel surprised that you don't see more people. That's all."

Outside, John heard the sound of the front door opening and shutting, and the sound of June's voice. A moment later, Alexander Layne's frame filled the bedroom door.

"Why are you here, John?"

"I'm just visiting your wife, Alexander. Is that a problem?"

"It might be. Don't you think you ought to give a man warning before you burst into his house?"

"I didn't burst in. Your daughter let me in. Now, will you tell me what's bothering you so much about me? I don't understand this."

"And neither do I, Alex," said Myrtle Layne. "John's a friend. You shouldn't talk so rough to him."

"Myrtle, you just hush. John made quite an accusation at me last night. I don't think I'm obligated to be kind to a man who would slander one of his oldest friends."

"Alexander, I'm sorry if I was out of line," John said. "I was just trying to understand why you were so cold toward me. I thought maybe, if it was you that accused Scruff, that my presence reminded you of all that had happened. I thought that was why you wouldn't talk to me."

"Did you hear that, Myrtle? He's accusing me of pointing fingers at folks—making me out to be something not much better than a murderer myself. I don't want him in this house."

"Don't worry," John spat out. "I'm leaving. I've done nothing to deserve this sort of treatment." He stalked out the bedroom door, June jumping aside as if she was afraid he would knock her over.

At the front door he turned. "But one thing I want you to know, Alexander—I'm convinced now that it was you who accused Scruff Smithers of killing my father. And I believe that you know as well as I do that he couldn't have done it." Then, slamming the door behind him, John stalked out.

And as he rode back toward town, he pondered why Myrtle Layne would tell him she hadn't seen Frederick Burrell, when the banker swore he had just visited her.

Like this whole confusing affair, it was an enigma he couldn't solve, and it bothered him.

A quarter mile from town, he heard the whistle of the train as it entered the valley. In a few moments, Sharon Bradley would be in Larimont and would be hearing that the uncle she came to rescue was dead and labeled a murderer. Just one more depressing detail in what was turning out to be a highly depressing day.

Chapter 5

Sharon Bradley took it rough.

John found her crying in Victoria's living room, with Victoria standing beside her, looking very guilty, as if having to tell this young lady about Scruff's death somehow made her partly responsible for it.

Sharon's face was tear-streaked and pale, and her hair was a mess from her having continually run her hands through it as she cried, but even in that condition she was a very beautiful girl, as John instantly noticed.

Sharon Bradley seemed somewhat embarrassed to meet John in her emotional state, and managed to stop crying, except for a few sniffles, as they exchanged their greetings.

After about an hour, the tension in the air had lowered a little, and John relaxed. Sharon seemed to be getting over the initial shock of her uncle's death, and John noticed that he was beginning to enjoy her company. There were not all that many young women to whom John was easily attracted. A fellow had to take advantage of opportunities when they came his way, he decided.

John had grown up with Sharon until she moved east with her family while still a young girl. John had scarcely noticed her absence, since at that age he couldn't care less about some skinny girl who lived on the other side of Larimont. The only thing about Sharon Bradley that stood out in his mind from those early years was the fact that she always seemed to have a runny nose, and that she wore her auburn hair long and usually tied in pigtails.

Her hair was still long and auburn; the pigtails were gone. The runny nose was still there, but only because she had been crying.

She was a couple of years younger than John. But as he talked to her, he discovered to his delight that she was quite an intelligent young woman.

Victoria managed to coerce Sharon, through well-worded questions, into confessing that she had no serious courters. John looked at Victoria out of the corner of his eye. She hadn't fooled him. He knew for whose benefit that question had been.

Victoria warmed up some leftover potatoes and beans and set a good meal. John was ravenous and ate heartily while Sharon picked at her food with an obvious lack of appetite. She was silent and apparently thoughtful for most of the meal, but at last began asking more questions about her uncle's death. John and Victoria answered them as best they could, and before long John was describing the events of the morning.

"I can't figure out why Myrtle Layne would lie to me," John said. "Maybe she'd just forgotten Burrell's visit...but the man had been there only minutes before."

Victoria began picking up the plates and carrying them into the kitchen. On the last return trip she said, "John, have you considered that maybe it was Burrell, not Myrtle, who lied to you?"

John pondered that one. "It could be, I suppose. But why would Burrell lie?"

"Burrell...he's the bank president?" Sharon asked, trying to keep up.

"That's right," Victoria said. She paused, then spoke again.

"I'm not sure this is something I'm right to bring up, but I haven't fully trusted Frederick Burrell the last little while. Bill confided something to me about a week before his death. Nothing real definite—just that he was suspicious about Burrell over something or other. I think that it had something to do with that bank robbery a few months ago, because I know that at the time Bill was thinking a lot about the robbery. You remember that robbery, John? I assume Bill must have written to you about it."

"I haven't heard of it," Sharon cut in. "What happened?"

"It was a daytime robbery," Victoria said. "About noon, when the bank was just closing for lunch, three masked men pushed their way in and robbed the place of several thousand dollars. It was well-timed, happening just when the bank had a lot of cash on hand. Nothing really happened—the robbers took the cash and left. No one was hurt."

John chuckled. "Maybe Burrell robbed his own bank," he said.

Victoria shook her head. "I happen to know from talking with Bill that Burrell took a big loss in that robbery. He replaced the stolen money right out of his own pocket, just to keep the bank afloat. He wasn't benefited by it at all—that's why I never really understood why Bill was suspicious about him...assuming that suspicion had anything to do with the robbery, anyway."

"And it doesn't explain why Burrell would lie to me today, either," John said.

"John, you might want to talk to Lawrence Poteet sometime—very carefully and very discreetly. Bill said that Lawrence was also suspicious about Burrell in some way, though the two talked little about it. I know that Lawrence likes you, John. I think he would help you out if you approach him right. It could be that all of those suspicions and that bank robbery tie in somehow with your father's death."

"Could be. I think I will talk to Poteet...this afternoon."

John took off his hat as he walked into the Larimont Bank. Turning toward Lawrence Poteet's office, he immediately felt his foot step down on something that definitely wasn't floor.

That something was David Burrell's foot. The young man, about two years John's junior, was Frederick Burrell's youngest son. An older son, Michael, had left home years before, going east to work in a bank in St. Louis. The middle son, Edgar, had hung around Larimont, becoming known as town trash and causing a lot of embarrassment for his father and providing a lot of the cause for the drinking problem that had nearly killed his mother.

David Burrell was his antithesis. Clean-cut and polite, the young man was never seen in any attire other than a tailored suit and tie, and his talk and general bearing were always stern and aloof. His reaction to John's clumsiness was in keeping with that image.

"Watch out, you oaf!" David bellowed, pushing John aside and striding out the door.

John would have been angry if he hadn't been so surprised. As it was, he merely watched the prim David Burrell stride haughtily away.

"I apologize for my son's behavior." John turned and saw Frederick Burrell smiling, extending his hand toward him. "David is sometimes less than tactful. I need to talk with him, I believe. Can I do something for you?"

"No, sir," John said. "I just wanted to have a word with Lawrence Poteet."

Burrell's eyes seemed to narrow slightly—or maybe it was just John's imagination. The banker's smile didn't fade.

"I'm afraid he's busy, John. Is it something I can help you with? If it's a banking matter..."

"It's not. And I think he's free—I just saw him walk into his office," John said, moving toward Poteet's office door. Burrell stared after him, his smile slowly fading.

"John—good to see you!" Poteet said as John walked into the little cubbyhole of an office that Burrell provided his vice president in the rear corner of the building. Musty and stacked with paper, the office—unlike Burrell's—was obviously that of a man who did a lot of work. Probably work that Burrell was supposed to do, John figured.

"Sit down, John. I just got some coffee off the stove in the back. Can I get you a cup?"

"No, thank you, Mr. Poteet. Just wanted to talk."

Poteet adjusted his glasses and squinted, puckering his thick lips at the same time. "Talk? What about?"

John looked out the open door of Poteet's office. Burrell had his back toward him and was shuffling papers in the teller's window, out of earshot.

"I wanted to talk about my father—and Mr. Burrell."

Poteet's ruddy face went pale, and his very official smile faded. His right hand, gripping his coffee cup, twitched convulsively, causing some of his coffee to splash over on his desktop.

"I don't understand."

"Mr. Poteet, I'm convinced my father's killing hasn't been solved. I think we both know that Scruff Smithers wasn't the sort of man to murder anyone. Which means that whoever did kill my father is still on the loose.

"You knew my father. You worked beside him, talked to him, and were a good friend. Maybe you know something about his last days, the days when he was bothered about something—Victoria told me that he was. She thinks it had something to do with the bank robbery a little while back."

Poteet shifted nervously in his seat. "John..." His voice was a whisper—a tremulous whisper at that. "John, this is hardly the time or the place to talk like that." He looked over John's shoulder, and John knew he was eyeing Burrell.

"Will you talk to me at all about it?" John asked. He knew he was pushing, and that he was making Poteet nervous. But this was a matter that deserved pushing, and he intended to get answers.

"I'm not sure I have anything to tell you—"

"Victoria told me that my father talked to her a while before he was killed, and that he said he was... curious, shall we say, about some details of Mr. Burrell's life. I don't know much more than that, but I think it had something to do with the bank robbery. And Victoria said that my father told her you had a few questions yourself. I want to find out about that. It's very important to me—more important than I can tell you."

Poteet glanced over John's shoulder once more, swallowing nervously. He lifted his cup and took a sip of coffee, and John noted that his hand was trembling.

"All right, John," he said quietly, looking down at his desktop. "But not here. Tonight, at my house. About eight o'clock. And try to be sure no one sees you."

John frowned. "You make this sound awfully secretive, Mr. Poteet. Do you know something that somebody doesn't want to get out?"

"I don't know anything," Poteet snapped quickly. Then his voice lowered. "But I...*wonder* about a few things. And maybe you have a right to know about it. Tonight, eight o'clock."

"I'll be there. Thank you, Mr. Poteet. Have a good day."

John walked out of Poteet's office, nodding at Burrell, who smiled back at him in a very hollow, artificial way. Then his eyes swung around and locked in on the nervous face of Lawrence Poteet, and the smile was gone.

Poteet delved into the papers on his desk, feeling sweat popping out on his brow, and hoping that Burrell couldn't tell how badly he was shaking.

Sharon Bradley felt a very unwomanly desire to curse. One wheel of Victoria's buggy, which she had allowed Sharon to borrow for a trip out to the Layne farm when the young lady had expressed an interest in seeing her old friend June Layne, was broken, thanks to an extra-large chuckhole right in the middle of the road. The buggy had gone as far as it would.

Sharon looked around her, wondering what to do. She considered trying to ride the horse back to town and getting John Kenton to come out and fix the buggy. But she was dressed in a long skirt—one of her best ones—and she didn't want to soil it. And riding with a long skirt was just about impossible anyway.

Only one thing to do. She would tie the horse in the woods nearby and hope that no one would steal it and set out on foot along the old trail through the woods between the Layne farm and Larimont—assuming that old trail was still there. The Layne farm was still quite a ways off, and she didn't want to risk walking all the way there to get help. It wasn't the Laynes' responsibility, anyway. She would get John to help.

Unhitching the horse, she led it into the woodland and hitched it in a small clearing beside a gully that had a little murky water in the bottom. Then she lifted her skirts and began walking through the woods, trying to avoid snagging the fabric on the protruding branches around her.

The old trail was still there, just as it had been years before. It was a handy shortcut, about a quarter mile shorter than walking back along the road, and it was wide enough that she didn't have to worry about tearing her dress.

Walking along the old trail that she had often traveled in her girlhood brought back a lot of memories. And it was reassuring, in a way, to think that in all the years since she had last seen Larimont, so many things were still the same. As she walked, she felt a kind of tingling, childish excitement.

She stopped in her tracks, suddenly holding her breath. Up ahead...had she seen someone moving?

She squinted through an opening in the brush alongside the trail. She *had* seen someone moving along toward the old Taylor shed—she had forgotten about that old hermit hideout—and it appeared to be a young man. She felt the impulse to hide. She couldn't tell who the young man was, with his back turned like it was. The only thing she could tell was that he was a fellow of average height, dressed in rather sloppy denims and a blue cotton shirt, with sandy hair hanging long and unkempt over his collar.

Forgetting about her dress's welfare, Sharon slipped as quietly as she could into the woods alongside the trail, settling down in a clump of young cedars.

It wasn't a moment too soon. Without warning, another figure came up the trail from behind. Sharon crouched down and held her breath, waiting for the figure to pass.

It was June Layne, walking alone. Sharon recognized her immediately, in spite of the fact that the last time she had seen her, both of them had been children. But those eyes were the same—there was no mistaking them.

Up ahead, the young man turned and looked down the trail. His face was vaguely familiar, but Sharon couldn't attach a name to it. When he saw June Layne, the young man waved and smiled. June walked toward him.

Sharon couldn't hear what they were saying—but the way he kissed June proved that the meeting was not accidental. And when the pair entered the old shed and closed the door behind them, Sharon realized that she had stumbled upon quite a clandestine affair indeed.

She slipped back onto the trail, moving swiftly in a crouch. She had lost the desire to walk back to town through the forest. When she greeted her old girlhood friend June, she didn't want it to be in such a clumsy situation as this. Some things were best kept secret.

She was already back on the main road again before she discovered that somehow, she had managed to tear her dress. And what's more, her monogrammed handkerchief, one her mother had given her the past Christmas, was gone, probably hanging from some tree limb in the woods back along the trail.

It was too bad. That was her favorite handkerchief. Maybe she would get a chance to come back and look for it, sometime when secret lovers didn't occupy the woods.

Chapter 6

Lawrence Poteet's house stood on the northern side of Larimont, a stark and oppressive structure that was far too large for one man. Behind it stretched only stubble-covered fields, then wild meadows that in the summer bloomed in a profusion of color that stretched to the base of the mountains. But at night, with the few lights that Poteet kept lit shining out of dusty windows and the wide front door dark like a screaming mouth on the house's face, there was no trace of anything warm or inviting about the dwelling.

John hated to admit, it, but it scared him. Though the night was warm, he shivered a bit as he walked up toward the gaping front door.

He knocked with the brass ring hanging on the thick door and imagined he could hear the echo ringing through the empty house—for Lawrence Poteet had little furniture, and little need for it. There was no answer, and John knocked again.

"Who is it?"

"John. John Kenton."

A pause. "You alone?"

"Just like we agreed."

John heard the banker fumbling with the bolt, then the door opened, and Poteet hustled him inside, hurriedly shutting the door. John took off his hat and began to feel even more uncomfortable. Poteet was nervous in even routine situations, but not *this* nervous. John began to wonder what he was about to hear ...and if he really wanted to hear it after all.

"Sit down, John," said Poteet. "Hang your hat here. Can I get you some coffee?"

"No, thanks, Mr. Poteet. I just had some supper. Where should I sit?"

"Here, anywhere. Just relax." Poteet took off his glasses and began wiping them. John found the man's nervousness to be contagious. He sat down in a stuffed maroon chair and immediately began fidgeting.

Poteet poured a glass of water from a pitcher on a low table in the middle of the room and downed it rapidly. Then he sat down across from John in a stiff posture.

"I'm not sure it was good for me to have you here," he said. "It might not be a good thing for me to say the kind of things I've been thinking..."

"Mr. Poteet, I'm only interested in understanding why my father was killed. You can understand why I need to know, can't you? I'm a discreet person, and I won't betray any confidences. I want you to know that."

Poteet nodded. John noticed he was sweating. "That does make a difference, John. It does."

John sat back, waiting for Poteet to begin. He didn't, so John asked a question.

"Mr. Poteet, what kind of suspicions did you and my father have before he was killed? Was it connected with the bank robbery?"

Poteet nodded. "It was. The best thing I know to do is to tell you about the robbery.

"It happened maybe three and a half months ago, about midday. We were just closing down for lunch—had just let the last customer out—when three men, seemingly young, though it was hard to be sure, came in and drew pistols on us. They were masked with old flour sacks pulled over their heads, holes cut for eyes. I couldn't tell a thing about what they looked like.

"The bank had a lot of money in it right then, and they got plenty of it. About seven thousand dollars, I believe. They tied all of us up and took off, locking the door. It took about a half hour for Bill to wiggle out of his ropes and turn us loose, then he took off and got the marshal. But it was too late then—they had gotten away, and nobody had seen anything that could serve as a clue about where they had gone.

"Well, we were all hot to get an investigation going—all of us except Burrell, at least. He seemed upset and angry, but he took it in stride, apparently, giving out little philosophical sayings about fate and so on. He answered a few questions for the marshal, but he didn't help any.

"Bill was the most anxious of any of us to find out who had robbed us, and for several days he was a regular firebrand, asking questions and so on. And every day, Burrell got a little more close-mouthed, a little more discouraging to the idea of tracking down the robbers. He never came out and said anything about stopping the investigation, but he did come close to that, and did everything he could, it seemed, to throw blocks in the path of the marshal, and of Bill, who was conducting as much of an investigation as the marshal himself was. Eventually, the discouragement had its effect on Bill. All at once he stopped asking questions. He seemed glum, even depressed. He had little to say to anybody—especially Burrell. I actually began to worry about him, but he shrugged off any friendly approaches from any of the bank staff. It was shortly after that that Bill was...was killed."

Poteet paused long enough for another drink of water. "I don't know what it was that affected Bill. It was as if he discovered something or figured something out. And I'm sure it had something to do with Burrell."

"Is that all you know?" John probed. "Nothing more specific?"

"Not really...but in a way there is more. You see, it's not just the bank robbery that Burrell seemed to handle differently than he would have a few years back. It's the man in general, his attitude, his work as a whole. He's hardly ever at the bank anymore, and when he is he shuffles most of his work off onto me or some other bank staff member. He goes out for days without explanation and will pack up and leave at a moment's notice and never tell where or why he's going. It's been that way for months now. I think—just conjecture, mind you—that maybe Burrell is seeing someone...a lady, if you take my meaning." Poteet dropped his head. He wasn't the kind of man to talk easily about such matters.

John shook his head. "Burrell having a love affair with someone... That's hard to conceive, somehow. Who?"

"I have no idea. And honestly, I don't know it has a thing to do with the bank robbery or your father's death. All these things may be unrelated. But somehow, I don't think so. Just a gut feeling, I guess. But I really believe there is some sort of connection."

John's voice was low. "Mr. Poteet...are you implying that Burrell had something to do with my father's death?"

Poteet jerked as if the question were a hammer blow. "No, John...surely not. Surely not. He couldn't do something like that..." Poteet's voice trailed off into uncertainty, and John's stomach did a slow turn.

"Mr. Poteet, I can't believe that Burrell would do something like that, either. But I confess I've never liked the man, and certainly had no illusions that he is a saint... But not even a man ten times as unlikeable as he is would be devil enough to kill my father."

"But *somebody* killed your father, John. And in a town this size, it was probably someone who knew him. Don't read too much into what I said about Burrell. I can't really believe he killed your father... I can't believe that, and I won't. But somehow I believe that the *situations* are connected—Burrell's actions over the last few months, his attempts to play down the bank robbery while your father wanted to play it up, Bill's strange change of heart at the end, the way he acted toward Burrell in those last days, the way he expressed suspicions to me—similar suspicions to the ones I've expressed to you—all of those things seem to be tied in. Just how I can't say. But they are...and..."

John waited. "And what?"

"Perhaps I shouldn't say this...but I'm worried."

"About what?"

"About my own safety, John."

"What do you mean?"

Poteet looked away, looking disgusted at himself. "I've said too much, John. I shouldn't have said anything."

"Mr. Poteet, I need to know what you meant."

"I meant nothing. Forget it." The banker refused to look again at John. "I think you should go."

John stood reluctantly. "If that's what you want. Thank you, Mr. Poteet. Maybe we can talk later?"

"I doubt it. Please, John—just go."

John walked to the door and took his hat from the hat tree. He slipped it on his head and stepped out, looking back over his shoulder at Poteet, who was sitting as if in deep thought, staring at his shoes.

Out in the night John walked along until he was on Larimont's main street, pondering the enigmatic things Poteet had told him. He was slightly disappointed at the vagueness of what the banker had said, but intrigued as well, and determined to delve further into the matter.

He could almost taste a solution to the mystery out there somewhere. He could feel it, sense that it was there. If only he could see into the right dark corner, turn over the right stone. He would find that answer.

And from now on his investigation would focus on one person—Frederick Burrell. It was there, he sensed, that the key to this mystery lay.

Lawrence Poteet was dreaming. Or at least he thought he was —in the half-drunken stupor into which he had drunk himself after John Kenton had left, it was hard to tell.

That noise—there it was again. And it was real, definitely no dream. Downstairs, a shuffling sort of noise, as if someone else were in the house.

Poteet felt his heart begin to race. The darkness suddenly became haunted and oppressive, the room intensely hot. His hand groped to his bedside and gripped the wooden handle of his Remington revolver.

Slowly he rose, cringing at the sound of the screaking floorboards at his feet. He moved silently to his bedroom door and, steeling his nerves, threw it open.

Only a dark hall out before him, and a staircase that faded into blackness at the foot of it, down in the living room where he had heard it...or him.

"Who's there?"

Silence. Silence and creeping fear.

"Who is it?"

Still no answer. But Poteet could feel a presence in the house with him. Stories of ghosts flooded in, and he began to tremble. Impossibilities suddenly became likelihoods.

Raising his pistol before him, he moved toward the staircase. After a long pause, he began creeping down the creaking steps, his heart hammering so forcefully that he could almost hear it.

"I've got a gun! I'll use it!" He was bothered by the weakness of his own voice.

He reached the base of the stairs and paused, looking all around. He saw the oil lamp on the table nearby but was too scared to take time out to light it. He would have to put down his gun to do that . . . and when the light filled the room, whom, or what, might it reveal?

Trembling, he moved toward the front door. Maybe the noise had come from outside, just a wind in the trees, or a branch rubbing a window.

Slowly he unbolted and opened the door. The night wind whipped in, rustling his nightshirt and raising chills up his back.

"Who's there?" he said softly.

No answer. He repeated the question, a little more loudly.

The gun was struck from his hand so swiftly, he couldn't even find the voice to scream. Something passed over his eyes, coming down from behind, and then his neck was being constricted, crushed by something rough and tight around it. Tighter, hurting...

The blackness rushed in, and he collapsed. Then a deeper blackness, and a numbness beyond anything he could ever imagine, and a sense of dying.

And then nothing.

Chapter 7

John had tossed nervously all night. His mind had raced, refusing to stop, and he'd suffered with a vague, tense feeling that something was wrong somewhere. He finally settled down to sleep about four o'clock and wound up dreaming he was in a railroad car that was bounding over the edge of a five-hundred-foot bridge, which caused him to jerk awake and wonder if he had yelled.

The darkness was making him nervous tonight, but he had too much pride to admit it to himself and light his bedside lamp. When morning finally seeped in through the gap between his curtains, he relaxed and drifted off to sleep.

He awoke a couple of hours later with the sun much higher and the noise of the street filtering through his slightly open window. There was the creaking of wagon wheels, the music of a woman's voice, the steady *whisk-whisk* of somebody sweeping off a boardwalk. He sat up and rubbed his eyes, yawning. He felt a bit foolish; in the sunlight the phantoms of the nighttime seemed terribly unreal.

John stretched his arms straight up above his head, then stood and rose on his toes, making his ankles pop, stretching his sleepy muscles. He walked over to the ceramic washbasin and splashed his face with water. Rubbing his whiskers, he pondered for a moment the idea of growing a beard, then shook his head. Some other time, maybe. He took a quick and painful cold shave.

John combed his hair and dressed in his last pair of clean trousers, making a mental note to ask Victoria to do some laundry for him today. He hated to push such a menial task onto her, but he would have more important things to occupy him.

John walked out into the hallway and turned the key in his lock, then headed downstairs with his mind on sizzling bacon and coffee. The lobby was empty except for the desk clerk, who was sitting with a cigar in his mouth and a month-old copy of a San Francisco newspaper in his hands. John walked past him, cutting through the heavy haze of cigar smoke and out the front door onto the boardwalk.

Leaning up against a porch column was a woman John didn't know. She was crying.

John slipped past her, looking at her out of the corner of his eye, pretending he didn't notice. He walked into the Rose Cafe and slipped into a seat at the table nearest the door. At the next table sat two men, both sipping coffee and talking in low voices. Without meaning to, John found himself listening to them, at first indifferently, then with sudden interest.

"Hard to believe he would do it. He never showed no inclinations to do such a thing, to my knowledge."

"Must have been awful lonely, more than people figured."

"They said he was hanging from the stair landing, like he'd tied a rope 'round his neck and the other end to the banister, then jumped. Snapped his neck bone like it was thin ice."

"Burrell's closed the bank, I reckon?"

"I reckon. Saw a wreath on the door a few minutes ago."

Elijah Smith, the owner and only waiter of the Rose Cafe, came over to John's table, coffeepot in hand. He poured steaming black liquid into John's mug while John kept his eyes fixed on the two men at the other table.

"Elijah, did something happen last night?"

"I reckon it did! Old Lawrence Poteet...he hung hisself. With your pa gettin' killed and old Lawrence dead, I reckon there must be some kind of curse or somethin' on that bank. Yes, sir—hung hisself."

John felt the color drain out of his face, and suddenly he had no desire for coffee, food, or human company. Without a word he rose and stepped out the door, feeling weak. Elijah Smith looked at him curiously as he left, then shrugged and took John's coffee for himself.

John walked over to the livery stable and sat down on a discarded wooden crate, feeling almost ill. Lawrence Poteet, dead. And by his own hand. That was hard to take in, especially without warning like this.

Without warning...

John frowned down at his boot tips. What was it that Lawrence Poteet had said, just before he rushed John out last night? Something about feeling he wasn't safe...

John jerked to his feet. With a staunch assurance he felt suddenly sure that Lawrence Poteet hadn't hanged himself at all. For one thing, he himself had given John a hint that he wasn't safe, and second—and most important to someone who knew Lawrence Poteet for as long as John had—Poteet would never, if he had a hundred years to try, be able to work up the nerve to snap his neck in two in such an unpleasant way as that man in the cafe had described. No way.

John entered the livery, saddled up Kate, and began riding at a good pace to Victoria's. He wanted to have a talk with her and Sharon, and quickly, for there was apparently a lot to talk about.

If Lawrence Poteet had been killed last night, it was possible, maybe likely, that it stemmed in some way from the fact that he had talked to John about Burrell. John mulled it over until his mind was a thunderstorm. When he rode past the lone tree in the middle of the main street, he felt a vague disgust for Frederick Burrell; by the time he dismounted in Victoria's front yard, he hated him. For it was clear to him now that if the evidence pointed toward any individual in Larimont, that individual was Burrell. Frederick Burrell, leading citizen, dignified banker...murderer?

John grunted a greeting to Victoria and pushed past her into the house, plopping down in a high-backed stuffed chair, with a dark expression on his face. Sharon walked in from the kitchen. John could tell from her looks, and those of Victoria, that they had heard the news already.

"You know about Poteet... Who told you?"

"Mrs. Chaffin next door. She came over right after breakfast with the news."

"Do you believe he hanged himself?"

Victoria looked noncommittal. "I don't know. Do you think he didn't?"

"I was over at his house last night, talking to him. He told me that he was suspicious of Burrell—he never spelled it out, just said he was suspicious. And he was scared and said that he wasn't safe. I don't think he killed himself, Victoria—he couldn't have. He didn't have that kind of courage...and he was truly scared."

"This is horrible..." Sharon sank down in a chair. "This is so terrible. I came and found that Bill Kenton was dead, that my own uncle was shot to death and labeled as a killer—and now *this*."

"Settle down, both of you," ordered Victoria. "It looks like there's something very dangerous and very underhanded going on around this town. We know that Bill was murdered, we know that Scruff never could have been the killer. And now it looks like Lawrence Poteet was murdered as well. Let's talk this over...put together what facts we have."

She pulled up a straight chair before John and motioned for Sharon to pull in closer. The group formed a triangle all around the low, central table in the room, and Victoria sat back and crossed her arms in a no-nonsense pose.

"We've got a few facts," she said. "Let's piece them together.

"First, we know that Bill was suspicious of Burrell in his last days of life. And we know that someone killed Bill—not Scruff Smithers, who could never have done such a thing. And now Lawrence Poteet is dead, probably murdered as well. And he, too, was suspicious of Burrell.

"All of that points toward a quite obvious suspect—Burrell himself. As for his motive, I have no idea. And whether he did the murder himself is something else we don't know. He could have hired it out."

"The motive is the big question," said John. "Why would he do it?"

"John, what did Poteet tell you about his suspicions toward Burrell? Bill never would describe his in any specific way."

"He said, for one thing, that he believed Burrell was having some sort of hidden love affair with some woman in this town," John said. "Such things as that can become motives for murder, you know."

Victoria was intrigued. "A love affair! That *is* interesting! Do you have any idea who?"

"Not a clue. I don't even know it's true," John said.

Victoria suddenly became thoughtful. "John, you recall your visit with Myrtle Layne the other day, and how she said she hadn't seen Burrell in three weeks, and he claimed he had just visited her? Have you thought that out?"

"Victoria! You don't believe Myrtle Layne and Burrell—"

"Don't be ridiculous. But think...Myrtle Layne isn't the lying type—she probably was telling you the truth about not seeing Burrell. And obviously Burrell didn't see Alexander Layne, because he was away from the house. So who does that leave?"

John's eyes widened. "June Layne!"

Sharon gave out a sudden, involuntary yelp, and all eyes turned toward her.

"What is it, Sharon?" asked Victoria.

"I'm sorry. It's just that I...well, I know at least a little something about June Layne, something I didn't plan on telling anyone. I mean, it didn't seem to be something I should say...but I suppose I must.

"I saw June Layne yesterday, just before John came out and fixed the buggy wheel. I was walking through the woods, heading back for town, when I saw her meeting a man at the old Taylor shed. They went inside—I know I ran in on a secret lovers' meeting. It was obvious."

"Burrell?" John queried.

"No...a sandy-haired, sort of sloppy-looking fellow. Long hair."

Victoria's mouth dropped open. "Edgar Burrell!"

"That's sure who it sounds like," said John.

"Edgar Burrell?" Sharon said. "Isn't that Frederick Burrell's son?"

"It sure is," said John. "Do you realize what this means? It means that if Frederick Burrell is having a love affair with June Layne, then his own son is having an affair with the same woman. Now, doesn't *that* throw some interesting possibilities into the ring!"

"And it also establishes a tie between Burrell and the

Layne family. Wasn't it Alexander Layne who accused my uncle of murdering your father?"

"Indeed, he did," John said. He rose. "I think it's time I had a good, thorough talk with the marshal. To me, this is some interesting evidence. The law needs to take a very close look at Mr. Frederick Burrell, and waste no time about it."

An hour later, John was sitting in Drew Roberts's office, doing his best to keep from losing his temper as the marshal took what he'd given him and tore it to bits.

"Evidence? You don't have any," the lawman said around the butt of an unlighted cigar. "Think about what you're saying. You're accusing one of the most prominent men in this town, a man everyone respects and who has no criminal record of any sort, of being involved in some way in murder. Now, think this out, John. You've got Scruff Smithers's niece there willing to do anything at all to make her uncle look better. And let's face it—you've got yourself trying to prove some fool notion that somebody else killed your father when all the evidence points to Scruff. You've got an isolated event or two with the Burrell family—which may or may not be true, and even if they are don't show anything conclusive.

"John, I appreciate the fact that you're angry about what happened to your father, and the fact that because you're helpless to do anything about it you want to stir up something just to make yourself feel better. But this is an agency of law, and I can't just go out and make an accusation against a man like Frederick Burrell based on speculation.

"Like your notion that Lawrence Poteet was murdered— good Lord, man, the evidence all points toward suicide. So that's the way I have to treat it. I have to follow the evidence. Now, is there anything else I can do for you?"

There wasn't. So John left, feeling strangely abashed, and

somehow sad—mostly because the marshal's words had halfway convinced him that perhaps he was wrong after all.

John stalked on out the door and into the street, not even noticing the figure that sat sprawled on the bench on the front porch of the jail, a newspaper raised before him. As John walked down the street to where Kate was hitched in front of the gunsmith's shop, the paper lowered, and bleary, pale eyes stared after him.

———

Frederick Burrell peeled off two twenty-dollar bills and handed them to the man before him. Callused, nervous hands grasped the bills as if the man feared someone would get them before he could.

"Thank you, Jesse. I appreciate you keeping your ears open. You were right to come to me."

"You're welcome, Mr. Burrell. And I'll tell you anything else I hear. That I promise."

"You do and you'll get more of what I gave you," said Burrell with a smile. "It could be a lot more."

The man nodded and scurried toward the door. Burrell watched him head for the saloon, until a figure stepped into the open doorway, smiling at him.

"Edgar—what do you want?"

"Nothing, *Daddy.*" The word had a contemptuous ring. "Just interested in what your little friend said."

"You've been eavesdropping? What in the hell makes you think that you can—"

"Sounds like John Kenton may be trouble for you, don't it, Daddy. Real trouble."

Frederick Burrell stood silently for a moment, stewing in anger at his son. Then, suddenly, he seemed to decide it wasn't worth it.

"Looks like it," he said. "Looks like it."

Silently, still grinning, Edgar Burrell slipped out through the door again. His father bit his lip, then moved over toward his office, where he shut the door behind him.

Chapter 8

That night John ate supper alone in the Rose Cafe, pondering the things the marshal had said, looking hard at himself to see if all his checking and suspicions and questions had come not from any real case against Frederick Burrell, but from some hidden desire to undo what he couldn't undo, to bring a man back from the dead.

Throughout the meal he really began to think that possibly that was it. It was when he stepped out in the moonlight and felt a cool breeze from the mountains whip against his face that he knew it wasn't.

There really *was* something here that was beyond the obvious. He wasn't digging in a dry well. Frederick Burrell had something to do with his father's death—he sensed it, he knew it. And no matter how long it took, he would prove it.

Back in a city many miles from here a job was awaiting his return, and a daily cycle of life was waiting to be resumed.

It would just have to keep on waiting. There was a more important job to be done here, and it *would* be done.

John walked around the town, enjoying the feeling of his muscles stretching and his blood racing. The night air was delicious, like a refreshing drink, and the darkness was restful. The confidence he had lost earlier at the marshal's office began to return. Before John realized it, he had walked away the entire evening. Feeling pleasantly weary, he returned to the Donaho and climbed the stairs to his room.

He thrust the key in the lock and pushed open the door. He stepped inside and sensed the other presence there only a moment before the universe came crashing in on his skull and he collapsed in a senseless heap on the floor.

Back in her room at Victoria's house, Sharon Bradley was dreaming about a cat.

It was an especially large cat, and a mad one. It was standing with its back arched high and its fanged mouth spitting, and it faced a man with claws for hands and the face of Frederick Burrell.

The cat leaped with a squall on the figure, and for a moment the world was a hurricane of fur and blood and wild screams, and then as suddenly the cat was gone and Sharon saw herself running through a dark forest with Burrell on her heels, and she was having trouble keeping ahead of him.

She awoke trembling. With a slight moan of horror, she sat up in her bed, staring at the open door that led out into the upstairs hallway.

A figure was in the door—a large, black figure—and he wore a mask.

Sharon opened her mouth to scream, and hard though she tried, she found her voice was gone. And the figure was approaching her slowly, then with sudden, heart-stopping rapidity.

Rough hands grasped her wrists and forced her back down into the bed, and Sharon felt the roughness of the coarse cloth mask against her cheek. The weight of the man fell on her full force, knocking the breath from her and giving her a voice again.

She sent up a piercing, wailing scream, only to have a strong hand crush firmly and painfully down on her throat and cut off her voice.

"Give it up!" the figure growled in her ear in a voice that sounded like a lizard's hiss. "Give it up!"

Sharon's hands flailed at her sides like those of a person drowning, her right hand digging uselessly into the sheet, her left hand groping about for something, anything. The kerosene lantern fell to the floor, the chimney shattering. Something else clacked to the floor beside it.

A knitting needle...one of the needles Sharon had been knitting with just before she went to sleep...

Her hand flailed wildly in search of that second needle, but she couldn't find it. The figure was crushing hard on top of her, and it began to sink in just what he was going to do...

She found it. Her fist closed around the base of the needle, and with all the force that was in her she raised it high and drove the sharp point down.

The scream that erupted from the man atop her was agonized and horrible. The grip on her neck relaxed, and the figure pushed itself up. Sharon's hand slipped off the needle, and the figure rose to his feet, staggering toward the bedroom door, the needle thrust grotesquely into his back, rooted horribly deep.

The figure tried to reach behind as it walked, and its hands grasped the air in a vain effort to get hold of the needle. Like a fading nightmare the figure stumbled away toward the staircase, disappearing into the darkness. Sharon heard the sound of boots bumping roughly down the stairs, and the echo of groans through the house. Then came the noise of the front door opening, followed by silence.

She lay for a long moment in a strange paralysis, holding

her breath. Then something broke inside her and she screamed, long and loud.

Sharon leaped from the bed and ran out onto the staircase. Her foot squished in something warm and slick...blood. Ignoring it, she rushed down the stairs and into Victoria's room.

The moonlight streaming through the window revealed the older woman's form crumpled on the floor. Sharon gave a low, almost whispered cry, and moved to her side, almost afraid to touch her for fear she would find her lifeless.

"Victoria?"

She imagined she heard a faint moan. She touched Victoria's hand...it was warm. Touching her wrist, she felt a pulse.

Carefully she rolled Victoria over onto her back. She looked around the room, and her eyes fastened on a glass of water on Victoria's bedside table. She scurried over and grabbed it, dipping her fingers into the water and bathing Victoria's brow.

After a long moment the woman's eyes fluttered open. In the moonlight Sharon could see the dull incomprehension in those eyes liven to terror as Victoria remembered. She looked up into Sharon's face like an insane woman, her lips pulled back to reveal gritted teeth, then relaxed as she recognized the young woman.

"Sharon...oh, God..."

"It's all right, Victoria. He's gone...and we're all right."

Sharon sensed rather than heard the figure that loomed suddenly in the bedroom doorway. All her strength drained from her like water out of a broken bottle, and she turned a pale face toward the doorway.

It was John. It took almost ten seconds for it to really sink in.

John struck a match and lit the lamp in the room, flooding it with a welcome light. Victoria managed to sit up, obviously groggy, and Sharon collapsed into a heap beside her, breathing hard.

"Are you both all right?" John asked. "Were you harmed?"

"I'm fine," answered Sharon in a very uncertain voice. "It's Victoria I'm worried about."

"I'm all right," Victoria said. "I took a good blow on the head, but I'm all right."

"Where did he go?" John said.

"He went out the front." Sharon paused. "I stabbed him."

"You what?"

"I stabbed him...with a knitting needle. In the back."

John didn't quite know what to say to that. He finally managed to stammer, "Did you kill him?"

"No. He went out. He might be dead now. I think I hurt him bad."

John shivered. "I can't believe it. Who would have thought it would come to this? But you know, this proves there's something to what we've been thinking. Somebody knows that we're checking into all of this, and they have something they want to keep hidden very badly. I was attacked, too, in my own room. Someone is trying hard to intimidate us."

Victoria was beginning to come out of her daze, and as she did, she grew shaky and frightened. John helped her to the bed, where she lay down, pressing her hand across her brow.

"Don't you think we ought to get the marshal?" Sharon asked.

"No!" snapped John. "We don't want him involved in this. What could we tell him? We have no proof, now that whoever-it-was is gone. And I don't trust the marshal now, besides."

Sharon thought for a moment. "There's blood on the stairs. I stepped in it."

"Yeah, but whose blood? The way Drew Roberts feels about my notions and suspicions just now, I think he'd probably accuse us of setting the whole thing up just to make it look like whoever killed my father was still loose."

"John..."

"What is it?"

Victoria held up a torn sheet of paper. "Just now... I found this pinned to my gown."

John took the crumpled paper and unfolded it. On it were words scrawled crudely in splotched ink:

GIVE IT UP.

CHAPTER 9

Drew Roberts grunted as he thrust the shovel deep into the soft earth atop the grave and winced as a drop of sweat burned his eye. Tossing out the heap of red dirt to the graveside, he paused and pulled out a checkered handkerchief, with which he mopped his forehead.

Beside him stood J. W. Warner, caretaker of the church and cemetery. He leaned over the grave with an intent look on his face.

"Any sign of anything?"

"Not yet," replied the marshal.

It had been Warner that had called the marshal out of his bed this morning, excited and almost babbling. There was evidence, he said, of someone tampering with one of the graves in the cemetery—fresh dirt was heaped upon it, as if it had been dug into in the night.

Grave robbers, the caretaker theorized. A body had been stolen during the night.

Drew Roberts reserved his judgment until he saw the grave. Warner had told the truth. The grave had obviously been bothered. But the grave robber theory was doubtful, the marshal felt. Only one way to be sure, though. And so, he had started digging.

After catching his breath, he once more thrust the shovel into the slightly moist dirt. Warner leaned even farther over the grave, watching impatiently.

The marshal's shovel struck something soft and resilient. Puzzled, he pulled back the shovel and dropped to his knees, digging in the dirt with his hands.

As the dirt was pushed back, something beneath it began to take a shape. Frowning, the marshal scraped away at the shape, removing more dirt. And in a moment, he jumped back involuntarily, shocked.

A face looked back at him. It was a pale face, frozen in an expression of pain. It took him a moment to recognize it, and before he could say the name Warner beat him to it.

"Sherman Horner," he whispered. "Sherman Horner, dead and buried!"

"He wasn't dead yesterday," Roberts said. "I saw him myself about dusk. This happened last night."

He began digging further, clearing the dirt away from the body with both the shovel and his hands. In about ten minutes he had fully exposed the body, dressed in a checked blue shirt and faded work pants. The boots were gone.

"Help me pull him out, J. W.," the marshal said. Reluctantly, the caretaker, who had always been a little squeamish around dead bodies, stepped down into the open grave beside the marshal, trying to avoid stepping on the body.

The two men grasped the figure and pulled it upward. Dirt flaked off the corpse, whose mouth dropped open as the head tilted grotesquely back. After the body was free of the dirt, the pair heaved it up and out of the grave, plopping it face down on the grass. It was then that the deep red splotch of blood on the corpse's back became visible.

"Look at that!" exclaimed the marshal. "He's sure enough been stabbed!"

J. W. Warner wasn't looking. His face was pale, and he was feeling quite weak, so he looked away from the body and down the road. He noticed a figure approaching and elbowed the marshal.

"Somebody's coming."

The marshal turned and saw John Kenton walking through the gateway of the cemetery fence. The lawman pursed his lips and muttered a very quiet curse.

"Marshal, I never thought I'd see you robbing a grave," John said. The derisive tone in his voice was apparent to the marshal, but it didn't bother him. He disliked John Kenton as much as the young man disliked him.

"Official business," said the marshal. "I'm going to have to ask you to leave."

"That's Sherman Horner, isn't it?" said John. "What killed him?"

"I asked you to leave," the marshal said. "And I'd advise you to get rid of that gun."

John glanced down at the Colt strapped to his hip. He had owned the gun for years, but this was the first time he had ever worn it. After the prior night's attack, he didn't plan to be without it, marshal's orders to the contrary or not.

"A lot of men in this town wear guns," John returned. "There's no law here that says I can't. It looks to me like Sherman has been stabbed...and I take it somebody buried him in this grave. That's real interesting. Sherman Horner...he's an old buddy of Edgar Burrell, isn't he?"

"I told you to leave, Kenton," the marshal snapped. "You'd best do it now, before I start wondering just how much you know about this body here."

"Sorry, Marshal," John said. "You've already convinced me that I don't know a thing about investigating crimes. You know, I think it's too bad old Scruff Smithers is dead...he would have been a handy peg to hang this murder on. Or do you think maybe it's suicide? Maybe

Sherman stuck himself in the back and buried his own body."

John's sarcasm was eating at the marshal, and he stepped forward. "You'd best watch that mouth, Kenton. You're on the verge of getting locked up."

"Don't worry, Marshal. I'm leaving. I'll leave you to figure out what happened to old Sherman. But if you want a tip from an old armchair detective like me, talk to Edgar Burrell or Jerry Horner. I've got a feeling they'll have something to tell you about this."

John turned and stalked away, knowing that he should have kept his mouth shut. But the marshal irritated him, and he just hadn't been able to restrain himself. And besides, finding out just who it was who broke into Sharon and Victoria's house last night put a whole new twist on things.

The Horner brothers, Sherman and Jerry, had been friends of Edgar Burrell for many years. It was obvious that more than one person had been involved in last night's incident, for some second intruder had knocked out John in his hotel room, and someone had buried Sherman's body.

It was, John felt sure, either Jerry Horner or Edgar Burrell. Most likely both.

Edgar Burrell. Jerry and Sherman Horner. Three men. Just like the three men who had robbed the Larimont Bank. It was intriguing. A whole new twist on this business was becoming apparent.

If Edgar Burrell had robbed his own father's bank, as unbelievable as that sounded, that would provide a good explanation for why Frederick Burrell had squelched an investigation of the robbery. If Burrell knew that his son was responsible, he might want to protect him.

But somehow that didn't sit quite right. Burrell had never been known as a man with a lot of affection for his middle son. In fact, his low treatment of him, along with a few public slurs about Edgar's general "sorriness," as folks put, it, had made the rounds of Larimont gossip many times over the years. Burrell had often publicly stated that he figured Edgar would wind up either breaking rocks or stretching a rope. It didn't make sense that he would be protecting him.

But apart from that, there was yet another possibility that this opened up, and an even more important one.

It might not be Frederick Burrell who was behind the deaths of Kenton and Lawrence Poteet. It might be the Horner brothers, or perhaps Edgar Burrell. Perhaps all of them together.

John was lurched out of his thought by a tall figure that stepped out before him from the door of the hardware store. It was Frederick Burrell, and his expression was stern.

"John, I need to talk with you," he said. "Now."

John looked at the banker with an expression of contempt. His own nerve was surprising him today.

"What's the problem?" he said.

"You're the problem—or rather, some of the things you've been saying. Let's go to my office and talk."

"No."

"*I* beg your pardon?"

"I said no. If you want to talk to me, then I'm here. Talk."

The banker's eyes snapped. "I'll not listen to impudence, you slanderer! I should have you thrashed for what you've said, accusing me to the marshal of being a murderer!"

John smiled coldly at the banker. "Now, I find that interesting. How do you manage to know what's told to the marshal in confidence?"

"Voices carry past closed doors—especially through open windows. You were overheard by a friend of mine, and I've got plenty of friends in this town. I'm afraid you might find yourself in a state of isolation here if you persist in spreading slanderous rumors."

"I'll persist in investigating the death of my father, and of Lawrence Poteet, sir," John replied. "And I'll do it no matter what the cost to myself. If you're innocent, you have nothing to fear. But if you're guilty, then I'll find you out."

Burrell was silent for a moment. "I can see that there is no point in continuing this conversation. You're mad. Literally mad."

Burrell pushed John aside and walked past him. A few steps down the boardwalk, he turned. "And as for the death of Lawrence Poteet, everyone knows that it was suicide."

"Oh, really? Like my father's suicide? That's what some said at first, you know."

"So I heard." Burrell turned again and walked away. John watched him, then continued on his walk, trying to piece together in his mind all he had found out so far.

"Old Pa really gave you a talking-to, didn't he, Kenton?" came a voice from an alley to John's right. John was slightly startled to hear the unexpected voice, and even more startled when he turned and looked into the face of Edgar Burrell.

Edgar was a sandy-haired, unkempt sort of fellow, whose hair was always a shade too long and shaggy, looking as if he combed it mostly with his fingers. His face was rather broad and full in the jaws, and always present was a disarmingly friendly smile. His eyes were narrow and edged with slight wrinkles that were all the more prominent because of his smile, and his shoulders were broad and muscled—a phenomenon John couldn't account for, since Edgar Burrell was known to have never done a day's work in his life.

He was about John's age and height, and had a sort of easygoing, slump-shouldered bearing that made him look like the kind of fellow it would be easy to like. But John—and the rest of the population of Larimont who had known Edgar Burrell any length of time—knew that Edgar's true personality was not as pleasant as his appearance might initially indicate, and that in all the Larimont Valley there wasn't a lazier, more generally worthless bum than he was.

"Hello, Edgar."

"And hello to you, John Kenton. Long time no see. You want a beer?"

"It's a bit early. ..."

"Hell, live a little! I'll buy."

John shrugged and accepted the offer, thinking to himself that he might uncover something informative by talking to Edgar Burrell.

Together they walked across the street to the Larimont Saloon. The saloonkeeper, Ebenezer Drury, met them at the door with a full dustpan and a broom.

"Howdy, fellers. Sorry, ain't open yet."

"Eb, you'll let me in, won't you? I'll pay you extra for a good beer for me and my friend here. You remember John Kenton, don't you?"

Old Ebenezer squinted in John's face. "Well, I'll be! Good to see you, John. Sorry about your pa."

"Thank you, sir. But look, if you're not open for business, we can move on elsewhere."

"Nah, come on in," the other said. "I'll give you a beer in memory of your pa and all the business he never gave me. Never did see that man take a drink. A dry, dry man where liquor was concerned."

Edgar and John followed Ebenezer into the saloon and sat down at a table beside the front window, a red-checkered affair about halfway up, something like a stained-glass window. The light streamed in above, illuminating dust particles stirred up by Ebenezer's sweeping of moments before.

The saloonkeeper brought out two beers in heavy glass mugs and sat them before them on the table, then shuffled off to the rear stockroom, where he began banging around on some unknown but noisy task.

"Pretty little lady you been running around with," said Edgar, grinning at John and taking a deep swallow of beer. He wound up with a foam mustache, which he didn't bother to wipe off.

John felt irked at Edgar's comment, and suddenly defensive of Sharon. He wasn't about to engage in a leering conversation.

"She's pretty. That's true."

"I reckon! What's her name? Sharon something?"

"That's right."

"Real fine-looking female, she is."

John stared coldly at Edgar. "Did you know Sherman Horner is dead?"

The smile didn't fade. "No... but then, I ain't surprised. Old Sherman, he probably tried to jump some old drunk or something ... is that what happened? Ain't hung around with him in four or five years."

A lie. John knew it, too, for his father had made mention of Edgar and his two cohorts in one of the last letters he had written him. And it was obvious that Sherman Horner's death was no surprise to the grinning young roughneck.

John took a sip of his beer, and decided that beer for breakfast was an idea unlikely to catch on. Edgar sat grinning at him, eyes crinkling. John stared back at him with hardly a blink. As defiant as he felt this morning, there wasn't anybody who was likely to stare him down.

"John, old friend, let me be blunt with you. I hear that you're accusing my old man of killing your pa or something like that. How much would it be worth to you to shut up and cut off all this checking around you been doing?"

So this was it. A bribe. John found Edgar's open dishonesty somewhat refreshing. At least one knew where he stood with Edgar Burrell.

"Is there something worth keeping hidden that you don't want me to find?" asked John, mirroring Edgars smile.

"Let's just say that nobody likes having his family probed into like you been doing," said Edgar. "I'm concerned that you don't go worrying my old man, you know. Fellow's got to look out for his own father, don't you see."

"Edgar, you intrigue me. And you sure make me feel certain I'm on the right track. As for your money, I don't want it."

Edgar Burrell reached into his pocket and pulled out a stack of bills, bound together by a paper wrapper plainly marked "Larimont Bank." John couldn't believe it.

Edgar read his expression of surprise, and apparently took it to be shock at the sight of so much money in one place, for he grinned even more broadly back at John.

"Sort of hard to resist when you see it lying out in front of you, ain't it?" he asked.

"Where did you get that money?" John asked.

"Got a rich daddy."

"Don't you keep your money in the bank? You always carry it around like that?"

"Don't trust banks."

"They can be robbed—right?"

"So I hear."

"Where did you get that band on the money?"

"Off my old man's desk. Listen—you want the money or not?"

"Did your father kill my father, or pay to have it done?"

"That's a hell of a question."

"I guess it is. How about an answer?"

Edgar reached out and retrieved his money, thrusting it back into his pocket. "You're a bigger fool than I took you for, Kenton. Terrible big fool."

John stood, making sure Edgar saw the Colt at his side. "No, Edgar. The fool is whoever killed my father—because one way or the other, I'm going to get him. You can bet on that."

John pushed out the door and into the sunlight. Inside, Edgar Burrell smiled and shook his head. He drained his beer, reached across the table, and took John's still-full mug and began drinking that beer as well, looking ever more thoughtful as he did.

It looked as if John Kenton was going to take a lot of convincing before he left Larimont. A lot of convincing.

Chapter 10

"The journal!" John exclaimed. "Why didn't I think about the journal?"

John leaped up from the table in Victoria's dining room and tossed his napkin down on the plate, while Victoria stared at him with wide eyes and Sharon froze in place with a forkful of eggs halfway to her mouth.

"What are you talking about?" Victoria asked.

"The journal...my father always kept a journal," he said. "He wrote in it daily, like clockwork. It was a pretty secret thing, too. He never let me see it, and he always kept it locked in his safe."

Victoria began to understand. "And if it was in the safe," she said, "then it might have survived the fire!"

"That's right," John stated. "And I'm willing to bet that it contains something of my father's suspicions about Burrell, maybe some things that we've overlooked or never known. It's worth checking into."

"But even if the safe is there, how can you get into it?" Sharon asked.

"Easy," said John. "My father gave me the combination years ago, so I could have access to it when he died. He kept his important papers there, or at least his more personal ones. The others are at the bank."

"I never realized that Bill kept a journal," said Victoria, looking wistful. "I wonder if he ever wrote anything about, well, about *me* in there?"

"He probably did," said John. "He really viewed that journal as a totally private thing, kind of the record of his most personal thoughts. You know, he made me promise once that when he died I would destroy it and never read it." John paused. "I guess I'll have no choice but to break that promise. I've got to. I won't read any more than I have to—to see if I can find some solution to this mystery in it. Then I'll destroy it, just like he would have wanted. I feel I owe him that much."

"Why would anyone write his thoughts down every day, only to have them destroyed in the end?" Sharon asked. "I've always wondered about that. I don't think I could ever keep a journal—if I did I couldn't be honest about all I put in there."

"Me either," said John. "But my father was different. He never kept the journal until after my mother died. It was a replacement of sorts for her, I guess. Something he could share with in a way he didn't share at any other time. It filled a need for him."

"I can understand that," said Victoria. "When Daniel died, I felt terribly empty—like I could never talk to anyone again. Then I met Bill, and things were different. When your dearest loved one dies, you have a void inside. Bill filled that for me. Now he's gone, too."

"But maybe, in his journal, he's left part of himself behind," John said. "I'm going to my father's house. I'll let you know what I find."

Slipping his hat on his head, he left by way of the back door to the stable, where he saddled and mounted his horse.

Kicking his heels into her flanks, he sent Kate down the road at a trot, her hooves kicking up dust behind.

He had moved into Victoria s house the night before, for after the attack it was obviously not safe for the two ladies to be staying alone. He didn't know how much safer things were with him there, but at least he felt more secure, both about them and about himself.

At his father's burned-out house, John dismounted and tethered his horse to a willow, then trotted toward the blackened structural shell. Skirting around the left side, he approached the portion of the house where his father had kept his safe.

It wasn't as badly burned as the other sections of the house, and a charred wall still stood there, for the most part intact. Stepping over the foundation, John stepped inside, his boot crunching ash beneath him.

He began to feel dismayed as he looked at the devastation all around him. The fire that had burned down this house had been a hot one—and although the safe surely must have made it through the blaze, there was no guarantee that the papers inside hadn't burned. What was more—and he hadn't thought of this before—the blaze might have melted the lock workings together, making it impossible to get into it without some sort of cutting equipment or dynamite.

Feeling less assured than before, John began moving aside burnt, fallen timbers and kicking away heaps of ashes. It took him only a little while to locate the safe, a blackened, rusty-looking relic of what it had been the last time he had seen it.

John knelt down before the safe, squinting as he peered at the combination lock. The paint had been seared off it, but he could still make out the numbers.

His fingers turned the dial. He frowned at the rough, jerky way the dial moved. Most likely the works of the lock had been damaged by heat.

In the forest about three hundred yards to the northwest, there was a rustling, almost slithering sound. John turned, but saw nothing except a movement in the branches of a young pine. Probably the wind or a dog. He resumed his work.

Breathless, he slowly lifted the handle of the safe door. With a rasping, creaking sound, it fought against him for a moment, then clicked completely up. John exhaled, smiling. The safe was open.

As he pulled open the door, a shower of ashes were sucked out around him. His heart fell. The papers inside were a black heap of useless ash.

He delved into the heap of black material, and his hand touched the edge of a book. Pulling it out, he recognized a now-seared copy of *Pilgrim's Progress* that his father always kept locked away, convinced that this particular edition was rare enough to be valuable. If it had been, it was no longer. John tossed it aside.

Reaching again into the pile of ashes, he felt a slimmer volume beneath the spot where the previous book had been. He pulled it out and dusted it off, and a smile broke across his face.

The journal. One corner burned off—the last few pages missing, but for the most part in one piece. He touched the cover, starting to open the book.

There was a sudden cracking sound from somewhere behind him, and immediately the safe rang out and John felt an uncomfortable concussion.

For a moment he sat staring almost stupidly at the safe door, wondering what in the devil had happened.

A shot. A shot had struck the safe door. . . .

Instinctively he rolled to the side just as another shot ripped above him and plunked into a blackened wall stud that poked out above the foundation. John was covered immediately with black, gummy ash. Diving behind a heap of rubble, he drew his Colt.

He had seen the powder smoke of that last shot. Someone was firing at him from the forest. Popping up like a gallery target, he fired a quick shot toward the spot from where the fire had come.

His bullet ripped harmlessly through the trees. Immediately two other quick shots rang out from some distance over, and John felt the lead sing past his ear. He dropped down again, teeth gritted. That had been far too close.

"Who are you?" he hollered. "What do you want?"

The only answer was silence. John figured that whoever was in the forest was probably moving again, trying to find a spot where he could get a better shot.

John looked around for better cover, struggling against panic. He saw the stones of the foundation sticking up behind him, and he realized the broken remains of the wall could serve as a protective screen.

Holding his breath, he leaped up, trying to move fast but feeling as if he was moving slowly, as in a dream. His foot slipped on the ashes beneath his boot, and he almost fell. Another shot blasted from the forest, and another bullet zinged overhead. John regained his footing and leaped over the wall, dropping to the dirt.

Quickly he replaced the spent cartridge in his gun with a new bullet. Then he peered carefully around the edge of the burnt wall.

He caught sight of something moving in the thickness of the brush, and he squeezed off a shot at it. Whether he hit it or not he couldn't tell.

Three rapid shots exploded from the forest, and the wood in the wall beside him snapped and spat out splinters and dust as the hot slugs tore through it. He dropped to his face on the ground, feeling utterly terrified for a few moments, then so angry that his fear was overcome.

He jerked upright and emptied four cylinders of his

pistol toward the forest, squinting over the barrel with his lips pulled back in a tight snarl over his gritted teeth. And as he ducked again, he caught sight of a figure approaching from the opposite side of the farm, across the open area east of the road. The figure bore a rifle—and looked a lot like Alexander Layne.

John quickly reloaded, then rolled to the other side of the expanse of wall. Rising, he fired off a quick shot at the part of the forest he figured his enemy must have reached, and caught a glimpse at the same time, from the corner of his eye, of Alexander Layne dropping to his belly behind a boulder and leveling his rifle toward the forest where the hidden assailant was.

Toward the forest...

John realized that Alexander Layne hadn't come to help the hidden attacker but to defend John against him. John watched gratefully as Layne poured a withering, hot fusillade toward the forest. Judging from the steadiness of his fire, John figured that Layne, unlike himself, could see at whom he was firing.

John himself fired off two more shots. A sudden silence ensued, lasting about ten seconds. Then Layne's voice called.

"John Kenton! Are you all right?"

"Well enough! Who's shooting at me?"

"Don't know. Keep a sharp eye—I'm coming to join you!"

Layne leaped up and scurried, with his head low, toward the burned-out house. John expected to see more powder flashes from the forest, but none came. Layne dropped beside him, panting.

"Whew! I didn't know what would happen just then!"

Layne was different, John realized. Something had changed in his eyes, his speech, his manner, since the last time he'd seen him.

"What's going on here?" John asked. "Did you catch sight of whoever's out there?"

"Not enough to recognize him," Layne replied. "You know, I'm mighty glad I decided to follow you when I saw you ride past. Else I wouldn't have been close enough to help you out here."

John nodded. He looked carefully across the foundation wall toward the woods. Nothing.

After a long wait, Layne said, "Think he's gone?"

"Seems like it. Can't be sure, though."

"He might be moving around, trying to get behind us. We'd best get away from here."

"Where's your horse, Alexander?"

"On the other side of that rise yonder. I left him there when I heard the shots, and came on afoot."

"And my horse is over there," John said, pointing toward the spooked Kate, who pulled restlessly at her ties.

"We ought to make a break for it," said Layne. "A very careful break, with heads low. And if you would, I'd appreciate it if you'd give me a hitch over to my horse."

"I can do better than that," said John, and quickly explained a plan that had Layne nodding in agreement once he'd heard it.

John stuck the journal under his arm and held it tightly against his body. Together he and Layne came to their feet and darted around the edge of the house toward John's horse. No shots came from the woods. They reached the horse, and John quickly unhitched her.

He leaped astride the saddle with the dexterity of a Wild West showman, while Layne stayed on the ground, keeping the horse between himself and the woods. John sagged his body sideways, Indian-style, and kept as much of himself shielded by Kate's body as he could. He set Kate into a slow trot, praying the saddle cinch, and his straining legs, would hold.

Still no gunfire. Layne and John traveled, John swung to the right from his saddle and Layne keeping pace on foot, over the top of a gentle swell of land to the northeast, until they reached Laynes horse and were out of sight and range of whoever had fired from the forest. All was silent.

John pulled himself upright in the saddle and let out a long, low sigh.

"He's gone now, whoever he was," Layne said. "I suppose he didn't like the odds of two against one." Layne mounted. "What were you doing at the house, John?"

John hesitated, still unsure even after what had just happened that he could trust Layne.

Layne read his suspicions. "Don't worry, John. Things are different now. I'm not going to run and hide from you anymore. Not for any reason, or any person. You can trust me."

John paused, then decided that indeed he would trust Layne. "I was looking for my father's journal," he said, "hoping I could find something in it to give me a clue about... all of this."

"And did you find it?"

John pulled the book from beneath his arm and displayed it to Layne.

Layne looked at it and nodded. "Come to my place. Nobody will bother you there, and you can look it over. Do you trust me?"

John thought it over one last time. "I trust you," he said.

Chapter 11

June Layne met John and her father at the door. The look she gave the pair was peculiar. But she said nothing as the two men brushed past her and entered a spare room, pulling the door shut after them.

Layne motioned John to a chair and pulled up one for himself. John looked at Alexander Layne uncertainly, wondering again if he should really trust a man who had acted so strangely before.

"I know," Layne said, noticing John's look. "You want me to explain myself. Well, I suppose you have a right to that."

"Alexander, we've been friends for years. Why did you treat me like you did before?"

Layne smiled sadly. "A bad conscience. Guilt."

"Over what?"

Layne's voice was low. "Scruff Smithers. It was me that told the marshal I saw Scruff Smithers riding out to your father's house before the murder and riding back just before the fire started."

"Was it true?"

"Yes. I did see him. But I know as well as you do that he didn't kill your father. He couldn't have. Not Scruff."

"So the marshal twisted what you'd said?"

"Not really. You see, I told him that I tried to call down Scruff, and that he rode by me like the devil . . . and that he looked scared to death."

"And that was a lie?"

"Yes."

"But why, Alexander?"

Layne suddenly sounded bitter. "Because of Frederick Burrell, that's why! Because he told me what to say about Scruff, and I said it!"

John felt a chill. "I still don't understand."

Layne looked at the floor. "Burrell holds the mortgage on my land, John. And I haven't done well over the last few years, and with my wife sick and all, it's been hard. Burrell has been easy on me, letting me get by with late payments. I owe him a lot. And the way he wanted to let me repay him was for me to get Scruff accused of killing your pa."

John was stunned, and for a moment he could only sit speechless. "So Burrell does have something to hide! And it must have something to do with my father's death, something he doesn't want brought out."

John glanced down at the journal. "Alexander, I'm glad you told me this. What you did to Scruff was wrong, but what you've done today is right. Now, let's see what my father wrote in here."

The door burst open. In the doorway stood Drew Roberts, staring coldly at John and Layne.

Roberts said, "Give me that book."

"Get out of my house!" shouted Layne, leaping up and causing the marshal to step back, his right hand edging an inch toward his side arm. "I won't have you storming into my home and taking property that isn't yours! This is still a free nation, you know! A citizen has his rights!"

"Shut up, Alexander," said the marshal. "I'm in my rights. I believe that book contains evidence pertinent to an open case."

"I won't give it to you," said John.

"You'll give it to me or I'll take it from you," the marshal said flatly. "You can have it either way you want it."

John gripped the journal tightly. "This is my personal property," he said. "I inherited it."

"Means nothing to me. Hand it over." Roberts's hand moved a little closer to his gun.

"Very strange that you showed up just now," John said. "Very strange that you know what this book is. You wouldn't happen to also know something about someone shooting at Alexander and me back near my father's house, would you?

"Hand it over. I won't say it again."

"It was *you*, wasn't it! You're bought out by Burrell, just like some miserable hired gun hand! It was *you* who shot at us!"

Roberts lifted one brow. "That's a serious charge, Kenton. You'd best be careful about making it. Now, hand over that book!"

"He won't do it," Layne said. "And I believe he's right. It *was* you who shot at John from hiding, then took off like a coward when you suddenly had two instead of one against you! But you had just enough courage to follow us here. It all makes its own kind of sense."

Like lightning Roberts's pistol was out and leveled at John. "I'm tired of this babble. Give me that book now!"

There was no way out, and John knew it. Slowly, reluctantly, he handed the charred journal to the marshal. Just now he hated Roberts, hated him enough that he might have been able to kill him without much more provocation. But he wasn't a fool.

Roberts took the volume. "Now you stay clear of me," he warned. "Kenton, one more bit of trouble out of you, one more fool accusation against Mr. Burrell, and you'd best think about leaving Larimont quick. You understand me?"

John's gaze was stony. "If you've tied yourself to Burrell, then you'd best be the one to stay clear. I'll not back down until I know the truth about my father's death, whatever it takes."

Drew Roberts holstered his pistol and stalked away, saying no more. John watched him leave and felt the greatest frustration he'd ever known. He and Layne followed the marshal to the door, watched him go outside.

Roberts mounted his horse, then turned in the saddle and shouted back: "Layne! Mr. Burrell ain't going to be too happy with you for your part in this little turn of events. You know what I mean, I think."

John watched him until he disappeared, then turned to Layne. He was stunned to see the older man quietly crying.

"Alexander?"

"I've lost it all now," Layne said. "My land, my home . . . I'll lose it. Sure as the world, Burrell will take it all away."

John didn't know what to say. So he stood silently, feeling uncomfortable and not a little guilty.

To the side, unnoticed, stood June Layne, her eyes wide and an expression of thoughtfulness on her face.

Dusk started high above the mountains, a faint grayness around the edges of the clouds that darkened to purplish black on the horizon. Then the shadows set in as the sun turned bloodred and sank toward the west, silhouetting the gap in the mountains through which the railroad led into the Larimont Valley. Then the darkness fell and lights winked on in the windows of Larimont, and enticing supper smells wafted out into the streets.

Sharon Bradley stood alone and nervous at the corner of the street and the alleyway that ran beside the jail. It was profoundly difficult to look nonchalant, and as she imagined that the short glances she received from the occasional passersby were suspicious ones, she struggled not to squirm.

She had cause to be edgy, for inside the dark jail John Kenton was hidden, digging through the marshal's desk like a thief after jewels. What he sought was his father's journal.

John had no way of knowing if the journal even existed anymore, for it was possible that the marshal had destroyed it as soon as he had taken it. But it was the only shot John had at getting back what he felt might be a valuable clue in solving the mystery that was coming to so obsess him, and he was willing to risk the consequences of breaking and entering a lawman's office and rifling his personal papers.

For an hour he and Sharon had stood hidden in an alley across the street, watching the jail until the marshal left. And then they had casually walked across the street, and John had gone around the back—leaving Sharon as a guard—and pried his way in through a back window.

And then he had started the hurried, silent searching in the office, looking in heaps of paper, in the cubbyholes of the beaten-up roll-top desk in the corner, and at last in the marshal's own desk. And the journal was so far nowhere to be found.

For a moment John wondered how Sharon was doing outside, and if she would be able to give him warning if the marshal approached. Then he yanked open another drawer and began shuffling through another heap of papers. He could hardly believe he was doing what he was.

The darkness outside was complete now. Sharon pulled her shawl around her shoulders to fight off the faint chill in the night breeze.

"Howdy, little lady."

Sharon jumped. The voice had come from nowhere. She looked around her, suddenly very frightened.

From the shadows a figure stepped out. It was Edgar Burrell. As usual, he was grinning— and drunk.

"Hello." Sharon was perturbed to hear her voice give a squeak a little like a rusty hinge.

"Mighty nice evenin'," Edgar said. Sharon could smell the whiskey on his breath as he drew closer. "A mite chilly, maybe."

"A little." Sharon wished she could run away.

"You know me, honey?"

The uninvited endearment scraped across Sharon's nerves, but she ignored it. "I think so."

"Well, tell me who I am, honey!" Then he laughed, and his alcohol-reeking breath forced Sharon to look away.

"You're Edgar Burrell."

"That's right! And you know, you're Sharon Bradley, the one who's been running around with that Kenton and saying all sorts of nasty things about my sweet ol' daddy. Now, why you doing that?"

"Please, sir ... leave me alone." Sharon glanced at the jail. John still hadn't come out; he must be having trouble finding that journal. Sharon wished they hadn't tried to do this in the first place.

"Leave you alone?" he said in exaggerated shock. "My goodness! The little lady wants to run around town spreading lies about my daddy, and maybe even about me, and she wants me to leave her alone! Lord a'mighty!"

Sharon was beginning to feel a strong urge to run away, John or no John. But she couldn't do it. Sharon feared he would prance out innocently, not aware she had company, and incriminate himself and her right before Edgar Burrell.

"Mr. Burrell, please don't bother me. I'm not trying to give you any trouble. I'm waiting for someone here —please go."

"Waiting for someone?" he said. "You know, I think I'll just stand here and watch you. Like you do, y'know. Sort of peep at you."

Sharon had no idea what he was talking about, but his cryptic tone and manner worried her. "What do you mean?"

"Just this," he said, producing from his pocket a handkerchief, one that was terribly familiar to Sharon. It was monogrammed with the letters "S. B."

"That's mine!" she cried out, snatching at it. "Give it to me!"

"Yeah, it's yours," he said. "And you know where I found it, don't you! Out in the woods, near the old shed—"

"Give it here!"

"How long did you sit and watch me and June?" Edgar asked. "Not a very ladylike thing for a little prissy darlin' like you to do, was it?" He laughed in her face.

Sharon's hand flashed out and snatched away the handkerchief Then she turned and began to stalk away, worried for her safety, praying that by deserting her post she wouldn't put John in a bad position.

Edgar Burrell grasped her shoulder, wheeling her around to face him.

"I don't want you to be asking any more questions," he said. "You or Kenton either. No more questions. You understand that? You'd best understand it...'cause if you don't you might wind up in a hole like ol' Sherman Horner. Got it?"

With a rough shove he pushed her back. She staggered but managed to keep her balance. Edgar Burrell walked rapidly away, fading into the darkness.

"Sharon?"

It was John's voice. He came around through the alley, a smile on his face. He had obviously not seen what had happened.

"I got it, Sharon! In the marshal's desk. Had to bust a lock. Now, let's get back to Victoria's and read it!"

Grasping her arm, he pulled her along beside him to where the buggy was parked a few hundred feet away. The pair climbed into the seat and took off down the dusty road into the night.

Chapter 12

Around a glowing kerosene lamp in Victoria's back room they gathered, drawing close together and talking in hushed voices, not because there was realistic danger of anyone outside their group hearing what was said, but simply because the covert nature of what they were doing made overcaution seem natural.

John opened the charred volume and looked for a moment at the faces of Victoria and Sharon. Eagerness to hear what was written in the journal was evident in their expressions. John was eager too. Perhaps there would be an answer in this book.

The first pages of the journal were old, dating back over a year. John glanced at them hurriedly, occasionally catching an intriguing view of his father's thoughts on some subjects that he later had discussed with his son. Other entries were more routine, jottings about the weather, about a conversation held with some friend at the bank that day, about somebody down the road feeling ill. John wanted to linger at spots, for seeing his father's handwriting seemed to bring him closer, somehow. But he had promised that he would read no more than what pertained to the issue at hand, and he would keep that promise...he hoped. It wouldn't be easy.

"Do you see anything, John?" Sharon asked. "Not yet. Nothing but regular daily stuff... Wait a minute! He's writing about the robbery!"

"Will you read it? Aloud, I mean?" John glanced up at Victoria. He could see in her the same desire that he was having to suppress in himself—the urge to hear what the journal said as a means not only of gathering information but of bringing the memory of Bill Kenton a little more to life.

"All right. It's dated the day of the robbery."

John cleared his throat and began to read:

"'Bank was robbed today. It was the first such experience of my life, terrifying. It's an unusual feeling to actually wonder if you're about to be shot by some nervous, young, masked scoundrel with a pistol. I'm frightened yet.

"'They entered the bank—three of them—shortly after we closed for our midday break. All were masked, with sacks over their heads. They appeared young, but it was impossible to get a good look at them, the way they flitted around. And what's more, they forced us to lie on the floor, facedown, which made it difficult to watch them. That, I imagine, was their intention.

"'I did catch sight of the eyes of one of them—it was a close look. He walked up to me and thrust his pistol right under my nose. The look of those eyes sticks with me, and I can't get rid of the idea that I know whom they belong to. But I just can't put my finger on it, can't figure it out...

"'I'm anxious to investigate this robbery. Mr. Burrell sent us home early today, supposedly to let us get over the shock. But he had the marshal in at the time I left, and I assume they were going over what evidence they had.'"

John flipped across the next few pages of the journal. The entries were still about the robbery, and of how Bill

Kenton was growing restless to find the robbers. As John skimmed the writing, he read occasional excerpts aloud:

"'Still no progress in the robbery investigation. Burrell seems strangely uncooperative, refusing to say much and offering virtually no encouragement in the matter. Strange. He stands a greater loss in this than any of us, yet he won't do anything about it. I must trust him. Surely he knows what he is doing.'"

John turned a few more pages, scanning them. A few pages later, he found another entry on the robbery.

"'Burrell is covering something up. I'm sure of it. There is no other explanation for his reticence in this investigation. For days I've tried to talk to him about it, for I'm convinced that if we all put our heads together we stand a good chance of figuring this thing out. Poteet, too, has noticed Burrell's ways lately. He said as much to me today, though he didn't go into detail. I've determined to say no more to Burrell about the robbery. But I will watch him— as I have for months, since I've come to suspect he is having an illicit romance in this town. Wish I knew more. Crookedness in one area of his life might well lead to crookedness in another—like in the bank. And I want no part of that.

"'That robber's eyes—they haunt me. I know him. But who is he? If only I could recall.'"

"This is fascinating!" said John. "I wonder if he ever figured it out."

Flipping through the pages as fast as his eyes could scan the lines, he suddenly stopped. Aloud he read:

"'Sherman Horner.

"'The eyes that I saw were those of Sherman Horner. I have no doubt about it. And the possibilities that opens up are frightening.

"'If Sherman Horner is guilty of the robbery, then it is tremendously likely his brother, too, is one of the robbers.

And if those two are in on it, then surely Edgar Burrell is too, for that is a trio that is never separated.

"'A son robbing his own father! It is hard for me to conceive. I'll go to the marshal with this information tomorrow.'"

John's eyes widened as he read that line. "He went to the marshal!" he exclaimed. "Victoria, Sharon—do you understand what that indicates? The marshal—who we know now is under Burrell's control—found out that my father had figured it all out. That means it surely got back to Burrell almost as soon as my father told the marshal. And if Burrell wanted badly enough to keep it all quiet, then he could have killed my father himself, hired someone to do it, or even had the marshal do it. Then Scruff was set up to take the blame. It hangs together."

"There are other possibilities, too, John," said Victoria. "What if Edgar Burrell or one of the Homers killed Bill? They may have gotten word that he suspected them of the robbery and then set out to shut him up. To me that makes more sense than saying Burrell did it. You see, we all know that Burrell wouldn't have a man killed just to protect Edgar. He doesn't care that much about him. But Edgar would protect himself, and we know that the Horner brothers were out to keep us from checking further. And he's the kind that would be capable of murder, I believe."

"There's more," cut in Sharon. "I ran into Edgar Burrell tonight. I haven't had a chance to tell you all until now, though."

Sharon outlined her encounter with the drunken young man outside the jail. When she was finished, John nodded.

"It does make sense—Edgar Burrell does seem to be a chief candidate for murderer in this case. But that leaves a few gaps—like why Frederick Burrell tried to squelch the investigation of the robbery, if in fact he wasn't trying to protect his son."

John picked up the journal again. "I'll see if there are any further clues in here."

He scanned the pages again. He noted a new sullenness in the writing. Some days had scarcely ten words as an entry, while others appeared written in a fast and angry hand, even though the subject matter was often innocuous. Bill Kenton's very writing was showing the growing dissatisfaction and anger that had marked his last days.

At last John's eyes fell on the last entry in the journal, written the day of the murder. Swallowing down the lump in his throat, he began to read.

"'Same as usual at work today, though Burrell had nothing to say to me. Looks at me strangely when he thinks I don't see. I don't trust him.

"'Saw Edgar Burrell today, and it was all I could do to look at him. I have no doubt of his guilt. Word has gotten around that I suspect his involvement in the robbery, somehow. The look he gave me was frightening.

"'Feel depressed tonight. Scruff Smithers was by, and I gave him that gold watch he had long admired. I don't know just why I did it—it was a momentary impulse.

"'I plan to retire early. I feel quite tired, and I want to—'"

"That's it," said John in a whisper. "That's all it says. It was as if he heard something, stopped in midsentence, and locked the journal away in the safe in a hurry."

"Something, or someone?" Sharon asked. "Looking at that journal may have been the last act of his life."

John closed the volume and pushed it away, a choking feeling making it hard to breathe.

And he was vaguely disappointed. The journal hadn't revealed the final clue that he had hoped it would. Unless it was that cryptic comment about Edgar Burrell.

Edgar Burrell. More and more John was beginning to think that Victoria was right. If anyone in this town had killed Bill Kenton, it seemed likely it was Edgar Burrell. It was all there—the motive, the ability, the character of a killer.

Victoria rose, breaking into John's thoughts. "I'll make some tea," she said quietly. "I think we could use it."

"I'll help," said Sharon. Quickly the pair slipped out of the room, leaving John alone to drop into thought once more.

Thought of one name, one face...Edgar Burrell.

CHAPTER 13

Frederick Burrell was in a foul mood. He walked alone along the wide alleyway that was Larimont's version of a backstreet, his eyes cast downward, and his forehead creased in thought.

Young Kenton was causing trouble for him. Just as his father had in the last weeks of his life. Burrell had friends in this town, and he knew the questions Kenton and that Bradley girl—hard to believe such a pretty thing was Scruff Smithers's niece—were asking around. And the hints of guilt they had been dropping didn't sit well with the banker. Something was going to have to be done. That was sure.

But what? Burrell had a reputation to uphold. What could a man like him do to stop the rumors that were arising without incriminating himself?

It wasn't an easy question, and the more Burrell reflected on it the gloomier he became. He began walking more rapidly, his hands behind him. An old dog sauntered out across his path, and he kicked it away with a curse.

The figure that stepped from behind the next building startled him, and he reacted visibly. When he saw it was June Layne, he relaxed.

"Hello, June," he said, speaking low and looking around. "This is a surprise." He smiled. "A pleasant one, I might add."

"Stop it," she said. Burrell's smile faded. "I need to talk to you—seriously. And right now."

Burrell cocked his head. "Well, now! What's your problem?"

"It's not really mine," she said. "It's my father. And it concerns you, Fred."

"How so?"

"He's frightened, Fred. Frightened of you, and what you will do to him. Ever since Drew Roberts took that journal that Bill Kenton wrote, my father has been miserable, just waiting for you to foreclose as a punishment. I've come to ask you to not do that. Please."

Burrell smiled. "June...you know I don't want to do anything that would hurt you." He reached out to her, and she drew away. His expression chilled into cold stone.

"I'm serious about this," she said. "You mustn't do anything to hurt my father. I care about him."

"You're confusing me, June," he said. "Why do you think I would hurt your father? What does that journal have to do with me?"

"The fact that you know about that journal proves that it has to do with you, Fred," she said. "I know more than you think I do about your doings. I know that you're the one who had my father implicate Scruff Smithers, and that Drew Roberts is under your thumb. And that John Kenton and Sharon Bradley and all their questions have you worried."

Suddenly, without warning or change of expression, Burrell slapped June hard. She gasped and stepped back, staring at him in shock, her hand to her cheek.

"Don't you ever talk to me like that again, girl. I've treated you well, paid you well. And I've gone easy on your father and let him off dozens of times when he couldn't pay me. And half of that has been for your sake.

"But your father hasn't shown his gratitude very well, has he? Helping somebody like John Kenton, who wants nothing more than to see me hurt. What kind of man is that? And why should I do anything for him? Why should I be concerned about giving him extra time to make payments, when he obviously doesn't care what happens to me? Answer me that, June!"

June's eyes blurred with tears, and she sensed that she was losing. "Fred... I'm sorry. Please...don't hurt my father for what I've done. He needs help now, with Ma sick and all..."

"I won't hurt your father, June. Not a bit. I'll just start treating him fairly under the law, as I could have done anytime up until now, and let him hurt himself. That's all it will take. Your father will destroy himself—he already destroyed himself, in fact, the minute that he crossed me."

June stood silent, tears streaming down her cheeks. She had failed. Not only failed, but perhaps made things worse.

"You'd best get home, June. Your poor old sick mother might need you. Good day." He turned and walked away, then turned again.

"There's only one thing that will make me change my mind about this," he said. "If John Kenton calls off his dogs and quits asking questions I don't like; if he quits trying to slander me and make me out a murderer, then perhaps I could be persuaded to go easy on Alexander. Just maybe. If you can work that out, then we'll see. We'll see."

He stalked off down the street and disappeared, leaving June alone with a feeling of hopelessness.

To persuade John Kenton to quit asking questions about his father's death—that was a hard bill of goods to deliver. Perhaps an impossible one.

Then the guilt came, flooding over her like a river pouring out of its banks, and she began to cry all the harder.

It was a hard decision. But once it was made, he felt he had no other choice.

Sooner or later, they were going to uncover the truth. It was obvious. No amount of persuasion had averted them yet, and there was only one other form of persuasion left. The hardest, the most final.

He slipped the last cartridge into the Winchester and hefted it to his shoulder, taking a practice aim in the mirror. Then he lowered the gun and stared at his reflection.

He would do it. Tonight, after dark. And then maybe all of this would stop.

It had to stop.

Sharon answered the knock on the door with the same caution she had used in all her actions in the last few days. She swung open the doorway following a careful peek outside and looked with frank surprise at June Layne.

"June? I'm surprised to—I mean, why don't you come in? It's good to see you."

June walked through the doorway, smiling uncomfortably at Sharon. Sharon sensed a humbleness, even a fright, about June that had not been there before. Closing the door, she frowned slightly.

"Sit down, June. I'll get you a cup of tea. I just brewed some."

"Thank you, Sharon." June sat down near the cold fireplace. Victoria stepped into the kitchen doorway and looked out at Sharon's visitor, confusion evident in her expression.

Then she stepped out into the room, wiping flour from her hands onto an apron. She smiled at June.

"Hello, dear. I haven't seen you in quite some time."

"Hello, Mrs. Rivers. Have you been well?"

"Fine." Victoria glanced at Sharon. This wasn't the same June Layne she had known for several years now—a brash, defiant young lady who rarely showed respect for her parents or any of their friends. This June Layne was quiet, humble, even scared.

Sharon went into the kitchen and returned a minute later with three cups of hot tea. She sat down near June and handed her a cup, then waited for the young lady to explain her visit.

"I have something to ask you," June said. "Something that's very important."

Go on.

"I've come to ask you to stop."

"Stop? What do you mean?"

"Stop what you are doing... Please, I don't mean to be pushy, and I'm not trying to tell you what to do. I'm just asking—and not for my sake, either. For my parents. You see, I...love them, no matter what some folks say about the way I act."

Sharon looked confused. "June, I'm not sure I understand what you mean."

June sipped her tea, and her hands were shaking. "I mean that I'm asking you, as honestly and as humbly as I know how, to stop asking questions about Bill Kenton's death. Quit trying to dig up anything about it. It's very important."

Sharon's countenance grew only the least bit stern. "Is there something that we shouldn't find out?" she asked.

"There's people, good people, who will be hurt," June answered. "I can't say much, but it will bring harm to my parents if you continue."

"Is it because your father helped John find the journal?"

Sharon asked. "Is somebody trying to hurt him because of that?"

"Please don't ask me for specific details," said June, growing somewhat upset. Her hands were shaking so badly now that she had to put down her tea. "My father had nothing to do with what happened to John's father. I want you to know that. But there is somebody who will hurt him if you all keep on probing in wounds like you have. I don't want to see him hurt. Or my mother."

"Is it Burrell?"

There was a pause. "Please—I can't say anything right now. I just can't."

"And I can't stop asking questions. And neither can John. If he was here, he'd tell you that, June. You see, my uncle was a good man, too, in his way. And he doesn't deserve to have his memory blotted with a smear like it has been. And Bill Kenton was a good man—and he certainly didn't deserve to die. That's why we *have* to ask questions. Do you understand?"

"Yes—yes, I understand. But I don't think *you* do! There's no justification for you both hurting innocent people just to find out what's past and done and unchangeable! Can't you see?"

"I can see that if a person is really innocent, then he shouldn't fear our questions. We don't want to hurt somebody that has done nothing. But we do want to see the guilty one uncovered, and justice done. And I can't go back on that."

June stood suddenly, upsetting her teacup. The night wind whistled in through the open window, suddenly chilling the room.

"I don't want to see my father put off his land, hurt by—"

Simultaneously with the blast of a rifle outside, the window shattered. June Layne fell back over her chair, landing faced own on the floor. She groaned once, tried to push herself up, then collapsed.

Suddenly weak, Sharon stood. She stared down at the form on the floor, then at the shattered window. She fainted just as Victoria's hand grasped her to pull her down to the floor, below the level of the windowsill and out of the line of any further fire from outside.

Slowly, a red pool formed around June Layne's body, and the only sound was the wind whistling through the empty window frame and the noise of rapidly retreating footsteps outside in the darkness.

Chapter 14

"She wants to see you," the doctor said to Sharon. "She's insisting. Has been for some time."

Sharon had been trembling for two hours now. She didn't feel anywhere close to getting over it. Alexander Layne was in worse shape; he sat in the corner of his living room with his head in his hands. His wife sat beside him, all the more drawn and ill from the shock of it.

"Try to be strong when you talk to her," the doctor whispered in Sharon's ear as she moved toward the bedroom door. "That was a rifle slug she took, and it hurt her bad. I don't know how I'm going to tell Alexander, but I don't expect her to make it. But there's always the chance that she will—if she really believes she can. That's crucial. I want you to help her believe that, if you can."

"I'll try, Doctor," said Sharon. "I just hope I don't break down."

"If you feel that coming on, then get out of there," the doctor said. "Don't break down in front of her, whatever you do."

John caught Sharon's glance as she passed him. He smiled at her in a sad way, and she understood the meaning.

June Layne lay on her bed, propped up by pillows, her face pale, her eyes closed, with deep circles beneath them. Her chest was bandaged beneath her gown.

The doctor drew near June and bent down. His voice was gentle.

"You have a visitor, June. Sharon Bradley. Just like you asked."

June's eyes opened, fluttered, then focused on Sharon's face. She smiled.

"Thank you, Doctor. I need to talk to her...alone."

Sharon could tell from the strain in June's voice that she was in pain. Fighting back tears, she sat down in a cushioned chair beside the bed. She reached out and took June's hand.

"I'm so sorry, June. So sorry this happened."

Behind her the door closed as the doctor stepped out of the room. June's face seemed to relax as she was left alone with Sharon.

"Sharon, I need to talk to you. I don't have much time, and—"

"Hush that kind of talk!" Sharon cut in. "You'll be fine."

"I'm dying, Sharon. I know I am. And there's some things I have to talk about before it happens. Things I have to set straight. Will you listen to me? You're the only one I can tell."

Sharon nodded tensely, not sure she really wanted to hear what June had to say. A deathbed confession of some sort...that was a frightening thing to have placed on her.

"I'll tell you as straight as I can what has been going on. What you do with this information is up to you...but I've got to get it out.

"I've been with Edgar Burrell a long time now. I mean that I've loved him, been close to him, been his lover. No one has known, except Edgar and me, and probably the Horner brothers. My mother and father, they've had no idea. They wouldn't approve of Edgar. He's not got a good reputation in this town—and I'll admit, he deserves that." There was a long pause. "And I know a lot of people frown on me too. And I deserve that. Far more than most would think.

"You see, Edgar had an idea, something we could do together that would make us both money. I knew then it was wrong, but Edgar persuaded me. I've never told anybody until now...

"I've been...selling myself—you know what I mean—to Frederick Burrell for months now. It was Edgar's idea, though his father doesn't know it. I approached Frederick Burrell about it the first time, and he snatched up the offer. He's a perverse man, and an evil one, Sharon. But I went ahead with it, for Edgar, and for the money.

"Edgar and I would split the money that Frederick paid me.

"I know that it's wrong. I knew it all along—but I just couldn't stop, somehow. Edgar wanted me to do it, and I needed the money. And I think that my relationship with Fred was part of the reason he didn't foreclose on my father's farm long ago."

June had been staring at the ceiling throughout her talk, but now she looked over at Sharon.

"There. I've told you what's going on—what *has* been going on, I should say. But there are parts of this that even I don't know. And there's a connection to the death of John's father, I believe.

"You see, hardly more than a few hours ago Fred told me he was going to foreclose on my father's farm unless I could convince you to stop checking into Bill Kenton's death. That's why I came to you, asking what I did. It's obvious that Fred Burrell was involved in some way, directly or indirectly, with Bill Kenton's murder. Else why would he want to stop the investigation?"

Sharon nodded. "That's a good question, June. But do

you think he's the one that shot you? And why would he do that?"

"I don't know who shot me," June answered. "But don't you see—they weren't after *me.* "

Sharon felt a sudden chill. "What do you mean?"

"They were trying to kill you, Sharon. Somebody wanted you to stop the investigation—very badly. But they missed you and got me."

"Frederick Burrell?" Sharon whispered, her throat dry.

"I don't know," said June. "Why would he do a thing like that before he even gave me a chance to try to stop the investigation like he wanted me to? It could have been him, I guess, but I don't think it was."

Sharon forced herself to ask the question. "June, could it have been Edgar? He asked John once to stop the search for Bill Kenton's killer. He even offered him money. Do you think he could have—"

"I don't believe it," said June. "That's one thing I won't let myself believe. I won't." She looked to the ceiling again.

"I'm sorry, June. I had to ask," Sharon said.

"I know."

Sharon ventured another question, noticing that June was beginning to appear tired. "June—why would Burrell try to blame Bill Kenton's murder on my uncle?"

"To divert the blame from himself. That's obvious. Your uncle was an easy out for him, and he used my father to implicate your uncle. Fred Burrell is like that—he uses people. He used me."

Sharon touched June's hand again. "Thank you for being so honest with me. I truly appreciate it. And don't worry—you'll be well soon. I know you will."

June looked unsmiling at Sharon. "I'll die," she said. "I'll die within hours. And the worst part of it is, I won't see Edgar before it happens. He won't come. They wouldn't let him in here if he did." The girl's eyes flooded with tears.

"I'm tired," she whispered. "I want to sleep."

"Goodbye, June," Sharon said, fighting back tears. "I'll come see you in the morning. I promise."

Then she was gone, getting out of the room as fast as she could, trying to hold back her weeping until she could get outside.

She pushed through the crowd in the living room and on out into the porch. Grasping a porch column to support herself, she cried like a child. John slipped out of the house and put his arm around her shoulder, feeling helpless and strangely bothered to see Sharon like this—bothered more than he could account for.

He looked into the yard for no particular reason, and his eyes locked onto the face of Edgar Burrell.

The young man stood beside a maple in the yard, staring blankly at John. The smile was gone. Edgar Burrell was changed. And beneath the blankness of his expression there was turmoil.

John sensed it all in a glance. Then Edgar Burrell turned away, mounted his horse, and rode off. John watched him until he was gone.

Shortly after midnight, the doctor walked out of June's room and informed her parents that she was dead.

Chapter 15

"I've figured something out, I think," John said.

He had been sitting for several minutes with a cup of coffee in his hand and a thoughtful look in his eye. Victoria was seated, looking out a window, and Sharon seemed to be in sort of a weary trance. Since word had come of June's death, she'd hardly spoken.

John's words brought both her and Victoria around to reality again.

"What have you figured out?" Victoria asked.

"Burrell's motive for covering up the facts of the robbery," John said. "At least, I *think* I've figured it out."

"Let's hear it, then," Victoria said.

John took a sip of his coffee. "We've got a new twist to the whole business considering the information that June gave to Sharon," he said. "It puts everything in quite a different light.

"Let's review what we know. First, we know that Edgar was fully aware of his father's involvement with June. I mean, it was Edgar who planned that whole thing. Now, imagine with me for a minute that Edgar goes to his father, the rich banker, the man of high standing in the community, and Edgar threatens to reveal his father's affair with June unless Burrell squelches any investigation of the bank robbery, because the bank robbery was done by Edgar himself, masked, with the Horner brothers."

Victoria was intrigued. "You may be onto something, John. It would mean that Burrell covered up his son's involvement in the robbery not to protect his *son*, but to protect himself, his reputation! It makes sense."

"It does," John said. "And it would mean that Burrell would have a strong motivation to get rid of my father when he began growing too curious and inquisitive about that robbery. Because if my father had managed to figure out that Edgar Burrell had been among the robbers, and if he made that public, then Edgar would have spilled the beans publicly about his father's love affair with June Layne. Burrell's reputation, his standing, would have been hopelessly ruined. So Burrell had to make sure that my father never revealed what he'd figured out.

"Or maybe there's a whole different angle. Maybe it wasn't Frederick Burrell at all. Edgar probably knew about my father's questions and suspicions, just like Frederick Burrell did. And he, as one of the bank robbers, had every reason to want my father to keep quiet, too. So it could have been Edgar who killed my father."

Victoria said, "And poor Lawrence Poteet was probably killed by the same person who killed your father. And now it seems that someone has tried to kill Sharon as well, probably to scare all of us away from digging any deeper." She paused. "It's a strange feeling, knowing that someone out there probably would be glad to see us all dead."

"Yes and add to that the fact that the law here is corrupt and in Burrell's pocket, and you have to realize we have no protection beyond what we can provide for ourselves. We're in a tight and dangerous position, all of us. We'll have to closely watch our steps from here on."

"Yes," Victoria said. "Because we know that someone else already is."

"Let's consider what else we know," John said. "We know that it was Sherman Horner who attacked you and June, and it was probably Jerry Horner who attacked me and knocked me cold. And we know that Edgar Burrell tried to bribe me out of investigating further. Take those things together, and you've got some pretty good evidence that Edgar and the Horner brothers had something to keep quiet. Pretty much a confirmation, in my opinion, that they definitely were the masked bank robbers."

Victoria asked, "Who do you think is more likely to have killed your father, John? Edgar, or his father?"

Sharon jumped in with her own answer before John could speak. "I believe it was Burrell. Because whoever shot Bill Kenton is almost certainly the same person who shot June, and Edgar would never have shot the very girl he loved."

"Maybe he didn't love her," John said. "Maybe he didn't care about her at all except as someone he could use to his own pleasure and benefit. Good lands, the man was actually encouraging her to sell herself, like some cheap trollop, to his own *father!* It's atrocious. How much could he have loved her if he was willing to let her do that? On the other hand, maybe June was right and that shot through the window wasn't intended for her. Maybe it was really intended for you, Sharon, or for Victoria. June might have been mistaken for one of you and have been shot by pure mistake."

Victoria stood. "I think I'm going to go lie down awhile," she said. "I want to be sure I have the strength to make it through June's funeral. Right now, I don't even feel like I have the strength to make it through the day."

When Victoria was gone, Sharon looked at John and said quietly, "It's all very dreadful, isn't it?"

John nodded. "Yes. It's all very dreadful."

The church was half filled a full hour before the funeral was scheduled to begin, and the closer the start grew, the faster the pews filled. Soon not a seat was left available, and John, Victoria, and Sharon were glad they had been among the early arrivals.

Sharon looked around the rapidly-crowding room. "I suppose it adds a lot of curiosity to the situation when someone dies like poor June did."

"Morbidity," Victoria grumbled beneath her breath. "Pure morbidity! People will come any distance to gape at some person who has died in an unfortunate way. People love morbidity, and I despise the whole human race for it."

"It's why there's never a lack of a crowd at a good lynching," John said. "You know, if I could know for sure who killed my father, and if I could roust up a good lynch mob to take care of them for it, I'd welcome any crowd that wanted to watch the final disposition, morbid or not."

"In that case, John, so would I," Victoria said.

The preacher, a white-haired, humble little man with stooped shoulders and an eggshell voice that would be challenged indeed to be heard by a crowd as big as this one, shuffled to the pulpit to the accompaniment of a piano playing mournful hymns. The soft whispers and sounds of movement among the crowd slowly died away as he came to his place, leaned over the podium, and stared across the biggest crowd his church had seen in many a day.

"It's a sad thing," he began, "that often it is tragedy and death that bring us together in this way. How happy it would make me if many of you who have come here today to dwell on the sadness and sensation surrounding this untimely death would crowd these same pews on Sunday mornings to worship the Lord."

The crowd moved and fidgeted at this mild but unexpected scolding. Indeed, many of them there hadn't even thought of entering the church doors in years and wouldn't have today if not for the way June Layne had died, and the wild, hot rumors that circulated about what might have been behind it.

"Nevertheless, I welcome you all," the old minister went on. "You are always welcome in the house of God, and in his kingdom as well, if only you'll accept his invitation." He cast his eyes down onto the closed pine coffin that lay on a table before the pulpit. "And in the kingdom of God there will be no more death, no more tears...no more staring eyes and wicked hearts that are stirred to passion only by that which is sensational and grim."

More shuffling, scooting, mumbling. This wasn't the kind of thing most had come to hear.

The preacher opened his Bible, cleared his throat, and began to read from the Gospel of John. The devout listened, while the non-devout stared at the coffin and wished it were open so they could get a good look at the corpse. These were the same people who had done their best to obtain all the gory details about the things the fire had done to the corpse of Bill Kenton, and whispered among themselves the lurid, gruesome details of Lawrence Poteet's hanging and the stabbing and mysterious burial of Sherman Horner.

The funeral dragged on, and John's mind began to wander. It fell into familiar paths, often walked these past days. He pondered angles, twists, possibilities, put together the facts this way and that, trying to see if something he hadn't noticed before presented itself.

He was startled, with the rest of the congregation, when the back door of the church burst open loudly as the preacher was about to begin a prayer. Turning his head, John was surprised to see Edgar Burrell standing in the doorway, disheveled, red-faced and red-eyed, shoulders slumped. He wore a heavy Colt pistol in a battered leather gun belt slung loosely around his hips.

The preacher and congregation fell silent as Edgar simply stood there, obviously drunk, his bleary eyes sweeping over the assembly. His nose was crusted with old rheum and his face was wet with tears.

He stepped forward, walking down the center aisle toward the closed coffin.

"Young man," the preacher said. "I ask you, in the name of all that is holy, to respect the dignity of these rites."

"You can shut the hell up, old man," Edgar replied in a cracked voice. "You can just shut the hell up!"

John glanced at Victoria, then reached over and took Sharon's hand protectively.

Edgar Burrell reached the coffin. He stood looking down at it, shoulders beginning to heave. He reeked of liquor; the smell reached every corner of the sanctuary.

The preacher stared down, looking as if he might faint at any moment.

Edgar Burrell wailed aloud, so suddenly that again the entire assembly was startled. He turned his head up, eyes toward the ceiling, fists balled and shaking in the air before him, and let out a long, bitter howl of a man deeply suffering. Then he fell to his knees, leaned forward, and rested his forehead against the side of the coffin.

"I'm sorry, June... I'm sorry... I didn't mean for it to be like this..."

"Please," the preacher whispered. "Please...can't someone take him away?"

Men rose and went to Edgar's side. Gently they encouraged him to rise, to turn away. For a moment it seemed he would go along, but suddenly he swore loudly, shook them off, and stomped out of the church, still weeping.

The preacher stood there weakly after Edgar had gone

and remained silent because he simply did not know what to say.

At last, his tired voice could be heard. "Perhaps," he said, "the best we can do just now is simply say a prayer and lay this unfortunate young woman to rest as quickly as we can."

The burial was carried out in a tense atmosphere, everyone there fearing that Edgar might return and make a new and even worse spectacle of the affair. But he didn't return, and June Layne was given to the earth with at least a modicum of dignity remaining.

But Edgar wasn't through yet. A couple of hours after June Layne was buried, he showed up at the door of a local tavern. He was already quite drunk and belligerent, and infuriated when he found the tavern, which operated only in the late evening and night, hadn't opened its doors yet. He pounded and screamed and cursed at the doorway, until at last he received the attention of the barkeep, a quiet, easygoing fellow who lived in a room above the tavern.

The man tried to explain to Edgar that the tavern wouldn't open for another couple of hours, but Edgar would have none of it. He pushed his way in, and when the barkeep tried to restrain him, turned on the fellow and beat him almost senseless.

By now the matter had drawn attention, and someone called for the marshal. This display was too much for Drew Roberts to conveniently ignore, and Edgar Burrell found himself arrested and hauled off to the jail to calm down and sober up.

Not a soul in the town believed he would remain there long, nor see any official charges or legal retribution filed against him. He was, after all, Edgar Burrell, son of the man who ran Larimont, and Larimont's law.

Chapter 16

John stood in the shadowed, recessed doorway, his face turned slightly to the right, his eyes cut to the left so he could watch the doorway of the jail and the marshal's office. He'd lingered there for about a half hour and knew that he couldn't stay much longer without drawing someone's attention. But he had a feeling, just an intuition, that giving it a few minutes longer might pay off—and five minutes later, when the marshal's door opened and Drew Roberts emerged, hat on head, John smiled subtly. He watched Roberts stride down the street, heading toward the Larimont Bank. Checking in with Burrell, John assumed. Making sure the boss man understood why the marshal in his pocket had been forced to lock up his master's rampaging, drunken son, because to fail to do so would have destroyed any public credibility that his claim to be a fair and independent lawman might have had.

John waited until the marshal was well down the street before he stepped out of the doorway and walked casually toward the jailhouse. He was nervous, but also excited. Right now, the jail was empty except for its lone prisoner, Edgar Burrell, and the marshal had left his office door unlocked.

John stepped onto the jail porch, resisted the urge to glance around and thereby make himself look suspicious, and opened the door. He stepped inside and closed the door behind him.

Sure enough, the place was empty. John took two or three deep breaths, calmed himself, and went to the door at the back of the office. The door opened onto the little hallway that ran between the three cage-like cells of the jail, one big one on the left, two smaller ones on the right.

John passed through the door and spotted Edgar Burrell at once. He lay in one of the smaller cells, curled up on the wood-slab bunk, his back toward John. John wondered if Edgar was sleeping. Some tense quality about him made him doubt it.

"Edgar."

The prisoner jerked, maybe surprised to hear a voice other than Drew Roberts's speaking to him. He pushed up, rolled around, faced John.

"I'll be damned," Edgar said. "I didn't figure to see you here."

"Quite a show you made at the funeral," John said. "And quite a job you did on that barman."

"Yeah. Wish I hadn't done that. Don't reckon he deserved it."

John looked closely at Edgar, who had a defeated, unargumentative manner just now, something seldom seen in Edgar's case. "You been crying, Edgar? Your eyes are a bit red-rimmed."

"I loved her, John. I loved that girl more than I ever loved anybody."

"If you loved her, how could you have had her do what she did, with your own *father*? She talked before she died. She told it all."

"I was wrong to let her do that. I know that now. But it just didn't seem to matter. Me and my old man, we've never had no affection for each other. I let June do that because it put money in her hand, and because it gave me something I could hold over the old man. To keep him under control, you know."

John hadn't expected to get this kind of unfettered honesty out of the usually cagey Edgar. "Tell me, then, was it you who robbed the Larimont Bank? With the Horner brothers?"

Edgar stared at him, then chuckled coldly, saying nothing.

John stared back. "It was. I can tell just by looking at you. Edgar Burrell, robber of his own father's bank! And your father knew it, too. But he couldn't allow the truth to be known, could he? Not only would it shame the great Burrell name to have it known his own flesh and blood had robbed the bank, it would also mean that you'd expose to all of Larimont that he and June were having a love affair. You set it up very cleverly, that I'll grant you. But you didn't anticipate somebody like me coming along, or somebody like Sharon Bradley. Somebody who wouldn't back down. And that's why you and the Homers paid those visits to me and Victoria and Sharon. Am I right?"

"Smart man, you are. Smarter than God! Now go off and leave me be. My head hurts."

"So I'm right, then. It really was you and the Homers who attacked me and two innocent women. But you didn't expect Sharon to have the presence of mind to stab a knitting needle into the back of her attacker. So once again, your plan didn't quite work out, did it? And Sherman Horner paid the price with his life."

"Smarter than God, yes sir. Why don't you go figure out somebody else's business and leave me be?"

"What about Lawrence Poteet, Edgar? Did you kill him, too?"

Edgar looked John in the eye and spoke with conviction. "No. No. That one, I swear, I had nothing to do with."

"Then who did?"

"I don't know. I swear I don't."

"What about June? Did you fire the shot that killed her?"

"No! God, no. I'd have never hurt her."

"But you might have if you didn't realize it was her. If you thought the woman you were aiming at through the window was Victoria Rivers or Sharon Bradley."

"I didn't do it, Kenton. I didn't shoot June! I swear!"

"Then why all the guilt at the funeral service? All the crying and moaning?"

"Because I knew that it was me who had put her in the position to get hurt. Because it was me who had gotten her involved with my father and turned a good girl into something she never would have been if not for me. And in the end, it got her killed...but I swear, John Kenton, I *swear*, I didn't fire the shot that killed her!"

John gazed at Edgar, evaluating. If he was lying right now, he was doing a remarkably good job of it.

"One last question," John said, more softly.

"And this one is the most important of all. Did you kill my father, Edgar?"

"No. I vow to you, John, I didn't. I vow before God himself, it wasn't me."

"One of the Homers, then?"

"No. I don't believe so. I mean, if one of them had done it, I would know."

"I don't think I believe you. I think I'm looking at the murderer of my father right now."

"John, it wasn't me. I swear it."

"Why should I believe you?"

"Because I'm telling you the truth."

John locked a fierce gaze onto Edgar's face and held it in

silence for a long time. When he spoke, his voice was low.

"You're in this jail right now because you got rowdy and hurt a man. Minor offense. You'll be out again soon. And when you are, I'll be waiting for you. I believe you killed my father, Edgar, and I'm going to make sure that you pay for that."

Edgar said, "I didn't do it, John. I didn't do it."

"Later, Edgar," John said. He turned on his heel and left.

John strode down the street in a cloud of rage, sure now that he had solved the grim mystery. Now what remained was to respond. There would be no help from the bought-off law in this town. He'd have to look higher than that. To the state, maybe.

Or to himself. One to one, man to man. That was the way to avenge Bill Kenton.

He looked up and saw Frederick and David Burrell walking toward him. He paused, letting them draw nearer, wondering if they were approaching him purposefully, or if their paths had just happened to cross.

"Hello, John," Frederick Burrell said coldly. David Burrell, pompous as ever, said nothing at all.

"You have something to say to me, Burrell?" John asked, making no attempt to avoid rudeness.

"I have nothing to say to you. We're heading to the jail to visit Edgar, and to get him out, if the marshal will allow."

"The marshal will do whatever you want, and you know it. I hope you do get Edgar out. I'm eager to spend some time with him."

The Burrells stared at him, seemingly trying to figure out what that last comment had meant.

"Good day to you, gentlemen," John said. "Enjoy your time with Edgar. While you still can."

He pushed between them, roughly, and continued on his way.

He knew he'd said too much. But he hadn't been able to squelch it. Edgar Burrell had killed his father, and he intended to kill Edgar in turn. And just now, he hardly cared who knew it, or what consequences it might bring later on, once it was done.

"It's him, Victoria. It's Edgar. I'm sure of it now," John spoke furiously, pacing back and forth in Victoria's sitting room as she and Sharon Bradley watched him and cast quick glances at each other. "I knew it while I talked to him. He killed my father."

"But, John...how do you know?" Sharon asked. "I mean, what solid evidence do you have that—"

"Evidence? The evidence of my own intuitions!"

"Well, John, don't take offense at me saying this, but intuition and evidence are not quite the same thing..."

"Listen to me, I know what I know. Maybe I can't prove it in the legal sense...but I know."

Victoria stood. "John, would you like some food, something to drink, maybe sit down and settle your mind a little?"

John frowned at her. "Settle my mind? What are you saying?"

"Just that you're overwrought. Your feelings are running ahead of your common sense."

He frowned even more deeply. "You don't believe me!"

"No, quite honestly, I think I do. I can't think of a more likely candidate to have killed Bill. But the fact remains that you still lack *proof*."

"And what good is proof except in a court of law? And what good is a court of law in Larimont, where Frederick Burrell has bought the law for himself?"

"Not entirely," Sharon suggested. "I mean, the marshal did lock up Edgar for beating that poor man."

"Well, he hardly had any choice about that! Edgar's violation was too flagrant for him just to let it pass. He has to keep up his front before the public eye, you know. But Edgar will be out before you know it. He probably already is. The other Burrells were on their way over to the jail to try to get him out when I came out."

"John, listen to me," Victoria said. "You're beginning to let all this wear away at you a little too much. You're going to let yourself get emotional, make mistakes. You need to rest, to think. I suggest you go back to the hotel for a while, take your room again. Take a nap. See no one. And *calm down!* The last thing you want to do is run out of control, like some train leaping its tracks for going too fast. Do you understand what I'm saying?"

John fought back the impulse to be irritated at what Victoria said, because he knew she was right.

"I understand."

"Good. Of course, you can continue to stay here, too. You can go lie down in the back bedroom, if you like. Take a nap."

"No, no. I'll go back to the hotel."

"May I send you some food?"

"I'll get something at the cafe later."

Victoria went to him and kissed his cheek. "Good. Rest and a cleared mind is what you need. Then we'll gather again and talk about how to gather solid proof against Edgar...not just intuitions."

John smiled at her. A wise woman, like a mother to him. He was glad she was around to keep him from losing his moorings.

He said his farewells, left the house, and walked toward the hotel.

CHAPTER 17

Somewhere between Victoria's and the hotel, John grew caught up in a memory from childhood that arose at the sight of a long-legged pup that scampered to him from somewhere, played and bounced about his feet a few moments, then darted happily away down the street. It reminded him of a similar pup he'd picked up as a boy, only that pup had been injured in some manner, and homeless. He'd taken it in and raised it, with his father's permission and help. Old Toby. The dog had been his boon companion for almost a decade. He was buried now in an unmarked grave to the west of the black rubble that was all that remained of Bill Kenton's house.

John was mentally running through a field with Old Toby as he reached his room. His hand gripped the knob and he dug for a key, only to be surprised when the knob turned freely in his hand and the door opened, already unlocked.

John peered in cautiously, saw nothing amiss, stepped slowly inside, turned, and let out a gasp.

"Hello, John," David Burrell said to him. Edgar's dandified brother was seated very casually in a chair in the far corner of the room. "Glad you finally made it back. I was beginning to grow weary of waiting for you."

"What the devil are you doing in my room?"

"I told you. Waiting for you."

"How did you get in here? I left this door locked."

"Money is the key that opens all locks, John. I paid the hotel manager to let me in. Quite simple."

"You have no business here. Go away."

"Oh, John, John, don't start acting that way. Yes, I know I have no legal right to be here. Yes, I know you probably don't like me or any of my family. Yes, this is probably a bit frightening...but since I am here, can't we just talk for a moment? That's all I've come for."

John's heart was beginning to slow down a little. The shock of encountering someone in his room had sent it racing. But as he looked at David, he ceased to worry quite as much. The young man certainly wasn't acting threatening, and he'd never perceived the young swell as a dangerous type. Annoying and overbearing, maybe, but not dangerous.

"What do you want to talk about?" John asked tentatively.

David's manner changed in a barely perceptible way. He grew a touch less arrogant. "I want to talk about my family, and the terrible situations that have come up lately."

"The killings, you mean."

"Well...yes. That. And all the gossip and slander and so on. It's creating some...*problems* for the Burrell family."

"The Kenton family hasn't fared too well lately, either. My father was murdered, and a lot of effort has been made to make sure that no one asks too many questions about how it happened."

"Yes. I know. And I'm sorry about your father, John. I truly mean that. It was terrible that he died. He was a good man."

"Quite honestly, I'm surprised you even noticed. I've

always perceived you, to be truthful, as totally wrapped up in yourself."

David smiled. "I probably deserve that. Yes... I suppose I do. I must admit that I've always

been a proud person. Proud of my name, my family...all of my family, that is, except my brother."

"Ah, yes. Dear old Edgar. Tell me, did you get him out of jail yet?"

"Yes. He's free."

"You don't look particularly happy about it."

"Frankly, I have little regard for my brother. He's done more to ruin the Burrell name than I would have thought any one person can do. He shames me, he shames my family, and if he vanished from this world, it would cause me no great sorrow."

"Well, you're forthright. I'll say that for you. And I agree. I believe that Edgar murdered my father. I want to see him punished for it."

"I know you do. And I can hardly blame you for your feelings. I must admit that Edgar probably had the motive, the opportunity, and the character—or lack thereof—to do such a dreadful thing."

"Look, just tell me why you're here today."

"I'm here for myself, for my father, for my mother. For all the Burrell family members who don't really deserve to have their names ruined by the actions of my brother."

"The actions of your brother, you say. Is that your way of confirming to me that Edgar killed my father?"

"I can't prove anything one way or another. Suffice it to say I can understand and sympathize with your suspicions about my brother. Which leads me to why I've come."

David clamped his mouth shut and stopped speaking. John wondered, perturbed, why people always waited to be prompted at moments such as this. "Go on, then."

"I've come to see if I might not be able to persuade you

to let things go, so to speak...to perhaps accept the fact that nothing you or I or anyone else can do can bring your father back, and that to go on with the kind of inquiries and accusations you have will really only hurt a family that doesn't deserve it."

"Your own, you mean."

"Yes. But listen to me, John! Don't look at me like you are! You have to understand. My father is deeply hurt by all that's happened. Edgar has shamed him deeply. But worse than that, there's what's happened to my mother because of this. My dear mother, always a good, fine woman, but never strong... and now all the shame and whispers have ruined her. She's turned to drink. She never shows herself in public." All at once, all the haughty veneer was stripped away from David Burrell; he was plaintive and human, speaking from his heart. "I love my mother, John. She matters more to me than anyone else. I can't bear to see her hurt."

John, shocked to witness this baring of David Burrell's rarely seen soul, felt an unexpected burst of sympathy. Also, confusion. What was David asking of him?

"David, my purpose isn't to hurt anyone except whoever murdered my father. But you'll have to explain yourself a little more. What do you want from me?"

David Burrell's tongue snaked out and wet his lips. He cleared his throat, eyelids batting nervously. Reaching under his coat, he brought out a well-stuffed leather pouch. "Here," he said, handing it toward John. "Take it. There's money in there. Probably more than you've ever seen at one place. And it's all yours, if you'll only leave Larimont, quit asking all these questions...and let my family regain the peace that it's lost."

John stared silently. The silence became long enough to grow tense, but John showed no eagerness to break it.

"Well?" David Burrell asked. "Will you take it?"

"I should throw you out of here. And I ought to take your head off before I do."

David sputtered disbelievingly. "You're *refusing* me?"

"You think I'd let my father's murderer go unavenged just for a pouch of money?"

"What? I don't understand... I mean, look how much I'm offering you!"

"You really *don't* understand, do you? For you it's all about your family, your worries, your reputation. The great Burrell name! And the rest of us, well, we're just there to be bought off. Hustled out of the way with a few well-placed dollars. Do you think my own father means less to me than your mother means to you, David? Do you really believe that?"

David gaped. "You *are* refusing me!"

"Indeed I am."

David Burrell visibly withdrew, drawing into himself, his face masking over with coldness, his eyes narrowing. "You'll regret this, John. You should have accepted my offer."

"Get out of here."

"I'll tell you what. I'll give you one more chance. If you'll accept my offer, then I'll—"

"Out!"

David Burrell stood, threw his head back, nostrils flaring like a horse's, and stomped out the door. John slammed it shut behind him.

Two days later, Sharon Bradley went to Victoria Rivers, as the recuperating woman lay back on her big four-poster bed and spoke to her confidentially about John Kenton.

"He's changed, Victoria," she said. "Since Edgar Burrell got out of jail, John has shadowed him. And not secretly. Openly. He mocks Edgar, challenges him, insults him. Calls him a murderer and openly declares that Edgar killed his father."

"I've already heard this," Victoria said. "Three people have called on me, telling me the same thing, and worrying about John."

"I'm worried, too."

"No more than I am. John's lost his perspective. He believes that he's proven that Edgar killed his father, but he's proven nothing of the sort. What he has is intuition and a reasonable likelihood of being right. But we still don't even know that Edgar really did it."

"I'm afraid John's going to antagonize Edgar until Edgar gets angry enough to kill him."

"Or to try. Maybe that's John's thinking. He wants Edgar to try to kill him and give him the excuse to defend himself. Tell me, is John carrying his pistol all the time?"

"Constantly. And he all but defies the law to try to take it from him."

"Edgar will kill him. If this keeps up, it'll happen."

"Victoria, don't say that!"

"You fear the same yourself. You wouldn't be here if you didn't."

"But isn't there something we can do?"

"I don't think a thing we can say will persuade John to do anything differently than he is right now," Victoria said. "He's determined to avenge his father's death."

"Maybe Edgar will just get tired of it and go away."

"I don't know, Sharon. I wish he would. But Edgar Burrell doesn't seem the kind to run."

The next day, though, Edgar Burrell did run. The word spread through Larimont that he was gone, and Frederick

Burrell, though unwilling to answer questions, substantially confirmed the same in his silence.

When the news reached John Kenton, he was livid. He strode to the Larimont Bank even before it had opened its doors, and pounded on the door until Frederick Burrell, the only man inside, could no longer ignore it. He rose, left his office, and came to the door, staring at John through the glass.

"Open this door!" John shouted.

"The bank doesn't open for another half an hour," Burrell replied coolly.

"Open the door, damn you, or I'll kick it in!" John yelled back.

Burrell cocked one brow, sighed loudly, and twisted the latch. Then he stepped aside, wisely, for John shoved the door open so hard that Burrell would have been knocked down had he not gotten out of the way.

John had his pistol out and jammed against Burrell's chin even before he'd gotten fully inside. The banker kept his calm, that same haughty brow arched as he gazed at his antagonist.

"Well, John, are you going to murder me in cold blood, right in the doorway of my bank?" he asked.

"I should, by all rights. I consider you almost as guilty as your son of my father's murder. You're the one who squelched the investigation! You're the one who looked out only for yourself and your family and let Scruff Smithers take the blame for a crime he didn't do!"

"I believe you know a lot less about what happened than you pretend," Burrell said. "You've convinced yourself that you have all the answers, when in fact all you have are suppositions."

"The hell with this talk!" John bellowed. "Tell me where Edgar's gone!"

"I don't know. Edgar quit telling me his comings and goings many years ago."

"You're lying!"

"You think Edgar and I are close? You believe he'd come to me if he wanted to flee and not be tracked?"

"So that's what he's doing? Fleeing?"

"It would appear so to me. Please, John, can't you lower that pistol? I'm not going to do anything to endanger myself."

John chuckled bitterly. "No. I suppose you wouldn't." He lowered and holstered the pistol. "Self-protection. That's your forte. Now tell me where Edgar's gone."

"I told you already. I don't know."

"Then tell me where you think he might be."

"That's not anything I can guess."

"Has he run before, in the past?"

"A time or two he's had cause to make himself scarce."

"Where did he go then?"

"Really, I have no idea."

The pistol came out again and jammed hard against Burrell's Adam's apple. John shoved, sending the banker staggering backward. Meanwhile, John lifted on the barrel, making the sight dig into the soft flesh beneath Burrell's chin. Burrell, gagging and sputtering, had to tilt his head back and go up on tiptoes as he backstepped.

"Talk to me, banker! Tell me where Edgar Burrell goes when he's on the run!"

Burrell's voice sounded high and squeaking. "He...he goes to the mountains...he makes camp, stays there alone until the trouble blows over..."

"The mountains? Outside of Larimont?"

"Yes."

"That's a lot of mountain country out there. Where exactly does he go?"

"I don't know."

John clicked back the hammer of his pistol.

"To the bluffs! The bluffs! That's usually where!"

John smiled and nodded. He thumbed down the hammer again and slowly withdrew the pistol. Burrell grabbed at his neck and sank to his knees, panting and sweating.

"I'll see you dead for that!" he snarled at John.

"Maybe you will. But you'll see your boy Edgar dead first," John replied. "After that, you do what you want—or try. All I care about is evening the score with the man who murdered my father."

John turned and walked out of the bank, still holding the pistol. Drew Roberts was crossing the street outside, toward him.

"John Kenton! Surrender that weapon!"

John lifted it, aimed it at the marshal's head, and clicked the hammer.

"I suggest you run like the bought-and-paid-for coward you are," he said to Roberts.

The marshal stared at him hatefully, but only a moment. Seeing the better part of discretion, he turned and walked back the way he'd come, while onlookers all around chuckled at the sight. The marshal had lost the respect of his town as soon as it had become evident that he was in Frederick Burrell's pocket. What had just transpired had sealed that disrespect into permanence. John knew it and was satisfied. Drew Roberts, quite likely, would leave this town before the sun set again, and not return.

John cast his eyes to the mountains. And by then, too, he hoped, Edgar Burrell would be dead.

Chapter 18

The Larimont Bluffs.

It had been years since John Kenton had visited those sheer imposing cliffs, which stood in a semicircular pattern around a deep crevasse in the mountains northwest of town. When had his last visit there been? He thought hard, and remembered, and the memory brought him a sad smile.

He'd taken a young woman there, back maybe a year before he'd left Larimont. Ephelia Green...a simple but appealing young woman who had been the object of a deep crush on John's part at the time. Without the knowledge of her parents or John's father, he'd gone with her to the bluffs on a Saturday and spent far too long there, getting back home after dark and finding major trouble awaiting him and her at their respective homes. He'd never been scolded so thoroughly by Bill Kenton as he had that day. But it had been worth it. Not a thing that was out of line had happened with Ephelia that day in the mountains. It had simply been an innocent, fun outing for the pair of them, and the last time he'd spent any time with her. Though his crush had lingered, hers hadn't. Five months later, she'd married Jimmy

Frost, and a few months past that, John Kenton had packed his bags and left Larimont.

He rode now toward the Larimont Bluffs, the trail so familiar, hardly changed by the passing of years. He thought back to visits to the bluffs years before that outing with Ephelia. As a boy he'd loved to make this trip, and Bill Kenton had taken him often. Sometimes they'd packed rifles and made a hunting trip of it. Other times they'd gone merely to hike and climb and enjoy the splendor of the mountains.

John glanced down at the Winchester booted in his saddle. A new rifle hastily bought before he left town.

Today's journey to the bluffs was no mere hike, he thought grimly. This one was a hunting trip.

Secretly he was surprised at himself. This was out of character for him. He'd never been vengeful, never been prone to violence, never favored scoffing at the due process of law. Had some friend taken off on a similar course, he'd have tried to dissuade him. Told him to get a grip on his senses and not act like a fool.

Now the fool was John Kenton. And he didn't care. All he wanted was the satisfaction of vengeance. To take the life of the man who had taken the life of his father.

John rode on, well out of town, into the foothills and at last to the base of the looming mountains. The mountains had always seemed close enough to touch in Larimont; only when one actually journeyed to them did the several miles of distance between the town and the mountains reveal themselves.

By the time John's horse began plodding up the old, slanting trail toward the Larimont Bluffs, he was already weary, and the heat had gone off his anger. He paused a moment to let Kate rest, and to ask himself if he really wanted to continue. Might it be better to return to Larimont, make contact with a federal marshal or some state officer, and seek justice that way? That would be the more traditional route. The safe way.

Also, the wrong way. For all John knew, Edgar Burrell was planning to leave the state completely. He might not even be at the Larimont Bluffs at all. Every moment's delay might be giving him the chance to put extra miles behind him. No, John didn't have time to take the traditional, unsure route to justice—unsure because such a man as Frederick Burrell surely held the power to influence politicians and courts in secret ways. There was only one thing to do, and that was to bring in Edgar Burrell himself.

No, he corrected himself. Not bring in. Bring *down*.

He realized that fate might be doing him a favor, if Edgar really was at the Larimont Bluffs. There, no witnesses were likely. There, John could do what justice demanded without fearing the consequences.

The thought, contrary to his usual character and way of thinking, strengthened and energized him. He urged Kate ahead, wanting to get every mile out of her that he could before having to dismount and take the hardest part of the trail ahead on foot.

He dreaded the exertion of that climb, recalling how difficult it had been even in the days of light and limber boyhood. No boy of Larimont had ever been able to make the climb up to Larimont Bluffs without growing winded. Except for one.

Edgar Burrell.

Kate had been left far behind, hobbled in a grassy area and no doubt glad to be through with her part of this ascension.

John struggled on, leaning into the slope, panting and sweating and hurting from exertion. He'd not realized how much stamina the relatively easy world of newspaper work had stolen from him. Several times he had to stop fully and catch his breath, taking advantage of those moments to scan the landscape in hope of seeing a smoke plume, or a flash of movement or color against the mountainous backdrop, or hearing some sound, to reveal the camp of Edgar Burrell.

The farther he went, the more unsure of himself John grew. What if Edgar wasn't here at all? Maybe Frederick Burrell had bluffed for his son. Maybe Edgar was hidden away in Burrell's own house. Maybe father and son were having a good laugh together over fool John Kenton, hauling his weary self up a steep mountain in search of someone not even there.

John looked up. He'd reached that certain spot along this way, the place where the Larimont Bluffs suddenly presented themselves in all their daunting splendor—high, striated faces of stone, two hundred feet high at places and sheer all the way down. A place of legends and folk tales, where Indians once fought one another, and where an early settler of the region reportedly threw himself to his death after accidentally shooting his own son during a hunt. John suddenly remembered something he'd forgotten...a gang of boys, including himself, gathering around a dark spot on a stone to stare at it, while none other than Edgar Burrell swore to them all that the dark place was what remained of the bloodstains left by that legendary, suicidal early settler.

John caught himself grinning at the memory and made himself stop. He couldn't begin to think sentimentally, especially about anything involving Edgar Burrell. To do what needed doing, he had to keep his hatred pure and hot.

He put another foot forward and heaved himself farther up the trail, when a shot sounded, and a slug slapped through the tree-tops ahead and spanged against a boulder.

"You won't let it go, will you, Kenton?"

Edgar Burrell's voice echoed off the bluffs, making it hard to discern exactly where it came from. John, who had ducked instinctively when the slug passed over, looked wildly around but could see nothing of Edgar.

"Why don't you leave me be? I didn't kill your father! Go away and let a man have some peace!"

"I'll trail you until I bring you down, Edgar!" John yelled back.

Edgar's answer was a shot, even higher aimed than the first one.

"What's wrong, Edgar? Are you going blind in your old age? You're not even coming close!"

Another shot, just as wild. But John ducked all the same, and wondered what in the devil he was doing, taunting a man who was shooting at him. Maybe he was as crazy as Edgar himself.

"Go away, John!" Edgar yelled. "Leave me be! I want no trouble with you!"

John pondered this. Edgar was shooting at him, at the same time declaring he wanted no trouble.

But was he really shooting *at* him? Edgar was known as a good shot, even in boyhood. But these shots were flying very high, not really even coming close. And there was the fact that Edgar had fled Larimont rather than try to track John down.

Maybe he really didn't want trouble.

John peered about, looking for Edgar. *Whether he wants trouble or not, he's found it. I'll not let my father's murderer go unpunished.*

"You going to go away, John? Or am I going to have to kill you?"

"You got that wrong," John yelled back. "It's me who'll kill you."

Another shot, as high as before...but this time John saw

the powder flash and picked out Edgar's hunched-over form among the rocks on a rugged slope across the crevasse from him.

John rose and scrambled to a safer place, a plan forming in his mind. Edgar saw him and fired again, but once more the shot was very high.

You ought to do better, Edgar, John thought. *You ought to shoot me while you can...because when I get closer to you, your life is over.*

"John?" Edgar called.

John grinned. Edgar had lost sight of him. That was good. It would give him more time to find a place he could aim from, find the best shot...

Something in him faltered. Could he do this, really? Could he line his sights up on a man and squeeze the trigger?

He had to. This was the killer of Bill Kenton. This was a man who would probably escape justice forever unless justice found him right here and now.

"John? You hiding from me?"

John didn't answer. He kept climbing, his eye on a notched rock slightly to the right and above him. A good niche for a sniper.

The air was thin, and John's heart was already hammering from the exertion of the climb and the terror of being shot at, however indirectly. Still, he kept climbing.

He was careful as he crept toward the notched rock. At one point he'd inevitably be exposed to Edgar's view, assuming Edgar happened to look in the right direction at the right time.

John didn't want Edgar to see where he wound up. The key to a successful shot would be surprise. If he could make it to that rock unseen, he could end this business quite summarily.

John climbed on, carefully and far more slowly than he

wished he could. Edgar called for him, scanned the landscape, and fired the occasional skyward shot.

The Larimont Bluffs loomed above, their shadows moving and darkening as the day began to wane.

John realized he had to move faster. Darkness would fall fast here and rob him of his chance. He increased his speed, praying that Edgar would not see him.

He stayed in hiding as long as he could, then reached a place where he had no option but to cross over an open face of stone toward the notched rock that was his goal. He paused there, took three deep breaths, got a grip on his rifle, and began his scramble.

John was halfway across the stone face when Edgar's rifle spoke loudly. He felt a sharp sting in his right calf. His foot went out from under him, his balance vanished, and he tumbled to the right, down the slope, rolling and tumbling.

He lost his rifle somewhere along the way, hearing it clatter off down the stone slope. His head pounded hard against a boulder, and his body dislodged a mass of gravel that poured and danced down the slope all around him.

He thought, in the midst of it all, that he heard another shot but he couldn't be sure.

He tried to find a handhold and stop his tumble, but succeeded only in abrading his hands, scraping off hide to the point of drawing blood. Then his body pitched into open space, and he turned in the air, seeing the world open up below him, a seemingly vast chasm with no bottom.

He screamed as his body turned again and fell.

Chapter 19

His right leg, if not broken, was severely sprained, but John was hardly sensible enough to recognize the fact. All he knew was that he was lying flat on something hard, and in a most uncomfortable position. And he knew he'd fallen. Just how far, he wasn't sure.

He'd struck hard, and though he couldn't be sure of it, he believed he'd been knocked unconscious a few moments after the impact. Even now he wasn't fully aware, feeling stunned. It was difficult to think... but something nagged at him, telling him that he was in danger if he lay here much longer.

Danger...

He looked around, turning his head slowly because his neck, like most of the rest of him, hurt.

Something...a noise. Something drawing near...

With a wince he managed to turn his head, then to roll over. He let out a long, low moan, his leg throbbing with sharp pain as he turned. His new position, though, gave him a view up the long slope he'd tumbled down. He'd hit a lip of rock at the bottom that had pitched him out into open space, and he'd thought he was going to fall a long distance.

Instead, he'd landed on a wide ledge he'd not been able to see from above. It had saved his life, but not without leaving him quite battered.

Someone was coming down the slope, scooting and scuffing and sliding, with a rifle gripped in one hand.

Now he remembered what the danger was...who it was. Edgar Burrell.

Edgar, coming down the slope toward him.

John knew he couldn't remain where he was. If Edgar reached him, as he would in moments, he'd be a dead man.

Had to rise, had to find his own rifle. Had to defend himself...

John steeled himself, preparing for the pain he knew he'd feel. With a groan and superhuman effort, he pushed upright, pulling his left leg up and under him, and rising by its power rather than that of his throbbing right leg.

He was dizzy, dazed, and it was hard to remain upright. He staggered, and in so doing, put weight onto his right leg without meaning to do so.

He yelled and fell to the right, toward the sharp rim of the ledge.

"Hold still, Kenton!" Edgar yelled at him from halfway up the slope. "Hold still... I ain't going to hurt you!"

Of course, you won't, John thought. *You took how many shots at me, threatened me...and now you don't plan to hurt me?*

He tried to rise again, but it was harder this time. He accidentally rolled a little farther toward the ledge rim.

Edgar Burrell was much closer now, coming down faster, almost falling himself now.

John sensed the open space beside him and knew he must move away from it. He couldn't fall, not now, not after having come so close to that fate already.

He wondered where his rifle was. Maybe it hadn't been

as lucky as he and had pitched over the edge of the chasm already.

Edgar was closer now, shouting at him to lie still.

John would not lie still. He wouldn't die this way, just lying there, waiting for his fate. With another groan and effort, he pushed up...

The rim of the ledge, nothing but weak, fractured rock, gave way beneath him. He fell, groping....

Somehow, he caught himself. But the pain was unbearable. He was hanging now by his hands, holding to the unstable, thin edge of the broken ledge, his legs swinging out in space beneath him. His injured right leg throbbed even more painfully than before; his body felt as if it weighed half a ton and would at any moment tear his gripping fingers out by their roots.

He knew he shouldn't look down, but he did, and saw the ground two hundred feet below him. A sheer, straight fall, with jagged rocks below.

He looked up again, fighting a fast-coming sense of faintness. No, God. No. Not like this.

He looked up again. Edgar Burrell was coming down at a near scramble, barely keeping hold of his rifle. But he did keep hold, and in moments was directly above John, standing on the ledge, looking down at him as he swung over space. The rifle was still in his hands.

"So what will it be?" John asked, voice straining. "Will you shoot me, or just let me fall?"

"Neither," Edgar said, kneeling and laying his rifle aside. "I'm going to pull you up, John. Hang on."

John was so surprised, he almost let go. "What?"

"I'm going to pull you up! Are you hard of hearing?" Edgar lay on his belly, bracing himself by anchoring his feet between boulders. Reaching over, he grabbed John's wrists, wrapping his hands around tightly, just as John's fingers were about to let go of their own accord.

"You're going to drop me," John said, staring up at Edgar's face. "You're going to tell me to let go, then you're going to drop me."

"If I wanted you dead, I could have shot you before. Or I could have just left you hanging here so you'd fall when your strength ran out. I don't want to kill you, John."

"I don't trust you..."

"Do you have any choice?"

John knew he didn't. If he was to live, it would be through Edgar's efforts. If Edgar intended to let him fall, there was nothing John could do to stop him. And without Edgar's help, he'd fall anyway.

He had nothing to lose in trusting Edgar, and maybe his life to gain.

John let go of the ledge.

Immediately Edgar's face twisted into a grimace of effort as John's full weight transferred itself to his grip. John stared into that twisted face, wondering if at any moment it might break into a dark grin, then recede swiftly from him as he was allowed to drop. It didn't happen. Edgar, through gritted teeth, urged him to hang on, to find a foothold if he could, and to help him as he tried to pull John up.

It came to John quite clearly, as he hung there, that Edgar really was trying to save him. The same man who had threatened him and fired his rifle—the same man John himself had been eager to kill—was now trying to keep him alive. It made little sense.

John groped with his feet, seeking a toehold. Edgar's hands were beginning to tremble, his grip on John's wrists slipping slightly. John knew Edgar could never get him back on the ledge alone. He'd have to have help.

But the more John moved his feet—in actual fact, his left foot, for his injured right leg hurt far too badly for him to use—the harder it was for Edgar to continue to hold him. Meanwhile, a new fear arose. If the ledge had broken once, might it do so again, especially now that the weight of two men was upon it?

John's foot touched a rock, found a small crack. It slipped away from him, but he guided his foot back and managed to wedge the toe of his boot in the crack. Pushing up, he saw Edgar grin slightly, and they actually made progress, John edging up a little, and strengthening his hold on Edgar, and Edgar's on him, at the same time.

"We'll make it, John," Edgar said. "Just keep pushing."

Together they worked, John giving it all he had, Edgar doing the same. By inches, John moved up. Edgar, meanwhile, edged back, using his braced feet for leverage.

"Soon," he said. "Soon you'll be able to take hold and pull yourself over."

There was a cracking sound, a slight shifting of the rock of the ledge.

"It's breaking," John said, finding his voice a whisper. "The ledge is breaking."

"No," Edgar said. "No, John. It's just a crack in the stone, that's all. It's plenty strong enough to hold us. Come on, now. Pull!"

Then, with a mutual effort so great it drew a yell from the throats of both men, they made a great pull and heave, and the next thing John knew, he was holding to the rim of the ledge again, and Edgar was reaching over, gripping his clothing, pulling up...

John rolled over onto the ledge, lay there a moment, gasping for breath, actually fainting for a second or two. Then Edgar stirred him to rise, pulled him back to a thicker, safer portion of the ledge.

John lay on his back, blinking, looking at the sky, now beginning to darken.

"Why?" he asked. "First you shoot at me, then you save me."

"I didn't shoot at you," Edgar replied. "I shot above your head. I was trying to scare you away."

"I came here to kill you, you know. Even when I fell down the slope, I was trying to get to a place where I could shoot you."

"I figured. That's why I put that particular bullet a little closer to you."

"I thought you'd shot me. I felt a sting in my leg."

"I didn't hit you. Maybe it was some chipped stone from where the bullet struck."

John sat up and looked at Edgar, who was crouched, sweating and breathless, about four feet away, looking back at him.

"Edgar, my father—"

"I really didn't kill him, John. I'm not lying to you." He paused. "Do you believe me?"

John thought about it. "I didn't. Now, I think, I do."

"I hope you do. Because it's the truth. I've done many a wrong thing in my time. I robbed my own father's bank. I sent the very woman I love into a life little better than that of a common whore, and that with my own father. Me and the Horner brothers tried to scare you and Victoria and poor old Scruff's niece into letting it all alone. I tried to bribe you. But it was all to cover up the bank robbery and about June. That's all. I never killed your father."

"Why did you run out here to the bluffs?"

"I wasn't trying to run. I came here for the same reason I always have, all my life. To escape for just a little while, and to think. To try to figure out what I need to do." He paused. "And what's really going on. And after I got here, I realized I've got a lot to make up for. I've done some foolish and wrong things...and in a way, all this is my fault. None of it would have happened if me and the Homers hadn't decided to rob Pap's bank." He chuckled. "It seemed quite a joke at the time. Rob Pap's bank and leave him in a situation where he can't do anything about it without having the whole world learn that he's been dallying with a gal young enough to be his daughter." In the gathering gloom, Edgar paused and looked down. "Poor June. She'd do anything I asked of her...and I asked all the wrong things. God forgive me."

"Why the change of attitude, Edgar?"

"Because of June. When she died, that changed everything. It took me some time to see it, but everything was different. It was the end."

"Edgar, if you didn't kill my father, if it wasn't you who shot through the window and killed June... then who did?"

"I didn't know... I think I do now."

"Tell me."

"I think it's somebody who cares a hell of a lot about the good name of the Burrell family."

John paused. "David."

"Yes. And if I know David, he's probably still worried about our precious family reputation. And if he's gone this far to try to protect it..."

"Edgar...David is still in Larimont. And so are Victoria, and Sharon."

"That's why we need to get back there and go pay a call on them. Before David decides to do the same."

"I can't walk, Edgar. My leg..."

"Reckon we'll have to splint it."

"But even then, how can I make it all the way back down?"

"I'll help you. Down's always easier than up."

"Edgar... I'm sorry I doubted you. I really thought you were the one."

"I'd have thought the same in your shoes. Now hush up and help me find something to brace that leg with. It'll be dark soon, and nigh on to midnight before we can make it back to Larimont."

Chapter 20

Victoria Rivers stirred in her bed, vaguely conscious of the clock in the hallway having just chimed midnight. And something else, too...something she couldn't quite grasp.

She rolled to one side and resettled her head in her pillow. The clock ticked repetitively, hypnotic and faint, and she began to sink farther into sleep. But a moment later, she heard, or maybe just sensed, something odd...and opened her eyes.

She sat up.

"Sharon?" she said softly.

There was no reply, but it seemed to her that something in the shadows beyond the open door of her room shifted and changed. There was a whisper of noise, almost below the level of hearing.

"Sharon, is that you?"

No answer.

"Sharon, are you sleepwalking?"

No answer again...but this time she was certain something moved out there.

Victoria's heart began to hammer. She stared out the

doorway, looking hard and listening, and trying not to breathe very loudly.

For a full minute she remained as she was, not moving, hardly blinking. Then slowly she turned her head to the left and looked toward her wardrobe in the corner. Beside it, unseen in the night shadows, leaned her shotgun. Loaded. Hardly ever touched, but always kept at that place, just in case she needed it.

She wondered if she needed it now.

Victoria snapped her head back around, having heard something beyond the doorway.

Reflexively, she held her breath.

But still she heard the sound of breathing.

It was all she needed to hear. Rising quickly, she ran toward the wardrobe and grabbed the shotgun, as through the doorway came a dark, phantom figure, racing toward her.

Her hand closed on the cold stock of the shotgun. She yanked it up, tried to turn, but a hand closed like an overtightened vise on her right shoulder and pushed her, making her stumble against the wall.

The man, whoever it was, shoved against her, slamming her against the wall panel, crushing her, muttering curses vaguely in a whispered voice that sounded familiar. She smelled his breath and the alcoholic stench it bore.

She was trapped, her hand still on the shotgun, but with no room available to let her hoist it.

She felt the man's hand grope down her arm, find her hand and the shotgun stock it gripped. He cursed again—and she knew who it was then—and took hold of the shotgun, pulling it away from her violently. He let go of her at the same moment and backed away.

"Please," Victoria said. "Please, David, don't kill me!"

David Burrell laughed. "Kill you. Why would I want to kill you, Victoria?" The shotgun was raised, aiming at her. She could barely make it out in the darkness. "Why would I want to kill someone just because they're determined to destroy my family and its reputation? What motive would that give me, hmm?"

His sarcasm deepened her fear. This young man was in a mental state that was quite dangerous. Victoria knew then, with certainty, that this was who had killed Bill Kenton. She knew why, too. Bill Kenton had dared to probe into a crime that had Burrell family fingerprints on it. And he hadn't backed away. He'd been ready to expose a bank robbery performed by Edgar Burrell, and in so doing, bring shame on the Burrell family's precious name.

Victoria wanted to cringe, to beg, to pray aloud... She wanted to scream for Sharon, upstairs, to come down and save her. But what could Sharon do against a man armed with a shotgun, and maybe other weapons besides?

She forced herself to maintain control...she had to think, to get out of this in whatever way she could. Cringing and begging wouldn't work.

"You should have left it alone," David said. "You should have never had anything to do with John Kenton. He's a fool. As big a fool as his father was. That's why I had to get rid of him, you know. Bill Kenton didn't have the common sense, the common *decency*, to leave a good family's reputation alone. He had to be gotten rid of, before he ruined everything."

Hard as it was to do, Victoria said what she knew she must. "Yes...yes, you're right, of course."

"You *agree* with me?"

"I...understand you. I can see why you felt as you did."

David Burrell's face was invisible to her, but she could sense the confusion it surely would have revealed had she been able to see it.

"You're trying to toy with me," he said. "You know I've come to kill you—you know I *have* to kill you—and you're trying to stop me."

He was certainly right about that. "David, you don't need to kill me. I can help you."

"Help me? How?"

"I can persuade John Kenton to stop asking questions. I can convince him that someone else killed his father. I can make him go away and stop bothering your family."

A pause. "You'd do that?"

"Yes, David. Of course, I would. I like you, David. I always have. I didn't realize we were causing you so much pain."

His voice sounded weak, rather pitiful. "There has been pain. So much. But not all your fault, or even John Kenton's. That I have to admit."

She sensed something in him growing calmer, less dangerous. Thank God. She'd try to keep him talking...for when he was talking, he was unlikely to be shooting. "What do you mean?"

"My father, and Edgar...both of them should be ashamed of themselves. The things they've done! The risks they've taken with the family's good name." He paused. "My father was doing a very wrong thing, you know. With June Layne...the harlot!"

"Oh. I see."

"Yes. It was shameful. I don't think he knew that I knew. But I did. And I was so ashamed... I despised what he was doing. If word had gotten out, can you imagine what that would have done to our family's reputation? Can you *imagine?*"

He was beginning to sound worked up again. *Please, David,* she thought, *stay calm. Please.*

"*I* had to kill Bill Kenton. But my father never knew. I never told him."

Victoria felt she should speak but knew nothing to say.

"Father has thought all along that Edgar killed Bill Kenton. Did you know that? It's true. He assumed that

Edgar did it, and so Father forced Alexander Layne to tell the story against Scruff Smithers, to keep himself safe, and to keep his love affair with June Layne a secret. That was Father's motivation, you see—looking out for himself. He doesn't really care much about Edgar, but he did believe that if Edgar was arrested for the murder, he'd reveal the truth about June Layne and Father. And he couldn't have that. No, indeed."

David had lowered the shotgun a little, but not fully. Victoria was feeling weak, faint, but dared not move from where she was.

"You know," David mused, "this whole sorry business has about exhausted me. I've been so busy, lurking around in the background, watching, doing what had to be done to protect my family. When John Kenton showed up, asking his questions, poking his nose into my family's business, I began to follow him. Everywhere he went, whatever he did, I was there, watching. It was hard, sometimes, to do it without being detected. But I succeeded. There was hardly a move he made, hardly a place he went, that I wasn't watching, and following...and doing whatever needed doing to try to stop the terrible damage he was doing. I watched him almost constantly.

"And I watched the people he talked to. Like Lawrence Poteet. I saw the way Lawrence was beginning to act, his suspicious manner, those shifting, worrying eyes of his... I knew he was becoming a threat. And when he took John into his home, talked to him, I knew he had to be removed. So I removed him. Hated to do it, really. I've always been fond of Lawrence." He paused; she sensed him looking at her. "I've always been fond of you, too."

Under the circumstances, she found little comfort in that.

"David," she suggested, "would you like to move elsewhere, someplace we can be more comfortable while we talk?"

"I'm fine where I am."

"But I'm not... I was injured recently, you know. I've been mostly bedfast ever since, and it's hard to stand here."

To her surprise, David Burrell laughed. "You looked plenty strong enough when you sprang out of that bed and ran for the shotgun."

"I was scared, David. You frightened me. I'm still scared."

"I'm sorry it has to be this way."

"It doesn't. I think I can help you, David. You don't need to hurt me. You don't need to hurt anyone else at all."

"Help me? How?"

"Come into the kitchen with me. I'll make us coffee. There's some bread in there, I think. Sharon baked two loaves this afternoon. We can eat and talk."

"How can you help me, though?"

"I can cause all the questions to stop. I can make John stop everything he's doing. I can make all this go away."

He paused. "No. No. It's too late. People are already dead because of this...people I've killed. Bill Kenton. Lawrence Poteet. And June. Poor June. I didn't realize it was her. As much as I despise her for the harlot she was, I didn't mean to kill her."

"Who were you trying to kill, then? Me? Sharon Bradley?"

"Either of you would have done nicely. And don't think ill of me for saying such a thing. It's not really my choice, you know. I've been forced to all this."

"Let's go to the kitchen, Edgar."

"No. We need to end this right now."

"Are you going to shoot me right in my own house?"

"No." He cracked the shotgun and removed its shells. Pocketing them, he tossed the weapon onto Victoria's bed. Reaching beneath his jacket, he pulled out something that

Victoria couldn't really see, though a sliver of moonlight caught it and she detected the fast gleam of shining metal.

"I have to be quieter than a shotgun would be," he said. "We can't awaken Sharon, you know."

He raised his hand, the unidentified weapon in it glittering again in the shaft of moonlight.

Victoria screamed, as loudly as she could, and ran straight at David Burrell with her arms extended. She hit him in the chest, knocking him down, then ran right across him.

He cursed and swung his weapon at her. It missed, but she heard a chopping noise as it struck the floor, like a blade sinking into wood.

Victoria ran, crying out for Sharon.

Just ahead was the front door of her house. She could exit the house, raise a cry outside and escape safely...

But she couldn't, not with Sharon upstairs, probably not fully realizing yet what was happening.

Victoria turned up the staircase, running and shouting. David Burrell came into the hallway below, cursing. His weapon was in his hand. Victoria glanced down as she reached the top of the stairs and saw, in the brighter moonlight in the front hall, that what he held was a meat cleaver.

She screamed again.

A meat cleaver. David Burrell had come here planning to hack her to death, then Sharon.

Sharon was already standing in the doorway of her room when Victoria rounded the corner toward her.

"Victoria, what is—"

"Go back inside!" Victoria yelled, hearing David coming up the stairs already. "Go inside and close the door!"

Victoria was almost on top of Sharon by the time she finished the sentence. Sharon backed inside quickly, Victoria bursting in past her, and slammed the door shut. Victoria turned and latched it, then twisted the key in the lock. Grabbing a chair, she shoved the back of it beneath the doorknob and jammed it in place.

"Victoria, what's happening?"

"David Burrell's out there... It's he who killed Bill, and Lawrence Poteet, and June—"

Something slammed hard against the door. David Burrell, throwing himself against the panels so hard that the door bowed and seemed about to pop off its hinges.

Sharon screamed.

"Pile more furniture against the door!" Victoria demanded. "Hurry!"

Together she and Sharon pushed a heavy chest of drawers toward the door. They jammed it hard against the edge of the door.

On the other side, David Burrell was cursing and pounding. Victoria and Sharon scrambled for other items of furniture, trying to increase the weight of the barricade.

A loud chopping sound echoed from the door, followed by another, and another, and suddenly the wood splintered.

David Burrell was chopping at the door with the cleaver.

Sharon screamed again, cringing back, falling to her knees and covering her face with her hands.

Victoria went to her, grabbed her, shook her. "Stop it! We can stop him if we keep our heads and work together."

"How? How?"

Victoria looked wildly around the dark room. Her eye fell on a pair of kerosene lamps standing on the mantelpiece.

The hacking of the door continued, splinters ripping out with each blow.

Victoria ran to the mantel and grabbed one lamp. She pulled the globe free and tossed it aside; it shattered on the floor. Yanking out the wick mechanism, she grabbed a block of matches off the mantel.

Sharon grasped what Victoria was doing and went

through the same routine with the other lamp, as the door continued to be hacked away.

She and Victoria moved together to the door. Though much of it was covered by the furniture they had put in place, a couple of inches of the base of the door were still accessible. Together they poured their kerosene onto the floor; it ran out beneath the door to pool around David Burrell's feet.

Victoria prayed that the young man, in his frenzy, would not notice the kerosene.

Breathing a prayer, Victoria broke off a match, struck it, and lit the kerosene.

Flame caught and traveled along the kerosene, passing under the door.

David Burrell howled like a wounded beast. The hacking on the door ceased. His screams continued out in the hall as he danced and slapped at the flames crawling up his legs.

Victoria looked at Sharon. Their plan had worked, but at best it would keep David Burrell back only a few moments. And now flames were crawling up the door. The same effort that had temporarily driven back David Burrell was also likely to trap them in this room.

The upper part of the door splintered seconds later. In one great burst, David Burrell had hammered the panel away. In the semi-darkness, illuminated only by infiltrating moonlight and the weird flicker of the kerosene flames, they saw him.

David Burrell ignored the flames now, clambering right through them, and through the shattered door, onto the top of the chest of drawers. He leaped from it onto the floor, the cleaver in his right hand. Cursing, he shoved aside the furniture that had blocked the door, strengthened by his fury.

A line of flame crawled up the left leg of his trousers. He noticed it, beat it out quickly, hardly seeming to care. He glared at the two women.

"You're dead. Both of you, you're dead. And when I find John Kenton, he's dead, too. None of you are even fit to live...spreading stories about my family, hurting our reputation, not caring how such things make my poor mother feel! I hate you! I hate all of you!"

He was upon them in a moment, shoving Sharon aside, making her fall. He tripped Victoria, came down hard upon her, pinning her with his weight. He brought up the cleaver and brought it down.

Victoria somehow managed to pull to one side and avoid the blow. The cleaver bit into the floor beside her. David Burrell cursed and pulled it free. He raised it again.

"David!"

David froze at the unexpected sound of the male voice. He turned, let go of Victoria, and came to his feet.

The flames had died away at the doorway, the wood having not fully caught. In that smoking doorway stood Edgar Burrell, rifle in hand. He stared back at his younger brother.

"No, David. No. Let her alone."

"Why the hell should I? Where did you come from?"

"From the Larimont Bluffs. Where I was trying to hide... But I can't hide anymore. The things I've done have cost the lives of too many good people, the best of them being the very woman I loved. No more of that, David. Let's you and me leave this be right now, and stop before things get worse."

"But the family, Edgar...the *family!* Do you not care about the things these people are saying, the way it hurts Mother, the way it ruins our family name? No, no. I suppose you *don't* care. You've never cared! If not for the way you've behaved, none of this would have happened. None of it."

"I know," Edgar said. "I know. And that's why I came back. Because I'm going to face what I've done."

A voice called from downstairs. Sharon glanced at Victoria. John's voice! Had he followed Edgar here?

"I'll kill you, too!" David said to his brother. "It's your fault as much as anyone's!"

He raised the cleaver and advanced toward Edgar.

Edgar backed up a step and raised the rifle. But he hesitated, didn't fire. David moved in, swinging.

Edgar screamed; the rifle fell to the floor, and with it, three of his fingers.

Clutching his blood-spurting hand, he scrabbled over the dresser blocking the doorway, backed off into the hall, and flopped down onto his rump. David advanced and began hacking. Edgar tried to get away, but David was relentless.

When he'd hacked his brother seven or eight times, he tossed the cleaver back over his shoulder into the bedroom, reached to Edgar's neck, and began to choke him.

Up the stairs came John Kenton, all but crawling, dragging his splinted leg, unable to move fast enough to reach the Burrell brothers.

"No!" he yelled. "No, David! Don't kill him!"

David jerked his head up and glared at John, his eyes wild in the moonlight, fired with hate...

And even as John watched, that fire died, instantly, as Sharon Bradley emerged from the bedroom with the cleaver in her hand, and brought it down with skull-splitting force onto and into the head of David Burrell.

He froze, the metal buried in his brain, gave one twitch, and fell to the side, dying with his eyes open.

Edgar Burrell, brutally cut, bleeding profusely, turned his head and stared into the open eyes of his dead brother. He drew in a deep, slow breath, let it out. He did not draw another.

CHAPTER 21

ONE WEEK LATER

John leaned on the cane that had become his steady companion over the last several days, as his sprained and bruised leg slowly healed. He looked at the gravestone of his father and thought of all the years past, and the years he'd anticipated he'd still have the pleasure of his father's company.

Life was a strange, unpredictable thing. A man never knew how long he'd be privileged to call his blessings his own.

John looked up and smiled at Sharon Bradley, who stood at the gate of the graveyard, respectfully giving John time alone with his father's memory.

If a man didn't know how long his blessings would remain his own, maybe the lesson to be learned was to waste no time in taking full advantage of them.

He hobbled over to Sharon, who slipped her arm into his and helped bear his weight as they walked together.

"Frederick Burrell is leaving town, you know. Taking his wife with him. I heard it from Victoria this morning."

"Yes. She told me, too. You know, I feel sorry for them, in a way. None of this was anything they planned to happen. Just a series of bad circumstances—one son being basically worthless and amoral, robbing his own father's bank, misusing his lover, the other son being, ultimately, a drunkard and near madman, obsessed with family pride and protecting his beloved mother's delicate feelings. But who would have dreamed he would go as far as he did?"

"I'm glad it's over."

"So am I."

"Where will you go now, John?"

"I don't know. I have a job to return to...if I decide to."

"Might you decide differently?"

"I could be persuaded."

"What are you thinking, John?"

"I'm thinking that maybe, just maybe, a small newspaper might be able to survive in Larimont. Not that I'd have much money to hire a staff of workers. Probably just me...and maybe one other person."

"I can think of a possible applicant."

John smiled and patted her hand.

"Coming home to Larimont... I should have done it sooner, while my father was still with me. So often we make the important decisions too late."

"And sometimes we don't," she replied.

They walked together, slowly, down the dusty road and toward the town. The breeze was rising with the sun. It was going to be, as best could be told, quite a fine day.

The Treasure of Jericho Mountain

To Matthew Cameron Judd

Chapter 1

A town of dust and shadows, of vacant windows and empty doorways. A street of creaking faded signs and unpainted lumber. This was the corpse of a town, an empty place that knew no life. There had been a time when the streets were living things and the buildings that now stood weather-beaten and empty had housed businesses that thrived and prospered.

Now the town stood empty, a memorial to times that had been and days that would never come again.

Into those dusty streets Jeremy Prine rode, and his eyes were alert and quick as he scanned the rows of ramshackle buildings. For days he had ridden this trail, and there were times when he had been unable to explain to his own satisfaction just why he was doing it. A single, cryptic telegram, a tantalizing message—that had been all that had moved him. When first he received it, he had tried to ignore it, but the message, vague though it was, had burned into his mind, stirring feelings that he had long forgotten—the sense of mystery, of adventure.

The first lines had been mere directions to this Colorado ghost town. Then the date and these words: "Important meeting, money to be gained. Arrive before nightfall. Thomas Stuart." That was all. Nothing specific, nothing to hint at what might be involved. But two things about that telegram had drawn his full attention and kept Prine from tossing it aside without a second thought.

Partly it had been the words "money to be gained". Money was one thing he did not possess in abundance right now, and he was interested in anything that might improve his less-than-satisfactory financial condition. There was little work for cowboys these days, especially aging ones. The open range was gone, lined by barbed-wire fences and crisscrossed by railroads. When cattle had been scattered across the range, it had been necessary to round them up, and that required men. Now that cattle ranged within the confines of fenced-in ranges, there was little need for men like Jeremy Prine.

But even more than the money, the thing that had attracted him had been the name on the telegram. Not the entire name—the "Thomas" meant nothing to him—but that last name, the name that called up memories of old friendship, of times good and bad, pleasant and disturbing.

Bob Stuart. Prine whispered the name to himself as his horse sauntered down the dusty and deserted street. How many times had he thought of that name since the days when the conflict between North and South was still raging? He couldn't even begin to estimate; Bob Stuart had been on his mind many times. It was hard to believe that they had lost track of each other; men who suffer together through an ordeal such as the bloody battle at Shiloh should not drift apart. Still, Stuart occupied Prine's thoughts, though now he did not know even if he were living or dead.

Perhaps now he would find out. The odds that the Stuart of the telegram was connected in any way with his old Civil War partner were remote, yet a possibility. At any rate, he would know soon. He had come as the telegram had directed, and if there were anyone else in the town a meeting would be inevitable.

Prine's eyes swept the bare street, looking for some evidence of the presence of another living human being. There was something ghostly about the place, and it filled him with a vague apprehension. He was not one to become frightened at a shadow, and superstition had never plagued him, but the emptiness all around him, combined with the sense of mystery and slight caution the telegram had produced in him, made him realize how essential alertness was right now. He looked carefully from one side of the street to the other, squinting his eyes slightly to look inside the dark interiors of the boarded buildings.

Was that a hoofbeat he heard behind him?

He turned in the saddle, every sense keenly alert. Behind him a shutter banged in the wind, its echo resounding down the street. Prine let out a low sigh and turned forward again.

"Mr. Jeremy Prine, I assume?"

The voice surprised him, causing his hand to drop instinctively to his side arm. Immediately his ears ascertained the direction from which the voice had come, and he saw a slender young man who looked back at him from the porch of a deserted hotel. The fellow had a grin on his face and an almost devilish twinkle in his eye. Prine was struck with the feeling that there was something familiar in the face of the young man and looked at him intently.

The man was posed casually on the roofed porch, leaning against the supporting post with his arms crossed in front of him and one foot cocked on its toe. He had apparently stepped from the inside of the building just as Prine's attention had been diverted by the loose shutter. He was dressed for riding, but the cut of his clothes was fancy, and even in his dust-coated condition he looked distinguished. His features were well formed, and his eyes were brown and clear. He held his pose only a moment, then walked lightly down the steps, his hand extended and his grin unfaded.

"Thomas Stuart, Mr. Prine," he said, his voice light and friendly. "I'm the man who sent you the telegram. I can't tell you how pleased I am that you responded. I've heard a lot about you."

Prine was somewhat at a loss at how to react to this fellow's friendliness. Stuart acted as if he had known him for years, though Prine could not recall where they might have met. The feeling that the young man's face was familiar continued, though. Prine felt slightly on the defensive.

The feeling of recognition only grew as Prine shook the extended hand.

"Mr. Stuart, who is your father?" Prine's words seldom failed to come straight to the point.

Stuart grinned. "So you've got it figured out already, have you? My father is—or was—Robert Stuart, the very one who you served with in the Confederate Army. It was through him that I heard of you."

Prine shook the man's hand again when he heard that, but a shiver of sadness rose in him. "You say he *was* your father—I guess that means old Bob's dead, doesn't it?"

Stuart nodded. "I'm sorry to have to bring you the news. From what Father said I gathered you two were pretty close back in the war."

Prine dismounted. "We were. Those weren't good times, by any means, but it was a time of good friendships."

Prine began walking his mount toward the deserted livery stable down the street. "I truly do hate to hear that old Bob's dead—I truly do. What of your ma, Mr. Stuart?"

"She's gone too, a year after Father. After he died, I don't think she cared to live anymore. He left her a lot as far as material things go—money, a good home—but it wasn't the things he could give her that meant much to Ma—it was Father himself. I did my best for her after he died, but I couldn't take his place. She followed on right after him, and in a way, I think that's just what she wanted to do."

Prine unsaddled his gelding in the shadows of the livery, putting the animal in one of the empty stalls. What remnants of hay that lay around on the floor were so old and dry as to be useless, but in a rain barrel outside there was water. Prine found an old, battered bucket and filled it, setting it before the horse. The only other animal in the building was a stallion; Stuart's mount.

Prine pulled a cloth tobacco sack from his vest pocket and poked it toward Stuart with a faint grunt. The other refused the offer politely, and Prine paused long enough to expertly roll a cigarette with experienced fingers. He lit it and drew in a huge cloud of fragrant smoke with a look of satisfaction on his face. The pair walked out of the livery into the light of the street.

Stuart led the way back to the hotel. "I brought a bottle of rye. Can I interest you in a drink?"

That was the best offer Prine had received in some time, and he told Stuart as much. Already he was beginning to like the young fellow in spite of his natural apprehensions, partly because he was Bob Stuart's son, and partly because of some unidentifiable something in his pleasant disposition and disarming smile. But Prine also wondered if maybe he were letting down his guard a bit too early. After all, he didn't even know what this man had in mind.

The interior of the old hotel lobby was like a faded photograph, a dusty relic. The furniture was still there, sitting as if the occupants had decided in one moment to walk out the door and never return. Dust coated the room, half an inch thick in some places, collected over a decade and undisturbed by cloth or broom. A few clean spots betrayed the areas where Stuart had been waiting. Prine wondered how long the young man had been there.

Stuart disappeared behind a counter and reappeared

with a bottle of rye whiskey. He popped the cork and filled two small glasses he had pulled from somewhere beneath the counter. Prine took his drink and drained a large swallow.

"The telegram mentioned a meeting. Is this it?"

"You might say this is the waiting period. There are still others to come." Stuart sipped his drink slowly and smiled. "I think you will be surprised—and pleased—when you see who they are."

Prine was intrigued. It was a tantalizing mystery, this strange man and his ghost-town meeting. But one mystery had been solved: the question of why Prine felt the fellow was familiar. It was because in the smile and crinkle of the young man's eyes he saw a reflection of the Stuart he had fought beside years before. The younger Stuart was in many ways the image of his father. It made Prine feel a little nostalgic to look at him and reminded him also of how many years had passed since he was this man's age. It made him feel rather ancient.

Stuart looked at Prine's face and read the question there. He flashed his self-confident smile again. "I'm sure you're wondering what this is all about. Before I fill you in, let me assure you that if you listen to what I propose, then act on it, you stand to make a good deal of money."

At that moment the neighing of a horse punctuated Stuart's words, and Prine's eyes flashed toward the open door to the street beyond.

"Ah!" exclaimed Stuart. "I think more of our party have arrived."

Chapter 2

It took Prine only an instant to recognize the bearded, gruff-looking man who rode down the street. The younger man by his side he couldn't place.

"John Ballard! You old devil! Who would have thought..." Prine's excitement got the best of his common sense, and he ran out into the street, giving his greeting with such vigor that the approaching riders' horses nearly reared beneath them. The bearded man sent forth a low curse and went for his gun, simultaneously trying to still his agitated mount. The younger man was so startled that he came close to losing his seat in the saddle, even without the help of his startled gelding.

John Ballard's gun was halfway out of its holster before he recognized the figure before him. His eyes changed. A softness came onto his features.

"Prine? Jeremy Prine?" The gun went back into its holster. The horse quieted, and the bearded man stared openmouthed at Prine. The younger man had more trouble controlling his animal, but when finally he succeeded, he looked first at Prine, then at the bearded man, with an expression of confusion.

In a moment, Ballard was out of his saddle and clasping the hand of Prine. Both men were smiling broadly, almost ridiculously, hands pumping and friendly arms clasping each other's shoulders. This was a reunion that neither was expecting but which both found intensely pleasant. Stuart stood watching upon the porch, the pose in which Prine had first seen him resumed, and a smile warmed his features. But unnoticed by the others, his expression grew colder when he glanced toward the young man who had ridden in beside Ballard. He glared at him silently.

"You old swamp rat!" Prine exclaimed, his grin still beaming. "I would never have imagined that I would see you here! I can't tell you how many times I've thought about you since the old days."

"Same with me, Prine! I figured I would probably never see you again. Oh, I planned to look you up a few years after the war was over, but you know how those things work out." He stopped and looked at his friend, as if the mere sight of him gave him immense satisfaction. "Jeremy Prine! Alive and kicking, and here in the flesh! I guess all the old Confederacy isn't gone, after all!"

"Ballard, that wouldn't be your boy there, would it? It seems I see a little of your good looks in his face."

Ballard grinned and glanced at the mounted young man. "That's my only boy, Prine, and I'm right proud of him. I didn't aim to come here without him by my side. Thad, get down here! I want you to meet an old war partner of mine—Lord knows you've heard enough tales about him! Come on, boy!"

The tag "boy" didn't fit the man; he was at least two or three years past twenty, every bit as old as Stuart, and very muscled. He dismounted expertly, then walked with a firm stride to where Prine and his father stood. His hand came out and Prine grasped it. The grip was strong.

"Pleased to meet you, Mr. Prine. Father's told me a lot of

tales about you and the rest of that wartime gang you all hung around with."

Prine grinned. "You can drop the 'Mr.'—Prine will be sufficient. It looks like old Ballard's got a good one to carry on after him. I'm proud to meet you."

"Well, it seems this reunion is more pleasant than I expected! It makes me proud that I brought you together."

The voice was Stuart's. Prine had almost forgotten the man's presence. Ballard eyed the young fellow strangely, as did Thad, but the pleasant grin remained on Stuart's face as he introduced himself to the newcomers.

Ballard's handshake was a good deal less spirited than it had been with Prine. His gaze left no doubt that he was wary. Prine expected that. Ballard had always been a cautious man in the earlier years, and the fact that he had not come on this journey alone was sufficient proof he had not changed.

But when Ballard learned the identity of Stuart's father, he softened a good deal, and his attitude became more open. And when Stuart offered the new arrivals a drink of rye, Ballard was almost totally converted. After seeing to the horses, he headed up the steps to the hotel in high spirits, with Thad close behind.

The quartet passed several long and pleasant minutes sipping whiskey and discussing bygone times before any serious conversation began. Prine had much he wished to hear from his old friend, and Ballard was every bit as curious about Prine's affairs. He was curious, too, about Bob Stuart, and he was saddened visibly when the younger Stuart related the same fact he had told Prine. Ballard looked down into his near-empty shot glass and sighed.

"It gets us all sooner or later. I hate to hear that old Bob's gone—I dearly would have liked to see him again."

When Prine asked Ballard about his activities since the war, the bearded man brightened and leaned back in his chair as he talked.

"After the war I headed down into Georgia for a while, but things were bad there. The war had pretty much demolished the land...there were homes burned, farms destroyed, just general ruin all over. I didn't stay long—there was no good way for a free-roaming man like me to make an honest living. I headed across the Mississippi, roamed a while. I wound up in Missouri and started farming for a feller. Pretty soon I had saved enough to buy a little land for myself, and I began farming on my own. Got married, had Thad here, and that's pretty much how it went. I never got rich, but then I never starved neither. My wife, she's gone now—it's been five, six years—but me and old Thad are still there, making a go of it. I guess I should be there tending to my business right now, but that telegram got my curiosity up and I had to find out what it was about." He eyed Stuart with open curiosity.

Prine told his own story then. "I never tried farming like you did, Ballard—couldn't ever stand to stomp through hog manure and get dirt underneath my fingernails any more than I had to. But after the war there wasn't nothing left for me, neither. I came to Kansas, then hit Montana as a cowboy. It was a good life for a while, but now there's just not much call for an over-the-hill cowpoke. Barbed wire and railroads have just about knocked men like me out of business. I've been riding the soup line for some time now, working at whatever kind of job I can pick up. It don't sound like much, but I guess in a way it suits me. I'm awful short on funds about now, but I reckon I'll live. 'Specially if Mr. Stuart's proposition is as good as he makes it sound." He glanced over at the young man, who sat casually sipping his drink. After the pause grew sufficiently long for Stuart to tell that the reminiscences were over, he set the drink down with a rather dramatic motion and looked closely at each of the men.

"Well, gentlemen, I can see that you're ready to discuss

the reason I called you here. I hesitate to do it just yet, though, for what I have to tell you is rather long and detailed, and there is one person yet to arrive. Do you have the patience to wait a while longer?"

"Just who are you expecting?" Ballard asked.

"Another of your war partners," he returned. "Silas Kent."

Ballard's expression was unchanged as he stated bluntly, "Kent is dead. He was killed in a Kentucky coal-mining accident two years ago. I got word through some kin of mine that knew him."

Stuart showed disappointment but brightened quickly. "In that case we can begin," he said. But then he stopped, and he looked as if he were struggling for words to say something that he found unpleasant and difficult. He glanced briefly at Thad Ballard.

"Gentlemen," he began at length, "I have no wish to offend anyone in this room. But, Mr. Ballard, there is something I must say. The proposition I have to discuss with you is of a unique nature, and you already realize from the telegram that money is involved." He paused, looking uncomfortable. "Mr. Prine and Mr. Ballard, I chose you because I knew from my father that you were men of absolute trustworthiness. Only because of your reputations are you here. It should be clear not only from the sketchy nature of the telegram, but also from this isolated meeting place, that this is a highly secretive affair. What I'm getting at, Mr. Ballard, is that—no offense intended—I hadn't counted on any of you bringing anyone with you. You must understand, I have to be totally certain that I can trust—"

Ballard seemed to grow taller in his seat, and his face became a thunderstorm of anger, his expression clouding and his eyes flashing lightning. His bearing was sufficient to halt Stuart's words in midsentence, and every eye turned on Ballard in anticipation of an outburst of fury.

Ballard stood, his hulking form rising to its full height, well over six feet. Thad looked humble, quiet. It was obvious that he had seen his father like this many times before and knew what was coming. Prine had seen it before, too, and waited expectantly for the bear to roar.

"Stuart, I am a man of family pride. Thad here is a Ballard. He's had honesty beat into him since the day he was born. Anywhere I go he goes—it's always been like that and it ain't about to change. After that no more need be said."

Ballard sat down again, glaring rather haughtily. Stuart returned Ballard's stare unflinchingly, in spite of the tirade to which he had been subjected. Prine sat to the side, trying to hide the grin that kept creeping onto his face. It had been a long time since he had seen John Ballard raging and it was good to see.

Stuart's words were crisp and articulate, delivered with biting politeness. "Sir, were you to understand the nature of what I have to discuss you would see clearly the need for discretion this affair warrants. Do not take my doubts as an insult to your family. I have interests to protect, and I intend to do it. I have no doubt that you have raised your son well. I will take your word that he will betray no secrets nor act in his own self-interest at the expense of the rest of us. Silas Kent is dead—your son shall replace him in this party. Is that sufficient to satisfy your 'family pride', Mr. Ballard?" Prine had never seen a man strut while sitting down, but Stuart had almost accomplished it.

The fire in Ballard's eyes had cooled slightly, and his only answer was a grunt that Stuart took as an affirmative reply. He looked slowly from one man to another, as if waiting for comment. Receiving none, he began to speak.

"Very well, then. But let us all understand that each of us, myself included, will act as gentlemen at all times. Once you hear what I have to say I think you will be glad you made this trip.

"But there is one thing that I must trust from each of you: absolute silence to anyone else about what I am going to reveal. Once I share with you the information I possess, I shall be, in a manner of speaking, at your mercy. I have called you here because I am totally convinced of your honesty. But can I have your word of honor that, whether you consent to my proposal or not, you will remain absolutely silent about anything I am about to reveal, and that you will hold in confidence anything I say?" He looked into faces that had become cold sober and intent.

Prine spoke first. "You have my word, Mr. Stuart."

"And mine." Ballard's words were low and gruff.

Stuart nodded, then looked at the last member of the party. Thad Ballard stared at him briefly, then nodded his head.

Stuart breathed deeply, as if in preparation for a statement of great import. He reached inside his vest and came out with an oilskin packet bound tightly with cords. He dropped it on the table with a dramatic gesture.

"Gentlemen, within that packet lies information that could make each of us a great deal of money."

Chapter 3

Ballard leaned forward, eyes shining.

"What are you talking about?"

"About money, Mr. Ballard. Honest money, and plenty of it."

"How much?"

"Fifty thousand dollars to divide between us."

Thad whistled and glanced at Prine, who lifted his brows.

"That's a lot," Ballard said. "Especially to come by honestly. What's in that packet?"

"Perhaps the best way to answer that is to tell you a story, one that leads up to where we are right now. It has to do with my father and an old outlaw named Wesley Stoner."

"I've heard of him," Thad said. "Robbed a lot of stages and trains back during the war."

"Yes," Stuart said. "And right after the war is where my story begins. Mr. Prine, Father never roamed like you did after the fighting ended; he headed back to Virginia and settled back into life on our old farm. The war had left it relatively untouched, which was both amazing and fortunate. Father became prosperous relatively quickly. He was able to buy out smaller farms around his, and in a few years, he had a spread of land to rival some of the Southern plantations before the war.

"Father used to ride the grounds of the farm, partly to keep up with crops and herds, partly because he enjoyed it. Many times, he would find small jobs to be done and do them himself, which made him come home late. Mother was used to that and didn't worry about it much.

"But on one particular August evening shortly before he died, Father was making his rounds when he heard a groan come from a woods alongside the road. He investigated and found a man propped up against a tree. He didn't recognize him. The fellow was mortally wounded, though; that Father could tell right away. Father was on horseback and had no wagon to haul the man in, so there was little he could do immediately except try to comfort and settle him and promise to go for help as quickly as he could.

"But the man wouldn't let Father go; he wanted to talk. He said he had been robbed along a public road nearby by some highwaymen who had taken his cash and watch. The man had crawled back into the woods to escape them. He moaned on about it being a punishment for his past sins, or something like that. Father thought the fellow was going out of his head from his wounds.

"The man said he had been traveling toward Washington to repay an old debt to the government. He talked about papers sewn into the lining of his coat. These were important and secret, he said, and related to what he was doing.

"Father was skeptical and asked the man why he would tell something like that to a stranger, if it were true. The man said that Father obviously had been divinely sent to him to finish the job he couldn't. Then he sang a line or two from a hymn, and Father was certain he was insane.

"I came by in a wagon about this time; I had been visiting a lady friend who lived a few miles away. I heard the man singing, and Father's voice, and found them in the woods. Father and I got the man onto the wagon and raced for the house, afraid he would die before we got him there.

"But he lived. Father sent a servant for a doctor, and we carried the man inside and tried to make him as comfortable as we could while we waited. Mother brought the man some wine, which seemed to relax him some. He began talking again.

"He claimed he was Wesley Stoner, the old outlaw, and that he was on his way to the capital to reveal the location of a federal gold shipment he and some cohorts had stolen years before. Some of the gold they had converted to cash and spent, he said. But the rest, Stoner told us, he had managed to get away from the rest and hide somewhere where it would never be found. Then he had successfully set about to murder his old companions to make sure they never got their hands on the gold again.

"Then something most unexpected happened to Stoner. He underwent a religious conversion, apparently a very sincere and thorough one. He put himself upon a quest to return what he had stolen and then give himself up to the federal government for whatever punishment they saw fit for him. He wrote a detailed description of where the gold was hidden and began his journey. He was nearing the end of it when he was robbed near our farm.

"He passed out when he finished his story, and though Father and I were bursting with questions, it was no use. He never woke up again. Without speaking of it, Father and I took his coat and hid it. The doctor arrived and pronounced the man dead, and later an undertaker carted him off. When we were alone, Father and I ripped out the lining of his coat. It was just as he had said—the directions were there. Now they are in the packet that you see lying before us.

"Father was excited by the whole affair, especially when some research revealed that a reward of $50,000 had been offered by the government shortly after the theft of the gold. We researched further and found the reward offer had never been terminated. You knew Father as well as I did—you know he would not keep stolen gold. But the reward was another thing entirely.

"Father and I checked and rechecked Stoner's story and found it plausible. We planned then to take over Stoner's quest, but with a different approach. Rather than simply give the government directions to where the gold was hidden, we would actually recover it ourselves and bring it in for the reward. But then Father took ill. A few weeks later he was dead.

"It was he who suggested to me that I contact you men to carry this thing through. You were the only men he knew, he said, who could be counted on to be thoroughly honest. And by the time Father fell ill, a situation had developed that we knew would require good and capable men to deal with. More about that in a moment. So I promised him that contact you I would...and I have.

"And that, my friends, is why I have called you here, and what I propose to do. I want you to help me recover that gold and get it into the proper hands, and we will divide the reward among ourselves."

Stuart stopped speaking, and for a time there was only silence.

"Well, it figures that old Bob would think of us, Prine. That always was his way," Ballard said.

Stuart looked at them intently. "There is more you have to know," he said. "Danger isn't merely a possibility in this venture—it's a certainty. Word of Stoner's quest apparently had leaked to people who should not have heard of it, and I think they suspect I have the packet. You should understand that this could be a deadly business. That's what I meant when I said the situation called for capable men. If there was no danger, I could simply go recover the gold myself." He paused. "Now I suppose it's up to you."

The time for decision had come, and the three men who would have to make it became silent again. The wind whistled around the eaves of the old hotel building. Finally, Ballard spoke out.

"Stuart, count me in. I guess I feel like this one is for old Bob."

"If my father is involved, then I'm involved," Thad quickly said.

All eyes turned to Prine. He grinned, shrugged, and said, "I reckon I'm too impoverished to say no. Besides, it's like Ballard said: This one's for Bob."

Stuart smiled broadly. "Friends, I think this calls for a drink."

Together the four men toasted the coming adventure. Stuart, with his big grin, looked more than ever like his late father.

Ballard drained his drink and slammed down the glass with a bang. "Well, Stuart, where's that gold?"

Stuart opened his packet. He pulled out a crumpled piece of brown paper covered with scrawled writing, and another upon which was drawn a map. Stuart held up the hand-scrawled sheet.

"This is Stoner's description of where the gold is hidden. It's three, three and a half days' ride from here. Have you heard of the old mining town of Jericho Creek? Above it stands Jericho Mountain. That's where we'll find what we're after. It should be relatively easy to get—if we can hold off the others after it."

"And who are they?" Prine asked.

"I told you about Stoner having his old partners murdered. One thing he didn't take into consideration was their families. The daughter of one of his old partners, name of Tate, discovered Stoner was behind her father's death and learned about the gold. After Stoner died, Father and I quietly made some inquiries to make sure his story held together. But we were not quiet enough, apparently, for somehow Tate's daughter—Priscilla is her name—discovered we had the information. I think she has pulled together a group of gunmen to track me down and get it. I have seen evidence recently that I'm being followed, by the way."

Ballard looked concerned. "Followed here?"

"I don't think so. I think I threw them off. Let's just hope nobody followed *you* for any reason."

The thought was slightly unnerving. The men pondered it a moment. Prine stood. "I suggest we get some sleep," he said. "I figure you're planning on a first-light pullout, Stuart?"

"I am."

The others stood. "The horses will need some grazing," Thad said. "There's an old fenced-in grassy graveyard on the far edge of town. I'll put them there."

"I'll lend a hand," Prine said.

The two walked out into the dusky evening. In the fading light, the old town seemed even more ghostly than before.

"This place is downright scary," Thad commented. "Puts a man on edge."

They got the horses and led them to the cemetery at the other end of the street. Beside the graveyard stood a small, crumbling church house. They worked open the rusty gate and turned the horses into the fenced lot.

"That ought to hold them," Prine said.

They returned to the hotel and found that Stuart and Ballard had brought in the saddlebags and bedrolls. Ballard already was spreading his roll. Stuart was standing beside the dusty window, looking out at the gathering night.

Ballard had just started to pull off his boots when they heard noise from the horses at the graveyard. Prine wheeled, drew his pistol, and went to the door. Ballard pulled on his boots and joined him.

"Somebody's down there," Prine said.

Ballard pushed past him and onto the porch. He stomped heavily down the porch steps to the street, his pistol out.

Down the street a rifle cracked, and a bullet slammed one of the porch columns behind Ballard, who swore and ran to the other side of the street. He dropped behind the end of a short stretch of boardwalk.

Prine and Thad exited the hotel, hugging the front wall, and ducked into an adjacent alley. They glanced at Ballard, who returned the look with a flashing eye. He was all right.

Stuart appeared. He drew another shot from near the graveyard; dirt blasted upward behind his heels. He backed against the wall.

"This thing we've gotten into might be a little more difficult than I anticipated," Prine said.

Chapter 4

Prine could just see about half the cemetery where the horses were fenced. They were still there, nervous and frightened by the gunfire—but the important thing was they were there.

Prine strained, through the thickening dusk, to catch some glimpse of movement that might indicate where the gunmen were hidden. He knew their approximate location, but the twilight masked their hiding place and made it impossible to get off a shot at them with any hope of accuracy. The only good thing about it was that the gunmen were having the same difficulty.

For a time, there was little sound from either end of the street. Everyone was waiting, trying to determine the location of the enemy. Prine wondered if their attackers were part of the gang led by the girl Stuart had talked about.

Something moved across the street; it was Ballard, creeping slowly in the shadows up to parallel Prine. Thad saw his father and quietly darted across the weedy dirt street. From the area of the church and graveyard came three blasts of gunfire—but Thad made it safely to his father's side.

More silence. Prine looked over at Ballard and Thad,

trying to communicate with them silently. Ballard looked back at him closely; the men tried to read gestures and expressions as best the light would allow. Somehow their silent communication came through, for they began moving together, very slowly, up the street, hugging the walls and shadowed places.

Prine noticed Stuart was gone, then almost immediately detected motion atop a building just down from him. He started and lifted his pistol, then saw Stuart's shoulders and head limned against the still-glowing, indigo sky. Stuart glanced down at him, lifting a thumb to indicate he was there for a reason. Prine thumbed back at him, then glanced across at Ballard and Thad—only to find Thad too was now gone.

He stopped a moment, wondering what had happened. But then Ballard gave him a thumbs-up and laid an upright finger over his lips. Prine nodded and waited. In a few moments, he heard someone else scramble onto the building just ahead; another form joined Stuart's atop the structure. Thad had recrossed the street far enough back to not be seen by the graveyard gunmen and had climbed onto the roof with Stuart.

Motion at the graveyard—then Ballard's pistol roared and spat fire. Prine, distracted, had not seen what Ballard had: One of the gunmen had darted from the graveyard toward a recessed door on the same side of the street as Prine, and about forty-five degrees across from where Ballard was. Because of the recess Prine could not shoot at the man, and because of the man's location Ballard was now hampered from further advance.

Prine, hugging the wall, leaned out a bit to try to get perspective, and the man in the recessed doorway suddenly leaned out as well and fired. Prine was almost hit; he pulled back flat against the unpainted board wall.

He didn't want to take any more that close. Prine

leaned out again, fired two quick shots to make sure the gunman stayed within his recess, and tried to move forward. But gunfire came from the graveyard at the same time, forcing Prine back. Prine might have taken a bullet had not Ballard joined fire then, quieting the blasts from the graveyard.

Prine realized now how perilous was Ballard's position, as well as his. The only hope was to get the man out of that doorway ahead, or Ballard would be bound to take a bullet sooner or later.

Suddenly Stuart and Thad fired simultaneous shots from the roof toward the graveyard, apparently having detected movement down that way. Prine both welcomed and feared the shots. It would be easy to kill the horses down there, shooting at mere movements. But in the darkness, there was little else to do.

In any case, the gunfire from above gave Prine his opportunity to move. He launched out, straight forward, then into an alley. There he stopped for a second, took a breath, and headed on toward the rear of the row of buildings.

He counted buildings as he moved along, looking for the one with the recessed door in which the gunman hid. He hoped there would be an open back way into the building so he could surprise the man from the rear. Reaching the building, though, he found the back doorway boarded up.

But there was also a window, and it was not boarded. Two or three of the panes were broken out. Prine hunkered down and sneaked forward to a spot just below the window, then carefully rose to peer over the edge of the rotting sill.

The darkness inside the structure was dense. But as Prine's eyes adjusted he began to make out a faint rectangle of light at the front end of the building. The front doorway, mostly glass—and in it the silhouetted black form of the gunman. Prine grinned.

He put the barrel of his pistol through one of the broken

panes and carefully sighted. When he had the man locked in, he whistled. The man heard it, spun, and Prine fired.

The glass in the front door shattered as the man jerked and staggered back into the street. Prine heard gunfire from Thad and Stuart's roof, as well as from Ballard's spot, and the man collapsed, punctured with multiple shots.

Then came Thad's voice: "Your partner's dead! Give it up and come out, and we'll let you live!"

Prine smiled and nodded. An intelligent fellow, that Thad. Just like his father. He knew it would be worthwhile to take the other gunman alive. Prine was sure that one gunman was all that remained; there had been no evidence of any more than two men. Prine wondered if the gunmen had attacked randomly, or if they were after Stuart's packet. He suspected the latter. Why would two men take on four unless driven by the strongest motivation? In Prine's experience, only two things had the ability to inspire that level of motivation: women and wealth.

Prine headed farther down the row of buildings to the end. The church house stood around the corner, diagonally from him and almost all the way across the street. The graveyard was on the side of the church that faced Prine. Keeping himself hidden behind the last building in the row, Prine carefully peered around the back corner.

He saw a man crouched behind a big stump. The man was aiming, apparently at Thad and Stuart. He fired off a shot that went high. Prine could tell the gunman was scared; he wasn't shooting well.

Suddenly Prine was startled, but then began to grin. He had seen a big shadow, like a bear, emerging from the darkness behind the remaining gunman. Prine would know that shape anywhere—Ballard. Obviously, Ballard wanted this man alive, too, for if he had wanted to kill him, he could have done so at any time since he had crept around behind him.

"Drop it," Prine heard Ballard say.

The gunman, startled, leapt up and dropped his pistol. He raised his hands high in the air. Prine grinned more broadly and holstered his own pistol. He stepped out.

"Good job, Ballard. You ain't lost the touch, that I can see."

Ballard was about to answer when a rifle fired on Thad and Stuart's rooftop perch, and the surrendering gunman shuddered and fell. Ballard swore and went to him; Prine was with him in another half second. Ballard felt the neck for a pulse, then shook his head and swore again. Suddenly Ballard stood.

"Thad! Was that you who killed this man?"

Thad's voice called back: "No sir. It was Stuart."

"Stuart, you fool, didn't you see he had given up?" Prine yelled.

"I certainly didn't. It looked to me like he was about to kill Ballard," Stuart shouted back.

"Then you're a blind man," Prine spat in return.

In a few moments, Thad and Stuart had descended from the roof and stood with Prine and Ballard beside the bodies, which now had been dragged together. Stuart looked upset. "I'm sorry," he said. "If I had realized you had him under control, I wouldn't have killed him. I simply couldn't see that well from where I was."

"That's a funny thing, then," Ballard returned. "You surely saw well enough to put a bullet between his shoulder blades at a dern long range!"

"A lucky shot," Stuart said.

"Unlucky is more like it," Prine responded. "We could have quizzed this man for information, found out if he and his partner were working alone or with that Tate female you talked about."

"I understand. I'm sorry," Stuart said. He looked sincerely repentant.

"Well, ain't no point in jawing over what can't be

changed," Ballard said. "At least we still got the horses. Maybe that's all they were after—stealing our horses. Maybe they didn't know about the packet."

"I don't buy that," Prine said. "You ever seen two men who would fight as hard as these did just for the kind of wore-out nags we're riding?"

Ballard eyed his old partner silently, seeing his point. For a time, everyone was silent, thinking it over.

"Perhaps we should ride out at once," Stuart suggested.

"Perhaps we should at that," Prine said. "There's a trading post and little settlement north of here a few miles. I suggest we make for it. We got moon to ride by and a trail we can see."

"What should we do with these men?" Thad asked.

"Leave them. If there's any more about here who are after the packet, our shooting might have drawn them. And I, for one, have no desire to become the newest dead thing in this dead town."

"Thad, let's go for the saddles," Ballard said.

Chapter 5

There was little talk as the group tensely saddled the horses. Silently they rode, every sense alert and every hand ready to drop to the butt of a pistol at a moment's notice. Ballard rode in the lead, followed by Thad, and close behind him was Stuart. Prine brought up the rear, aware that his position was particularly strategic, for if there were other men who sought after the packet, it was likely that they would approach from behind. Prine was very conscious of how good a target his back would make for anyone who managed to approach unheard from the rear. It sent a tingle through his skin.

For two hours they rode, the trail nearly invisible in the darkness. On either side the forest was dark and frightening. At almost any point they could be bushwhacked with scarcely a warning.

When Ballard reached a clearer spot on the trail, the moonlight streaming through the branches above him, he turned, guiding his horse into a small gap in the brush to the left of the trail. The others followed; no one questioned Ballard's move. Prine knew what the husky man was doing—his sharp eye had spotted a good spot for camping somewhere off the trail, someplace that would hide them and at the same time give them a fairly clear view of the woods around them, at least as much as the dim moonlight would allow. Prine had always envied Ballard for his catlike ability to see in the darkness.

They dismounted, hobbling their horses in a patch of coarse forest grass. The sound of a nearby bubbling spring reached them. Ballard had chosen an excellent campsite.

The conversation was scant as the group cleared the ground and laid out bedrolls. Thad took first watch, and throughout the remainder of the night the men alternated at sentry duty. When the sun at last filtered through the trees the next morning, casting a green glow upon the camp, all the men were rested.

They dined on jerky and water from the spring. They didn't have an abundance of food, only what each had brought for himself. Ballard grumbled because of the lack of coffee, but he knew as well as any of them that building a fire would be dangerous.

They had found and brought with them the horses of the men they had fought, eliminating the need to buy pack mules and giving them a chance to switch mounts and rest their own horses. Prine now rode on a big dun, a strong animal, though more unruly than his usual mount. Stuart rode the smaller dun that they had inherited from the men they had battled.

After an hour's ride the trail was wider, the trees thinner, and the woods filled with grasses and saplings. There was less tension amid the group, and Prine allowed himself the luxury of whistling beneath his breath. Still, though, he found himself continually glancing over his shoulder.

They reached the trading post at noon sharp. The sun was hot, beaming directly above, and there were not many trees to shade them. The post was a low, squatty, ugly place with a smattering of houses and businesses nearby.

They ate a poor dinner in the post's cafe, and at last Ballard got his coffee. They were alone, seated around a large table and saying little, but Prine fancied that the man behind the bar gave them a searching look. He wondered if perhaps the fellow knew something about who they were, maybe even what they were carrying. He hoped not. If the packet were that well known, then there would be more threat than just the Tate gang.

They paid their bill and stepped out into the street. The light was almost blinding after the darkness of the cafe.

"Let's you and me go after some supplies," Ballard said to Prine.

"You want us to go with you?"

"No, Thad. You and Stuart stay here and look after the horses. The less show we can make out of this the better."

Ballard and Prine walked across to a shabby building with a faded sign that read DRY GOODS, GROCERIES, HARDWARE. The interior was dark and cool, and smelled of dust that had not been swept out since the year before.

"Pick and shovel? I got plenty of both, right in the back." The keeper looked as grubby as his store. He leaned across the counter smoking a cigar and watching the two men with strange interest.

Ballard picked the best of the tools the store carried and moved them to the counter. Prine had already gathered foodstuffs and other supplies. Ballard pulled a small roll of bills from his pocket and paid the storekeeper. The man handed him his change, puffing the cigar through yellow teeth.

"You men from around here?"

"Why do you ask?"

"No reason. Just nosy, I guess." Then he looked at them as if he were sizing them up, the cigar sending out a steady flow of strong-smelling smoke. He spoke again.

"There was a good-sized group of men in here yesterday

asking if any others had come through lately," he said. "I told 'em no. Think they might be looking for you?"

Ballard shot Prine a quick glance. "I don't reckon so. Did you know any of them?" Ballard asked the question a bit too quickly. The grubby storekeeper noticed, but he said nothing of it.

"Nope. Never seen any of 'em before. I tell you one thing, though—they were sure a rough-looking bunch. Not the kind that I like to deal with." He handed the tools across to Ballard. "You be careful. I don't know you from Adam, nor what your business is, but that group might have been highwaymen looking for easy victims. Pardon me if I've got into your private business a little—I just thought you deserved fair warning."

Prine looked the fellow over. He seemed trustworthy.

"'Preciate it."

He and Ballard moved on out the door and onto the porch. The man called to them from inside.

"There was something unusual about that bunch."

"What was that?"

"Had a girl with 'em—pretty and blonde. She seemed to be part of them."

Ballard and Prine both knew full well the significance of that.

From Ballard's fast stride Prine could tell he was nervous. He didn't blame him.

They walked back over to where Thad and Stuart waited. The two young men appeared restless and uncomfortable.

"Let's get out of here," Thad said as the men approached. "We've been getting some strange looks. I don't like it."

"Neither do I, Thad," said Prine. Quickly he related what the storekeeper had told them. Stuart grew agitated.

"They really are looking for me, then," he said. "Let's go."

The storekeeper stood on the porch of his store, still puffing his cigar and watching the leaving riders. They rode with their backs toward him, disappearing into the woods just beyond the outskirts of town. He stayed there for a while longer, then turned and walked back into his store.

Chapter 6

The land cleared and widened, giving a good view in all directions. This was big land, open land, the kind that had always made Prine feel glad to be on the move.

But today he felt differently about it. There was danger from the rear; he sensed it, as surely as if a band of armed riders were galloping up within full view. In a paradoxical way Prine almost wanted some sort of attack to come, just to relieve the tension of expectation. It would be better to fight openly than to ride and wonder how many and how strong the enemy was.

Prine was in the rear again. An almost military order had set itself up in the group with no conscious design by any of them. Ballard rode in the lead, and his instincts were trusted by every member of the party. Stuart rode in the middle, accompanied by Thad. Prine followed, riding with ears listening for any surprises from behind.

Prine said nothing of his apprehensions to the rest of the group. Probably Ballard felt the same thing already.

All day they rode, hardly stopping, except to spell the horses and take a smoke beside the road. They made good time, for the travel was steady and the trail was well worn.

When the sun began westering, Ballard started searching for a campsite. Before them was another stretch of woods. Into it they rode. The trail wound beneath the dark trees.

Ballard located a clearing and there they stopped. The sunlight was not entirely gone, but the forest was darker than open land.

It was a cold supper again. Prine sat beside Ballard as he ate and spoke privately to the man.

"We're being followed."

"I know it. I've known it all day. I expect whoever it is will try something tonight."

"I never saw nobody, so I can't figure out how many there are. Could be anywhere from just a couple to the whole Tate gang. Somehow, I think it isn't the gang, though. That storekeeper said they were there yesterday, so that should put 'em somewhere ahead of us."

"They could have doubled back. I figure we'll find out tonight."

The pair agreed that Thad and Stuart had best be warned, so they told them of their suspicions, and were mildly surprised when the two younger men told them they had felt the same way all day.

"We figure they'll try to take us in our sleep tonight, Pa," said Thad.

"I'll sit first watch," said Ballard. "And we can stuff some packs into Prine's bedroll to make it look like he's sleeping, then he can hide off in the woods somewhere nearby. Between the two of us we should be able to spot something. You fellers only pretend to sleep. You'll never wake up in time if something happens quick. I saw too many throats slit at Shiloh to think otherwise."

It was still too early to turn in, though the darkness of the woods made the hour seem later than it was. Prine and Ballard talked along the line Ballard had brought up: the

Battle of Shiloh, where they had lost many companions and seen much death during the three-day conflict.

"Ballard, I recall a tree down close to the pond. The first part of the fight it was leafy and green. I saw the same tree after the battle. Not a leaf on it, and hardly a branch. And the pond was as red as blood where men had been washing their wounds. There were bodies all around. It's a sight I don't ever want to see again."

Ballard looked thoughtful in the growing darkness. "That's for sure, Prine."

Prine chewed on a twig. "You know, I hoped my lolling days were over when the war ended. And they were, up to now. It's a painful thing, killing a man, even when there's no choice. I hope that nothing happens tonight. I saw enough death at Shiloh to last me the rest of my days."

"There's things that are worth killing for, Prine," said Stuart. "Don't you think a pile of money is worth a few dead outlaws?"

Prine studied the young man. "You're young, Stuart. Things seem different when you're young. Men were meant to live, not to die."

Stuart looked into Prine's face, then turned away without a word.

The night grew thick and black, though the moon managed to filter a little light between the trees. The men made out their bedrolls, cursing the lack of fire and light, and Stuart and Thad crawled in, adjusting themselves as Ballard had instructed. Prine thrust his saddlebags into his bedroll, moving them around until they approximated the shape of a sleeping man. Then he took his rifle and pistol into the woods nearby as Ballard sat down on an old stump, his shotgun across his knee.

Prine sat alone in the woods, staying out of sight but keeping an easy view of the camp. He could see Ballard's face through the leaves. His friend looked much older than when he had known him years before, his eyes weary and his skin weather-beaten. But still he was a strong man, perhaps even stronger than in his youth. He could hear the faint sound of the man singing.

> *My own true love is gone away,*
> *Across the rolling water,*
> *And now I wander all alone,*
> *But I shall roam no farther,*
> *But I shall roam no farther.*

The tune was soft and sad in the darkness and made Prine feel old and tired. Suddenly he wasn't sure why he was there. Maybe it was because of Bob Stuart—yes, that was it. This was not for money, but for his old friend. It was a last tribute to his partner and a way of standing defiant in the face of time and death. Perhaps he wouldn't survive this quest, but even if he died it would be as he wanted it— fighting to the last, in a paradoxical way victorious in defeat.

His thoughts were interrupted by a rustling in the woods on the other side of the camp. Then there was silence, long enough to make him suspect that he had only imagined the disturbance. But it came again, at a slightly different location. Someone was there. Someone was moving about in the brush, trying to remain unseen. Ballard sat unmoving, as if he had heard nothing, but Prine knew better. His friend was as aware of the location of the noise as if he were looking at it. Prine saw Ballard's finger settle on the trigger of the shotgun.

Prine rose silently and began to move toward the other side of the camp, circling the clearing. He trod lightly, trying to make as little noise as possible. He wanted to surprise whoever was hidden across in the brush. His hand crept to the knife in his belt and unsheathed it. It felt good in his hand, sharp and well balanced.

His progress was slow. Ballard's back was still turned toward the hidden intruders, but when Prine had circled far enough to let him see the husky man's face, he saw alertness in his eyes. Stuart's face was also turned toward him, eyes open and muscles tense, though he kept the posture of a sleeper. Thad was no doubt as alert as the others.

Closer he crept, hoping he would give no sign of his presence. Perhaps he could get close enough to whoever it was to jump him, take him alive, and make him talk. Then the moonlight shimmered on the barrel of a revolver muzzle thrust out from the brush, pointed at Ballard's head.

That was it. Secrecy would be impossible if he wanted to save his friend's life.

Prine cried out a warning as he threw his knife hard at the spot just above where the barrel protruded from the leaves.

CHAPTER 7

There was great confusion immediately after Prine's throw. Ballard ducked quickly and rolled. The knife passed over him and thudded into something in the bushes. There was a groan and the sound of a falling body. Prine's blade had struck home.

Just as Thad and Stuart leapt from their bedrolls there was a scurrying, rushing sound in the woods, the noise of snapping branches and disturbed bushes. Someone was running away. Probably there were two of them, one either dead or wounded from Prine's blade, the other running for his life through the dark forest.

Ballard leapt up and ran along with Prine into the woods after the fleeing man. Prine mouthed quick instructions to Stuart and Thad.

"Head off and circle around right, toward the west. We'll try to head him off in that direction." The two young men obeyed, disappearing into the thicket.

Prine and Ballard gripped their rifles and ducked low branches, straining to see in the darkness. They couldn't let their prey escape; they needed to know how much information he possessed about their mission, and mostly if he were involved with or knew anything of the Tate gang. They had lost their previous chance for that type of information when Stuart killed the gunman in the ghost town.

There he was, heading around a thick clump of undergrowth. Ballard was quick as a running deer, an amazing achievement for a man of his size. Prine was growing hot, his brow covered with beads of sweat and his hair disheveled from brushing against unseen branches.

They lost sight of the man again. Perhaps he was hidden, trying to let them run past him. They stopped, panting and listening intently for some indication of where he might be. There was only the sound of their labored breathing and the night breeze in the treetops for a long while; then suddenly, several yards off to the left, they heard breaking branches and hurried, heavy footsteps. They took off in that direction.

He was heading up a wooded slope not far ahead. They could have dropped him with a shot, but that could have foiled their plan of taking him alive. And if by chance there were others in this forest, it might have drawn them.

Like a pounding buffalo Ballard dashed up the slope, Prine beside him. This must be a young fellow they were chasing; he seemed fleet and swift. But he was also scared, for he would never have been so loud in his escape had he been thinking clearly.

They crossed the crest and stopped again. Prine was out of breath, and his face and arms were bloody from many scrapes with brush and briars. He tasted sweat in his mouth, and his lungs ached as they sucked in the cool night air. But he couldn't stop now.

Farther off they heard him, running as swiftly as ever and heading west. Prine drew a deep breath and took off again, and Ballard thudded along beside him, his heavy strides shaking the ground.

They reached the spot where they had heard the fellow, but he was gone. On the ground Prine found a portion of the man's shirt, ripped from his sleeve by a protruding branch. He fingered it as he looked around, trying to guess which way the man had run.

It was more chance than anything else that led them off toward the southwest, dodging the smaller saplings that filled this portion of the woods. They ran for several minutes before Prine began to suspect that the man had not come this way. He stopped and conferred with Ballard.

"We'd best be careful—we might lose our way if we don't watch where we're going. I thought he came this way, but now I ain't too sure."

"Let's head due west. I think I heard something over there a minute ago."

Prine listened. Ballard was right—there was noise from the west. But from the sound of it, it wasn't a running man. Maybe he had slowed down, thinking that he had evaded them. Now would be the time to surprise him.

They headed in that direction, trying to keep their heads low and the noise down. It was hard to do; the leaves and twigs beneath their feet were invisible in the darkness, and at times they would step on some dry branch that would snap noisily beneath their weight. And now, fatigued as they were, it was hard to not gasp loudly for breath.

They moved down a few more yards, and then suddenly Ballard stopped. Prine didn't understand his friend's action, but he stopped beside him, tense and listening intently. Ballard's face showed sudden concern, as if he had heard something that disturbed him.

Prine heard it then, too. Men talking, and not in low voices. Then through the woods he saw the faint flicker of firelight. A group was camped about a hundred yards away, and from the appearance of things, was making only a token effort to remain unseen.

Ballard crouched. Prine did the same. "Who do you think...?"

Ballard shook his head. The two men sat still, listening. They forgot the man they were chasing, for this discovery was a development they hadn't anticipated.

"Sounds like several of 'em—maybe five or six," Prine said. "It could be more. Do you think we should get closer?" Prine wasn't sure whether his friend would want to draw nearer and risk discovery. But Ballard nodded at the suggestion, and the two men rose, two dark and silent ghosts of the forest gliding toward the flickering light some distance away.

They were almost to the very edge of the camp when the thicket before them burst to life, moving suddenly and loudly. Prine hissed beneath his breath, startled like a man who unexpectedly hears a rattler at his feet.

But this was a human animal that made the noise, apparently the same one they had been pursuing, for he ran like a man in blind panic off to the left, leaving them too stunned to move or say a word.

"What was that? Somebody's out there!" The voices came from the camp, and there was sudden movement from that direction.

"Lord, this is a fine fix!" Ballard snorted low as he darted for cover. Prine jumped down beside him, and they hid behind a rotting log, thick bushes covering them on all sides. There was scarcely room enough for both of them, but there was no time to look for a better hiding place, for suddenly the woods began filling with armed men.

Ballard and Prine were on the very edge of the camp. Looking across the log they could see right into the clearing. Men were moving out of it with guns in their hands, scouring the forest in all directions. There was a blazing fire in the midst of the clearing, and the tantalizing smell of hot, boiling coffee reached them. But they took no notice of the aroma, for what they saw beside the fire caught their attention and confirmed the suspicion that had been growing in their minds.

A girl—a pretty young blonde. And she held a gun and looked around at the dark forest. Prine could read her fear. Her hands twitched nervously on the butt of her pistol. She started occasionally when one of the searchers in the woods made some unexpected sound.

It could be no one else but Priscilla Tate. They had stumbled right into the camp of those they least wanted to meet.

Prine thought of Thad and Stuart, out there alone and unaware of the armed men who searched the forest. What if they should stumble right into their hands? It could be death for both of them.

Prine glanced over at his partner. Ballard was staring into the camp, watching the young girl—she seemed much younger and more delicate than Prine had anticipated—and the big man's expression was grim. His face showed fear, but Prine knew the fear was not for himself but for his son, who was out there somewhere and probably unaware of the danger.

Brush moved close beside them. A man was approaching, a pistol in his hand and his free arm knocking aside the brush as he searched. In only a moment he would be upon them.

Chapter 8

One bush stood between them and detection. Prine gripped his rifle; that fellow might find them, but he wouldn't live to announce his discovery to the others. Not that it really mattered—the shot would draw them anyway—but Prine would not go to his grave without taking someone with him, nor would Ballard.

He prepared to fire as he saw the hand come around the bush, gripping the branches to push them aside. But before that fateful move was made the unexpected roar of a shot, then another, came echoing through the forest from some distance away. The hand withdrew suddenly, and the man moved away at a run. Prine and Ballard were saved from discovery, at least for the moment.

But neither took time to ponder their good fortune, for they were filled with concern about those shots. At whom had they been aimed? Thad and Stuart? Prine hoped not, but it was hard to feel optimistic. Ballard must be in a horrible turmoil right now, Prine thought. His son was out there in the forest, perhaps wounded or dead.

They could hear voices coming loudly from the darkness behind them. The girl still crouched beside the fire, listening.

Prine looked at her face. What he saw wasn't what he expected, based on what Stuart had said. She didn't look like the kind of girl to be riding with a band of killers, searching for stolen wealth. Prine had expected to see hardness and cruelty in her, but he could detect only fear. She reminded him of a frightened fawn. And she was very pretty.

The men were moving as a group toward the camp now, carrying something between them. They strode past Prine and Ballard into the circle of light around the campfire. On the ground they dumped their burden. A body. The dead face fell toward Prine and Ballard.

It wasn't Stuart or Thad. It could be no one else but the same man who had earlier tried to get the packet, the man they had chased only minutes before. He was stone-cold dead. There was a spot of deep crimson on his chest.

"There he is, ma'am. We found him trying to hide in a clump of cottonwoods. You needn't worry about him no more."

The girl said, "Did you have to kill him? I didn't want anything like this."

"What did you expect us to do, lady? Shake his hand? This fellow double-crossed you. You hired him, then he and Thaxton decided to get it all for themselves, just like Bryant and Allen. He deserved just what he got."

The girl covered her brow with a slender hand. "I'm just not accustomed to this. I didn't think it would come to murder."

"Murder, you say? No, ma'am—this was just and fair execution. I'd say if there are any murderers in the light of this fire it's our dear departed friend Orville Beecher here. We found no trace of Thaxton. Likely as not Beecher killed him so he wouldn't have to split the take. It would be like him to do that. That's murder, lady—not this." He turned away. The girl said nothing but looked despairing.

Another man spoke, "Do you think there could be

others out there? There was an awful lot of crashing around a minute ago."

"I don't know, Harvey. Maybe. But they'd be long gone by now."

Another of the men was laughing, apparently drunk. Prine looked closely at the group. Not until then did he notice the careful, exaggerated movements of men that have had too much to drink. Apparently, they had been tipping the bottle for quite some time now, for many of them staggered slightly and others sat quietly in a kind of daze. The man who had laughed spoke out in a loud voice.

"Ol' Beecher here was a bad sort, I reckon, but even a dog deserves a funeral—and a wake! Buster, get out your fiddle! We'll have the derndest wake that ever was—and then you'd all best settle back, for I aim to preach me a sermon!"

Hooting and laughter came in response. The one called Buster moved over to his pack and brought out a dirty flour sack. From it he produced a battered fiddle, and he plucked the strings, twisting his face in concentration as he turned the pegs and brought the instrument into some semblance of good tune. Then he tightened up a bow that had as many loose hairs as good ones and drew a cake of rosin across the taut horsehair. He dragged the bow across the strings with a scratchy sound that quickly melted into the smooth, mellow tones of an old fiddle tune.

He began tapping his foot and sawing hard on the catgut strings. Not ones to worry about hiding themselves, this bunch! They were singing, some dancing, and the whiskey was flowing freely. And off to the side sat the young, pretty Priscilla Tate, apparently disturbed by it all, and looking out of place.

Prine realized how drunk these men were, and the amount of liquor they were consuming would only make them wilder. Several were dancing crazily, reeling around the fire, hooting and stomping out of rhythm with the fiddle, making so much noise that the music was hardly audible.

"This is for you, Beecher!" one of them shouted. "Show some life, boy! Get up and dance!" They laughed hard at that. Priscilla Tate buried her head in her hands.

"Why, boys, I don't believe old Beecher is aiming on dancing with me!" the fellow continued. "Somebody had best explain to him that that ain't nice! Harvey, give me a hand here. I'm going to teach ol' Beecher how to step to the music!"

Harvey quickly moved to the body and hefted it up. The head fell back, mouth open, as he dragged the gruesome corpse over to the dancing man and pushed it into his arms. He supported its weight and began moving about, holding the body around the waist. The feet dangled, swinging in a wild, loose parody of a dance. All the while the other men laughed and clapped, drinking from bottles, jugs, canteens, and anything else that would hold liquor.

"That's the way, Beecher! You sure know how to liven up a wake!"

"Step lively, now, Beecher!"

"Stomp them feet good, boy!"

The sight was appalling, but the men seemed not to notice or care. This was a rough, wild crew, and somehow Prine could feel only pity for the pretty young lady involved with them. It didn't seem natural for her to be there. She sat to the side, an image of dejection, as the wild celebration continued.

"Boys, I believe Beecher's getting tired of dancing!" the man shouted. He suddenly flung the body away from him, and the corpse fell limply and hard onto its back with a loud thud. One hand fell into the fire, but no one seemed to notice.

"That's right, Beecher. You rest a while. You've got a

right to be tired after dancing like that!" The fiddle screeched on.

After the party had continued for some time, the man who had originally started the celebration walked forward, raising his arms above his head and looking at the rugged assembly with mock earnestness. The fiddle screeched out a particularly grating note and stopped. Orville Beecher's recent dancing partner quit his wild gyrations. The men gathered around the fire, and the mock preacher moved over to the body of Beecher and looked down on him for a moment.

"My friends," he began in a tremulous voice, "we are gathered here in the sight of God and man to lay to rest the body of the poor departed Orville Myron Beecher Jr., a man known and loved by each of us here." He paused, and from the crowd came a muttered "amen" and "God rest his poor soul."

The preacher's hands moved to his chest and he stood with stomach protruding and thumbs hooked into his armpits. "A good, good friend he was, and a wonderful provider for his family, and he shall certainly be missed by all of us. But mostly he shall be missed by his two lovely babies and his lovely wife, wherever she is and whoever she is with tonight. But mostly, friends, all of us shall remember one thing about Orville Beecher: He was a truly marvelous dancer, a man with feet as light as sunrise and legs so muscled as to remind one of a buffalo..."

For long minutes the mock sermon continued. Prine lay there wondering how long this travesty would go on. Ballard nudged him and pointed over to the group of seated men. Two of them were asleep in a drunken stupor, and from the looks of the rest of them it would be a matter of only minutes before the same condition overtook the entire group. Even the preacher was tottering a little more with each word.

"...and so, friends, let our dear dead brother be a lesson to each of you...do not start on the horrid road of crime, for in the end it will kill you and destroy your soul..."

He was getting fired up now, his voice flowing like water over a mill wheel, spurred on with the enthusiasm of an old-fashioned pulpit-slapping preacher. All the while his congregation of ruffians were drifting off one man at a time into a deep, drunken sleep, their cries of "amen" and "you tell 'em, Preacher" growing ever fainter.

Priscilla Tate was on her side now, apparently dozing, though her hands were over her ears, as if to block out the sound of the funeral oration. The preacher was winding to a close.

"...and so now, friends, let us always remember our departed brother in love—good lands, Beecher, you've got your hand right in the fire...here, let me kick it out for you—and do what we can to ensure that his memory is always held dear to those who...who..."

From the sudden glazing of the speaker's eyes, it was clear what was coming. He swayed like a great oak in a storm, then stiffly fell, out before he hit the ground, landing directly atop the subject of his eulogy. He began to snore in deep, rich tones.

Prine and Ballard quietly slipped away from their hiding place and moved swiftly through the dark forest.

Behind them the campfire flickered fainter and quickly burned down to glowing red coals that cast a strange light on Orville Beecher, his unconscious mourners, and the lonely-looking lady with them.

Chapter 9

They found Thad and Stuart in a thicket about halfway back to the camp.

"I'm glad to see you!" exclaimed Thad. "We thought maybe they had shot you."

"It wasn't us they shot—it was that fellow we were chasing. We thought at first it was *you* they got. Stuart, that was the Tate gang. We saw Tate herself with them."

"That's what I figured. We saw them coming through the woods and hid out here. That's when we heard the shots. But why did they shoot that fellow if he was one of them?"

"Because he had cut out on his own," said Ballard. "That fellow Prine killed, and this fellow were trying for the prize themselves. The others made short work of him when they found him."

"At least he had a funeral."

Ballard flashed a sardonic glance in response to Prine's comment.

"Well, if the Tates are that close, then we should get out of here fast," said Thad. "They could find us before morning."

"We don't need to worry about them tonight, Thad,"

said Prine. "They're drunk as sailors, passed out on the ground. All but the lady herself. And they have no idea we're this close by, I think. If they did, they would sure have been more careful about their little party. The best thing we can do is get some rest."

They went back to their camp. In the brush beside the clearing, they found the body of the man whose life had been cut short by Prine's blade. Prine retrieved his weapon, cleaned it, and then joined Thad in dragging the body into the clearing

He didn't recognize the face. The fellow had a mustache and hair touched with gray. Prine glanced at Stuart.

"They said his name was Thaxton. You know him?"

"Never saw him before. I'm not acquainted with any of the Tate bunch except by reputation."

Prine said, "Just how much do you really know about this Tate girl, Stuart? She didn't look the type that you described. I had the feeling that she wasn't used to being around men of that type at all. In fact, she looked downright miserable about the whole affair."

Stuart shook his head violently. "Don't let appearances deceive you, Prine. She's as hard as they come. Why would she assemble a bunch like she's got if she weren't? She's a devil, one that will give us a lot more trouble before this thing is over."

The young man turned away, apparently and surprisingly perturbed, as if any hint of defense of Priscilla Tate, no matter how tentative and hypothetical, made him angry. Prine was taken aback by the show of emotion but said nothing as he began searching through the pockets of the dead man. Just what he sought he didn't know, but it made no difference, for the man carried nothing.

Ballard and Prine picked up the body, carried it off into the forest, and dumped it in a gully.

When they returned to camp, Thad was in his bedroll

and Stuart sat on the stump at guard duty. "You get some rest," he told them. "Ballard, you can replace me in a couple of hours."

Ballard lay quietly, not far from Prine. His eyes were sad, and his head was cupped in his hands. He stared up silently through the branches as he lay on his back. Above, the stars flickered in the blackness of the sky, and occasionally across his vision flashed dark things, creatures of the night, moving silently across the heavens in search of other night creatures that would become their prey. Ballard closed his eyes and tried to sleep.

Prine was awake, too, his thoughts occupied by the girl named Priscilla Tate. She wouldn't leave his mind for a moment. When he had looked at her from his hiding place beside the camp, she had looked like a girl trapped in something that was now beyond her control, and he could not view her as an enemy, no matter how he tried. He felt a strange pity for the young lady.

"I must be getting soft and old." He whispered the observation to himself, then hoped no one had heard him.

He rolled over on his side and stretched his tired muscles. Sleep began to steal over him, and soon he was slumbering. He dreamed later that night, seeing Priscilla Tate standing over him, a gun in her hand, preparing to kill him. Then, just as her finger squeezed down on the trigger, she flung the weapon aside and disappeared, leaving him alone and mystified. It was a strange dream and made Prine stir fitfully in his sleep.

Ballard still could not rest. He lay quietly, though, aware that even a sleepless man could arise refreshed if he avoided the temptation to tumble about all night. And besides, soon it would be time to replace Stuart at sentry duty, so sleep was somewhat pointless anyway.

Stuart. Now there was a man Ballard could not feel fully comfortable around, He was certainly a cocky and able fellow, yet mysterious too. Ballard's instincts had guided him accurately all his life, but now they seemed to be failing him, for he could find no category in which to place the young man. He found no obvious reason not to trust him, but still he was cautious, afraid to rely on him without reservation.

"You should be more trusting," Ballard's wife had told him time and time again. Perhaps she had been right, he thought. Maybe he was overly suspicious by nature. But still, caution had saved him many times from disasters of all types and trusting the wrong person could easily be a fatal move.

After several more minutes, came the noise of movement from the other side of camp. Stuart had risen, his rifle in his hands. Ballard started to rise to see what had stirred the young sentry, but then he stopped. He twisted his head slightly so he could see Stuart's form in the darkness.

Stuart was looking over the reclining figures before him, as if trying to decide if they were truly asleep. For a long time, he stood there. Ballard tried not to move. Stuart looked once more at each of the men, then turned and stared into the forest.

Lifting his rifle and holding it close to him, he stepped quietly toward the dark trees, as silent and sly as a cat. Now that was a strange move for sure, Ballard thought. He sat up carefully, now wide awake. Why would Stuart leave his post with such obvious stealth? And what could inspire him to head out into the woods alone at a time like this, leaving the camp unguarded?

Ballard sat listening. He heard the faint tramp of Stuart's feet on the forest floor, moving away toward the southwest. He was obviously not trying to be silent now that he was away from camp, at least not to the extent he had been before. Ballard was struck with a strong feeling of suspicion.

He rose from his bedroll and slipped on his boots, debating whether to wake Prine. He reached over to nudge the sleeping man, but suddenly he pulled his hand back, paused indecisively, picked up his shotgun and moved off alone.

He headed into the trees at the same spot he had seen Stuart enter. His eyes squinted in the darkness, and for a time he could see nothing. But to the southwest he thought he could make out a moving form in the darkness. He tried to remain silent as he headed toward it.

It was Stuart, all right. The young man gripped his rifle tightly, and from his crouched stance Ballard could tell he was again trying to move swiftly and silently. And what was more, he was traveling toward the Tate camp.

Ballard stayed behind in the shadows of the trees. There was only the noise of the night birds and the faint rustling of the wind.

What was that noise off to the left? Ballard heard it just as Stuart whirled around, and slid quietly behind a spruce as the young man searched the forest. Ballard stood like a statue, trying to breathe softly.

The noise came again, and Ballard saw a deer loping off through the night. Stuart saw it too, and relaxed. Stuart wheeled and began moving off in the same direction as before. After waiting long enough for Stuart to get some distance away, Ballard slipped from his hiding place and followed.

There could be no doubting one fact: Stuart was heading straight for the Tate camp. Why? Was he aiming to take on the whole gang at once? Then Ballard was struck with a sudden realization: The gang was asleep, and not with the normal, light sleep of men on the trail, but with a heavy, drunken stupor. And Stuart knew that, for they had told him. The horrible possibility of what Stuart just might be planning came to Ballard, and he was appalled. He remembered the way Stuart had cruelly shot one surrendering man. Killing didn't seem to bother the fellow. That put a bad taste in Ballard's mouth.

He couldn't let him do it. The men Stuart was seeking to kill were killers themselves, and heartless ones at that, but if Stuart were planning on shooting them in their sleep, he was no better than any of his prospective victims. Ballard wouldn't stand for it. He had to stop him. But how could he make his presence known without becoming the first victim of Stuart's gun?

That problem was suddenly eliminated, for a branch snapped loudly beneath Ballard's foot. Stuart whirled, his rifle up.

"Who's there?"

There was nothing to do but face up to him. "It's Ballard. Don't shoot!"

"Why did you follow me?"

Ballard's mind worked fast. "I thought I heard a noise, and I saw you get up to investigate. I thought you might need some help."

Stuart lowered his gun, but he looked angry. "Why didn't you make your presence known?"

"I didn't want to tip off anybody that might be in the woods. And besides, I wasn't sure it was you."

Stuart was cooling off, relaxing. Then he suddenly realized that he had some explaining to do.

"I heard a noise, too, and I thought some of those Tate gang members might have come up to camp. I would have woke you, but I wanted to be sure before I stirred everyone up." He approached Ballard as he talked. "I guess I was wrong. It must have been that deer back there poking around for food."

Ballard's instincts were sounding an alarm in his mind, but his voice remained calm. "Yep ... I expect it was."

Without another word the pair headed back toward their camp.

Minutes later, Ballard was seated on the stump with his shotgun across his lap, studying the sleeping Thomas Stuart, trying to piece together the strange puzzle of this man. Many of the pieces didn't fit, but a few were joining themselves together neatly. And the picture that came out made Ballard uncomfortable.

He resolved to keep a close eye on Stuart from that time forward. He would say nothing of what he had seen, at least not yet, for he could not be sure of the accuracy of his suspicions. But he would be watching, very closely.

CHAPTER 10

Sunrise sneaks in like a slinking cat in Colorado, and this morning the sun's beams shone down on a group of sleeping men. Ballard sat slumped over on the stump, his gun still across his knees, his snores low-pitched. Prine stirred fitfully, and Thad and Stuart lay almost as still as one Orville Beecher only a short distance away. The morning was heralded by the music of birds.

Prine awoke abruptly, conscious of the sunlight on his face. It wasn't a feeling he was accustomed to when waking up, for usually he rose before dawn and was at his breakfast when the first rays peeped over the eastern horizon. But he had been bone-weary when he retired, and fatigue had overruled habit. From the looks of the other men the same had held true for them.

Prine rubbed his eyes and looked around. He grinned when he saw the hulking bear-like form of John Ballard dozing at his post. It could have been a dangerous thing, he realized, but last night there had been no real threat to their camp—only a bunch of outlaws who did not suspect their presence, and who were so drunk that they wouldn't have known Prine or Ballard from their grandmothers had they stood before them.

Prine grinned devilishly. He looked around and plucked a small, feather-like leaf from a wild shrub growing nearby. He crept toward the slumped-over Ballard, carefully slipped the leaf beneath his nose, and began tickling the sleeping man gently.

Ballard snorted in his sleep, his broad nose wrinkling.

He rubbed a huge, hairy hand against his face, then with a canine woof awoke, leaping up and knocking Prine aside unwittingly. His eyes were bloodshot and bleary, and for a moment he looked like a man who had been suddenly set down in the midst of an unknown country. Then he saw Prine.

Prine was grinning like a cat with a blue jay in its jaws; Ballard scowled back at him and swore. His voice stirred Thad and Stuart from their sleep, and they sat up bleary-eyed.

Breakfast was cold and the mood of the men was generally far from pleasant. Prine was the sole exception; for some reason he felt rather jovial this morning, though it was a joviality built on a foundation of caution and a very real sense of the danger that they might face later. His mind wandered to the group that had presented such a drunken spectacle the night before. This morning there would be no laughing and singing in that camp—only the nursing of headaches as big as the Rockies.

Ballard and Stuart were strangely quiet and sullen. Prine fancied that they avoided each other's glance. Lazily he pondered the mystery, but it seemed a minor affair. Probably they were both still tired from the exertion of the day before, and the threat of the Tate gang had doubtlessly worn on their nerves.

Ballard was grumbling again because of the lack of coffee. Prine had to admit that it was one luxury he too was missing right now, but there was no point in dwelling on it, for there was certainly nothing they could do about it. By nightfall they would be in Statler, and there perhaps they could have coffee. And if the coffee they brewed there were half as powerful as the town's reputation, then that would be one mighty strong brew.

"Just how close do you reckon the Tate bunch thinks we are?" asked Thad.

Prine swallowed a piece of jerky that tasted like shoe leather. "I can't be sure, Thad, but I don't think they realize how close we are. My guess is they're heading for Statler, hoping to find us there."

Ballard finished his breakfast and pulled a twist of tobacco from his pocket. He bit off a large chunk and settled it into his jaw. "I expect we'll have some trouble in Statler. That's a rough town."

"Well, why don't we avoid it, then?" Thad asked. "Just bypass it and go on."

Prine shook his head. "That's not what we need to do. Right now, we got no gold on us, nothing but ourselves. If somebody is trying to give us trouble, now's the time to take care of them. The thing to avoid is letting them set the terms of the fight. In Statler we can set a trap and let them walk into it, instead of just waiting for them to jump us out in the mountains."

Thad looked concerned. "I was looking forward to Statler so I could get a hot bath and sleep in a read bed," he said. "Now I'm not so sure I want to go."

The men rode the rest of the day and did not encounter anyone. The country was wild and overgrown. The group fell into the same order it had followed during the preceding portions of the journey. Ballard was in the lead, and thus his face was invisible to the rest of them, but if any had been able to see it, they would have noted an expression of worry. Ballard's thick brows were lowered, and his mouth tightly set in a line. He could all but feel the gaze of Stuart burning into the back of his head.

It was about Stuart that Ballard was thinking. Particularly he thought about the strange action of the young man the previous night. Clearly Stuart had been lying when he said he heard a sound in the woods, for Ballard had been awake and knew there had been no sound. And the careful scrutiny with which Stuart had studied his sleeping companions was not the response of an alert sentry to a sudden noise; it was the calculated and careful move of a man doing his best to avoid detection.

Ballard figured that Stuart knew of his suspicions. Something in Ballard wanted to tell Prine about all of this, but he stopped short of that. This was not the time...not yet.

The trail was narrow here, and every man in the party was on edge. They knew the danger of these wildlands. There was never a time that bandits did not haunt this region. Perhaps they would be ambushed up ahead, perhaps not.

As the sun westered in front of them, shining deep orange into their eyes, they saw Statler appear down the slope, the main street opening to engulf them like a hungry mouth. Prine thought about Priscilla Tate and her men. It was possible that they were still behind them on the trail, but again they might have avoided the road and cut through the forest itself—a more dangerous but much shorter route. If that were the case, then they might already be there in the hellhole before them.

Statler was a town just waking up with the sunset. Saloons lined the streets, more than Prine had ever seen in one town. This was the last of the West's lawless towns, a throwback to the Dodges and Tombstones of years past.

Many were the stares that the men drew as they plodded down the street, and greedy and hungry were the looks of many of the watchers. How much did this town know of what they carried? No doubt the local thieves considered any new arrival as a potential gilded chicken waiting to be plucked. Prine hoped they did not realize just how valuable were these chickens' feathers. Ballard carried a sawed-off shotgun across his saddle, daring any of the onlookers to move.

Prine looked hard into the faces of the men who stood about them on the boardwalk. He thought of Priscilla Tate again. She would be here, in the midst of this hell town. It didn't seem right. Not for a pretty, young girl like her.

"Get hold of yourself, Jeremy Prine," he muttered beneath his breath, reminding himself that Priscilla Tate was probably a killer. It was definitely a group of killers with whom she associated. Her father had been a member of one of the West's most cruel and bloodthirsty gangs, and she herself sought to thwart a mission that was lawful and right. She didn't deserve pity.

But it didn't matter. Prine had seen the fear in her face last night in the camp, and he thought of her not as an outlaw but as a lady. And this was no place for a lady at all.

Before them was a hotel. It was a remarkably tall one for a town of this sort, three stories high and nicely painted. It looked out of place amidst the gaudy glow of the tawdry saloons and dance halls like a church in the middle of a circus. Prine tethered his horse in front of it and walked inside. Stuart went with him, while Ballard and Thad stayed outside with the horses. Ballard's sawed-off shotgun lay in the cradle of his crossed arms, looking deadly and threatening.

Prine and Stuart looked over the lobby of the hotel. It was fancy, almost elegant. The man behind the counter was dressed sharply, and his voice had an educated edge.

"Good evening, gentlemen. How many rooms?" He flashed an artificial smile that years of practice had rendered almost convincing.

"Two, please. Side by side." Prine glanced over at Stuart. "We need to stay close together."

"Fine, then. You'll have Rooms Five and Six, directly up the stairs facing the lobby. There is a connecting door between the two rooms."

Prine took the keys and looked upstairs. The doors to their rooms were visible from the lobby, opening right out onto the landing. The landing became a hallway off to the right, leading past one more door before making a right-angle turn toward the back of the building. Prine asked if anyone were in that third room and was pleased to receive a negative reply. He didn't want anyone close beside them during the night.

"I like this setup," he told Stuart. "Better to be facing the lobby than to be hidden away back in a corner like a rat in a nest."

The pair turned and headed back toward the street. Halfway out the door Prine turned and called back to the clerk: "You got a stable here, or do I have to use the town livery?"

"There's a stable out back, sir. And the watchman is an alert man and a teetotaler." The clerk flashed his imitation smile again.

Prine and Stuart stepped out onto the boardwalk and rejoined Thad and Ballard. Music carried to them from a myriad of saloons, mixing into a dissonant conglomeration of sound.

CHAPTER 11

Ballard pulled the door shut behind him and locked it. He turned to look at the others standing in the hotel room. Stuart and Thad looked wary and apprehensive. Prine's features were unreadable. Ballard sat down heavily in a chair in the corner.

"Well, Prine, what now?" An unspoken assumption seemed to have arisen that Prine was the man who made the decisions, at least in Statler.

He sat down on the edge of the bed. "I didn't see anyone out there that I recognized as part of the Tate gang, but I'm sure they're here. Whether they'll come looking for us I'm not sure, but it don't matter—I plan to draw them to us."

Prine rubbed his chin. "They know only you by sight, Stuart. We could always use you as bait, but I don't want to risk that. Ballard and me are more used to this type of thing, I think. I believe I have a plan that should draw them like bugs to a candle."

The men gathered as Prine spoke in low tones. The plan he outlined sent a prickle of fear down the spine of everyone there, but each recognized the logic of it. At the end there was general assent on the idea.

Outside, the town of Statler grew wilder, and the noise of a gunshot echoed down the street. Few of the stragglers in the street noticed, and none of them cared.

Ezekiel Statler had first built his trading post and saloon in these parts in 1847, and from that time on the place had grown. The men who came there were for the most part rowdy, strong characters, most just a shade on the wrong side of the law. But Ezekiel Statler had taken them in with no questions asked, and his trading post became the refuge for much of the scum of the West.

When the old man died, the tradition continued just the same, and the town that sprang up bearing his name remained a haven for drunkards, bandits, horse thieves, cattle rustlers, prostitutes, and card sharks.

It was toward the end of the nineteenth century now, and law was commonplace across the West. But not at Statler.

It had a sheriff, all right, just as legal as any other town. The only trouble was that the sheriff was also the town drunk, and his election had been pulled off as a joke. Many thought he didn't yet realize that he held office. He would sit in the back of the Black Ace saloon for hours, his head on the table and his hand wrapped around a near-empty whiskey bottle, and his badge shining from his tattered shirt. Occasionally it would fall off, but someone would, without fail, replace it.

Statler couldn't last. Everyone in the town knew that. It was the last of a dying breed of town. Already many of the wild cattle and mining towns were gone. Someday that would be true of Statler, but until that time the people there would continue to carouse drunkenly and toast the days that would never come again.

Four men sat in the Black Ace saloon, their faces hard and unsmiling. They had been on the trail for days, looking for the men who rode with Thomas Stuart.

They knew of the packet Stuart carried. They had followed his movements closely, and they were certain that he was here in Statler with his companions. But could they find them here? That was the one thing that worried them.

Except for the one named Buster. He was too worried about whether or not his fiddle was being stolen to think of anything else. He had left the instrument in the town livery, and from that time on he had worried about it. His laments were becoming an irritation to the rest of his friends, mostly because he refused to leave his liquor long enough to do anything about the problem.

The piano music was loud, and the flow of conversation and shouting made a steady hum in the place, occasionally rising to a roar. The men sat silently, except for Buster, watching the action all around them, and occasionally they would glance toward the door.

About ten o'clock two men walked through that door. Staggered, actually. One of them was a tall, powerful-looking fellow with dark hair and sideburns touched with gray. He was slender but had enough heft about him to indicate that he was no weakling. But he was dwarfed, almost, by the fellow beside him, a huge, burly bear of a man with a graying beard and broad face. Both men were middle-aged and appeared roaring drunk.

They were almost comical, holding on to one another as they moved into the saloon, the big one singing and the other waving to the crowd as if this were a party held in their honor. The big one was loud, his voice carrying over the noise of the other saloon occupants.

"Prine, my friend, let me buy you a drink! Then you can buy me one!"

The pair headed over to the bar, and the big man banged

the polished bar top with such force that it rattled every glass on it and some on the nearby tables. It got the attention of the barkeep, all right, along with that of everyone else in the building.

"Whiskey! Good strong whiskey! The kind that pickles your guts and burns out your hair from the inside! That's what I want! And a whole bottle!" the big one demanded.

He got it. The husky fellow paid off and headed back across the saloon with his partner. They found a table in the corner, not far from the Tate gang members. Then they started in on the bottle of whiskey.

The big man talked on a myriad of topics, and all the while his partner did his best to keep him quiet. He would frown at him like a mother at a child, whispering "Hush" and "Keep your voice down!" and finally "Stuart will blow your head off if you talk too much!"

At that the four men sat up quickly. The name "Stuart" had gotten their attention.

"Nonsense, Prine!" bellowed Ballard. "I'm not worried about that runt's opinions. I'll do as I please, and Stuart be hanged! And why do you keep on telling me to hush? There ain't nobody in here listening to us...see, I'll show you."

The big man raised himself up and looked around without discretion, eyeing very closely everyone around him. He appeared so drunk as to be comical. But the four men at the nearby table were not laughing, though they listened and watched intently.

"See, Prine...nobody heard me." He pointed at a man near him. "Did you hear me? Or you? See... I told you they didn't hear me!" He glanced around toward Buster and his group. His face twisted into an exaggerated smile, and he reached up to tip a hat that wasn't there. "Evening, friends!"

They looked back with cold eyes, but he didn't seem to notice. He filled his shot glass to the brim again and drained most of it at a swallow. He sang for a while along with the piano, then began a drunken oration.

"Prine, we're going to be rich! Rich beyond our wildest dreams! And it's all out there just waiting to be picked up."

The four men at the nearby table glanced at each other, and smiles flickered across their faces. They listened closely to the blabbering big man and the other fellow who was so unsuccessfully trying to keep him quiet.

For a long time, the show went on, the big one talking loudly and the smaller one trying to quiet him. Most of the men in the saloon paid no attention to them; most had not heard the big one's talk about wealth. But even the half-drunk Buster was paying close attention, though he tried to mask it.

One thing he didn't notice, though, was that after a full hour the bottle the pair were sharing was almost as full as when they began. His friends paid no heed to that strange phenomenon, either, not noticing that the sips taken by their drunken neighbors were quite small ones. Also unnoticed were the eyes of both men, eyes remarkably clear for men as drunken as these apparently were.

Abruptly the pair stood, walking away and taking their bottle with them. They moved out of the door of the saloon and on into the night. The four outlaws could hear their loud singing as they moved down the street. Then the immediate noise of the saloon drowned out the raucous music.

The four rose wordlessly, and followed the pair out onto the street. On the boardwalk they looked in the direction the two had taken. They saw them only an instant before they disappeared into the next saloon.

"The fat one had a lot of mighty interesting things to say, now, didn't he!" grinned one of them. "It looks like they're making every saloon in town. And judging from the direction they're moving, I'd say they started from back this way

—which means that they probably came from that hotel over yonder. Friends, I'd say that that hotel is where we'll find our friend Stuart—along with that map."

"Should we go after the two drunk ones, too?"

"Them two won't give us no trouble. And we should be able to handle the rest ourselves. Let's go."

They walked toward the hotel on the other end of town. None of them noticed the two men who stepped out of the saloon down the street, both cold sober. The pair moved like shadows after the four gunmen.

The whole scene was watched by Thomas Stuart from the alley window of Room 5. The building beside him cut off part of his view of the street, but when the four were almost in front of the hotel he saw them. And he also saw Ballard and Prine lurking behind them.

He dropped the curtain and moved quickly through the door that joined Room 5 with the next one. Thad was in there, busily at work on the thing they had been preparing since the two older men had left to act on Prine's plan.

"They're coming. Are you ready?"

Thad quickly finished his work. "I am now. Let's go."

The two young men headed back into Room 5 and picked up a chair. They sat it outside on the landing, facing the lobby, directly between the landing doors of Rooms 5 and 6. Thad sat down in it, his father's shotgun across his lap, his eyes fixed on the front door of the hotel. Stuart gave him a quick pat on the shoulder, then hefted his own rifle and stepped back inside one of the rooms, closing the door until it was only open a crack.

And then they waited.

Chapter 12

The hotel clerk was locked away in the back office counting his day's receipts, so he did not notice when four men entered the lobby with their pistols drawn. Had he seen them he would have done nothing to stop them, for he had been in this town far too long and knew too well the type of men they were. He was not a strong man, nor a brave one, and that was why he was still alive in Statler. He had always hidden away from danger like a mouse in a corner.

So the lobby was empty when the gunmen came in, crouched and scanning the interior of the hotel. It took only a moment for them to notice the young man who sprang from his chair on the landing with a shotgun in his hands. And it took only a fraction of another moment for them to react with gunfire.

The bullets smacked close above Thad's head as he ducked into Room 6.

In the hotel's back office, the clerk crawled under his heavy mahogany desk.

The four men scattered. One leapt behind the counter running parallel to the right wall and another hid against the opposite wall beside a heavy cabinet filled with fancy china and glassware. The remaining two headed immediately to the stairs and began running up toward the door Thad had entered.

They were halfway up the stairs when the short muzzle of a double-barreled shotgun poked out of the doorway and let go with a double roar. Two charges of shot ripped into the wall just above the heads of the two men, and they ducked, one of them losing his footing and tumbling down the stairs to roll out on the floor. But he was up in an instant, and he and his partner darted up the stairs and hugged the facing wall on either side of the Room 5 door. At a signal, both men leapt in front of the door and kicked it in.

A figure stood in the middle of the room, holding a rifle aimed directly at them. They opened fire immediately and riddled the tall form through and through with .44 bullets.

As the figure fell stiffly backward onto the floor, the men saw it for what it was: a dummy constructed on the back of a chair, set up in the middle of the room with a rifle in its lifeless arms. They had been fooled.

But another figure, this one very alive, bolted through the doorway in the back of the room that connected the room with the adjoining Room 5. In his hands was a sawed-off shotgun, reloaded and cocked. As he entered, the closet door on the other side of the room burst open and revealed another man hidden there, his rifle aimed at gut level toward the men.

The second of the Tate gunmen wanted to give up immediately, but was knocked aside by his partner, who made a desperate scramble for the doorway. He tripped and fell, and the other let panic override his urge to surrender and leapt across the fallen man onto the landing just outside the door. The downed man then leapt up and fired a shot that zipped close by Thad's head. In answer, a blast from the shotgun exploded, in unison with one from Stuart's rifle from the closet.

One man was caught full in the chest, the force of the shots kicking him up from the floor and sending him reeling backward onto the landing. He hit on his heels and staggered, the small of his back striking the landing railing. He fell over it backward, arms spread wide, flipped in the air, and landed face down on the floor below with a loud crash. He moved once, then no more.

Thad bolted to the door, thrust the shotgun out, and sent the remaining charge hurtling down toward the man hidden behind the counter in the lobby below. The man ducked, and the wall behind him shredded with lead pellets, just as two quick shots from the man who had just escaped the room sent Thad back under cover again. By now one gunman was hidden just around the corner down the hallway to Thad's left, and his position effectively sealed Thad in his room.

One of the gunmen hidden downstairs darted suddenly toward the storeroom beneath the landing and directly below Room 6. Thad saw it but was unable to get off a shot at the man.

In the storeroom the man listened to the sound of footsteps above him and aiming at the spot where their sound came from, sent two slugs ripping through the floor of the room above. He heard a startled and angry cry from above, and the sound of feet pounding away from where the shots had entered. He followed the sound and sent another blast angling off in that direction.

Suddenly he found his own strategy turned against him, for rifle slugs came ripping down through the ceiling of the storeroom to splatter into the floor all around him. One grazed the side of his head, almost costing him an earlobe, and he turned to dart out into the lobby again.

He caught himself short about halfway out the door, though, for he saw them suddenly: the same pair that had been in the saloon, bursting through the hotel's front door.

He ducked back inside the storeroom and heard his partner behind the counter open fire. He joined the effort, firing around the edge of the door, and the two intruders were forced back into the night.

He expected at any moment to receive more fire through the ceiling above, but it never came. And in a moment, he understood why, for he heard running feet on the landing above, and the blast of a shotgun, aimed, he guessed, at his partner hidden around the corner in the upstairs hallway. The pair in the rooms above were apparently trying to drive the man out of his hiding place, but the plan didn't work, for there was a return burst of fire, and suddenly the rooms above were occupied again.

The dark window of the storeroom shattered, and a big man came rolling across the floor toward him. The outlaw turned to fire at the man, but the shot missed by several feet, even though he was almost at point-blank range. He didn't wait for the rapidly rising bear of a man to completely gain his feet. He darted quickly across the lobby, bullets smacking around his heels, and threw himself over the hotel counter to join his partner hidden there. Bullets punctured the smooth and polished countertop, and he hugged the floor in fear.

Ballard stuck his head and arm around the side of the storeroom door and fired toward the counter and the man raising a gun from behind it. The bullet scarcely missed the man, but the gunman managed to squeeze off two quick shots at Stuart, who fired from the doorway of Room 5.

Ballard pulled his head back into the storeroom. He looked about the dark room. His eyes rested on a half-full kerosene lamp, and he was struck with a sudden inspiration. He grabbed the lamp, removed the chimney, and dug in his pocket for a match while cranking the wick out several inches.

Upstairs, Thad was reloading. He could do little to stop the man who fired at him from the corner of the hallway, for every time he tried to squeeze off a shot at him, he was caught in the fire of the men behind the counter. And conversely, whenever he fired at them, the man around the corner blasted away at him at close range. Stuart was in the same predicament the next door down.

Where was Prine? Thad had seen no sign of him since he burst through the door alongside Ballard a few minutes before. Somebody was downstairs, firing on the outlaws from the storeroom. Perhaps it was Prine, or maybe Ballard. He suspected the latter, for the crack of the pistol sounded like that of his father's Colt.

What then of Prine? Had he deserted them? It didn't seem like something he would do, judging from what Thad had come to know of the man so far. Maybe he had some sort of plan. Maybe he would show up unexpectedly. If so, Thad hoped he would hurry, for as it was now it was pretty much a standoff.

From below came a sudden flurry of gunfire from behind the counter. However, it was not aimed at Thad and Stuart, but across at whoever was hidden in the storeroom. There flashed across the lobby something flaming and glowing that Thad could not identify. A shot sounded below the landing, and the burning thing shattered in midair, sending a shower of flaming kerosene all over the counter and the area behind it.

With a horrible howl one of the men leapt from behind the counter, his left arm coated in flaming liquid, his right hand desperately pounding the flames. All about him on the floor was flaming kerosene. His partner remained invisible, apparently huddling away from the flames, making no attempt to help his endangered companion.

Thad was in a clear position to fire at the man, but he could not, for he felt pity for the unfortunate fellow. The man had dropped his gun and was exposing himself as a clear target because his pain made him forget the danger of such a move. Thad would not shoot a man who couldn't fight back.

The man ripped off the flaming shirt, casting it aside and saving himself from any serious burns. But he could not save himself from the slug that whistled through the lobby from Stuart's gun, killing him before he hit the floor.

Thad glowered. It had happened again. Stuart had again killed a man with no good chance to fight back.

The fight remained in full swing, and it would not stop until more men were dead or wounded. Thad knew it and accepted it. He thrust his shotgun around the corner of the door and fired off a blast in the general direction of the man hidden down the hall and around the corner.

The flames below had burned themselves out now, and the remaining gunman behind the counter began firing again. The death of the other man had changed little. It was still a standoff.

Below, Ballard was disgusted that his kerosene lamp ploy had been unsuccessful. He had wanted to force the men to surrender, but his plan had been foiled. He knew it was Stuart who had killed the man, for he had heard the crack of a Winchester when the shot was fired, and Thad was fighting with a shotgun. Rapidly Ballard's doubts and suspicions about Stuart were growing into certainties.

Ballard thrust his head around the door and fired a fast and ineffective shot at one of the two remaining gunmen. He heard Thad's shotgun blasting upstairs and the noise of shot ripping into the countertop.

Suddenly there was no more shooting. The silence was almost painful in contrast to the bedlam of the past few minutes. Ballard could hear the pounding of his own pulse in his temples. He took advantage of the stillness.

"You out there! We'll give you this one chance to surrender! The same goes for you upstairs! There's no point in anyone else getting killed! Give up and we'll let you go."

The only answer was a quick shot from behind the counter. Ballard felt the sting of wood chips against his face, scattered by the impact of the shot striking the door frame. He ducked back inside.

"All right. You just set the terms!" Ballard fired off a shot around the doorway.

There was a tremendous scuffling upstairs—shouting, gunfire, general confusion. And the gunman behind the counter suddenly ducked, cowering in his hiding place.

Then, landing directly in front of the doorway to the storage room, a body fell from upstairs. Ballard knew immediately the man was dead. It was the gunman who had imperiled Thad and Stuart from around the corner of the hallway.

Upstairs, Prine holstered his gun. He had entered through the back of the building, climbing in the second-story hallway window from the roof of the woodshed built between the hotel stable and the building itself. He had surprised the gunman from the rear, and when the fellow responded in gunfire, Prine's shots had driven him from his hiding place to fall over the railing and land beside his partner, who already lay dead on the floor.

"Don't shoot! Don't shoot! I surrender!" the voice came from behind the counter. Ballard saw a pistol fly over the countertop to clatter onto the floor. He recognized the voice of the man who had played the fiddle at Orville Beecher's funeral—the one they had called Buster. Quickly he moved out of the storeroom and into the lobby.

Buster stood behind the counter, arms high in the air. Ballard took the man prisoner at gunpoint, glancing upward toward the landing to make sure that Stuart did not kill this one too.

Thad stood directly in front of Stuart's door, blocking his view of the lobby. Ballard knew the move was deliberate, and he flashed a grin at his son. Stuart glared at Thad from the doorway right behind him, fingering his gun in frustration.

They had a prisoner at last, a man who could tell them more about this gang of killers that stalked them. Maybe now a few questions could be cleared up.

Ballard led the prisoner upstairs and into Room 5. Below, in the office, the hotel clerk still cowered beneath his desk.

CHAPTER 13

Buster's attitude changed rapidly from one of fear to a contemptuous, snarling defiance of the men who had captured him. That didn't bother Prine; all he wanted was information, and he intended to do anything short of torture to get it. He stood before the seated outlaw, looking tall and fierce, and his eyes said clearly that he expected no nonsense. Behind him on the bed sat Thad and his father, and Stuart stood behind them in the corner, his arms folded across his chest and a look of dissatisfaction on his face.

Prine gazed silently at the prisoner for a long time. "Well, Buster, your scheme didn't work out, did it?" The outlaw started noticeably when Prine spoke his name, and he said, "How do you know who I am?"

"Oh, Buster, we know a lot of things about you, things you would be surprised at. We know how many men you run with, who leads you, and what you're trying to do. And it looks like we've knocked a good-sized hole in your group." He grinned sarcastically. "You should be grateful to us, Buster. We could have killed you out there, but instead we were nice enough to ask you up for this little visit. Now you can repay our kindness with a little information."

"I'll say nothing," Buster said.

Prine slapped the man across his stubbly cheek, hard. The slap resounded in the room and Buster cried out sharply. Prine looked into the man's red-rimmed eyes. "This is no game, Buster. You're lucky to be alive. Now, you can talk decent, or we can flail you within an inch of your life. It's your choice." Prine punctuated the end of his sentence with another ringing slap that knocked the slumping outlaw back upright in his seat again.

"Now, friend, you can tell us the one thing we need to know—just exactly what your group has in mind. I want details, specifics about the whole thing. And no nonsense. None at all."

Buster flashed his version of a defiant leer into Prine's face. His voice sounded like that of a snake. "You just got three of us, mister, and there's more left. And before you leave Statler you're going to die, every one of you, from your fat friend over there to that rattler standing over yonder." His gaze fell on Stuart, who stood tense and angry, a killing glitter in his eyes. The outlaw's face became ugly with hate.

"What's the matter, bush baby?" Buster laughed. "Take a look at your friend over there, men. You know what he is?" Every eye turned to Stuart in instinctive reaction to the outlaw's words. "I'll tell you, he's nothing more than a bastard and a son of—"

Prine had seen fast draws in his days on the range, but never had he witnessed anything like what occurred at that moment. Stuart's hand disappeared, blurring into invisibility with sheer speed, as it whipped to the gun belt at his waist and drew out the Remington. Three shots exploded in the small room, filling the air with smoke and the acrid smell of burnt gunpowder. As the reverberations of the shots faded into silence Prine's gaze fell on the dead body of Buster, blown against the wall by the shots, the animal snarl still on his lifeless face. For a long, tense moment there was no sound but the faint hissing of Buster's last breath escaping his dead lips.

"You murdered him...shot him like a dog! You..." Ballard's voice failed him, and his rage found its outlet in the only way possible: He swung his huge arm and pounded his fist into Stuart's jaw.

The young man fell back on the floor, his gun still clutched in his hand. He came up quickly, cocking back the revolver's hammer. His face was red with rage as he aimed the gun squarely at Ballard's face.

Every man in the room froze. Ballard stared unflinching into the black eye of the threatening gun. Stuart trembled, almost tearful in fury; then slowly the gun lowered, and he slipped it into his gun belt. He strode to the bed and sat down on the mattress, his head dropping to his hands. Ballard looked at him coldly and said nothing.

Prine tried to break the tension in the air with soft words. "Why did you do it, Stuart?"

The young man looked up at the others. His expression was different now.

"Isn't it obvious why I killed him? Prine, didn't you see him moving toward you?"

Prine was incredulous. "Are you loco? He was sitting in this chair the whole time. He wasn't moving at me."

"I didn't see him move either, Stuart," Thad cut in. "All I saw was you killing a man because he insulted you. It was murder."

Stuart snorted in contempt. "Murder! If I hadn't done what I did you would have seen murder. He would have snapped Prine's neck in a second. But I realize why none of you saw him moving at Prine—when he started speaking of me you turned and looked in my direction, every one of you. I was the only one facing Buster, and so of course I was the only one who saw him move."

Prine realized that Stuart was right. When the outlaw

had begun his tirade against the young man, all of them had turned to face Stuart. It had been a natural thing to do, and it had given Stuart an alibi that could not be refuted. Prine knew that the young man was lying, but he could not prove it. Clever, this fellow.

"I don't care what happened—from this moment on Thad and me are out of this deal," Ballard said. "C'mon, Thad. Let's head for the stable and get our horses."

Prine looked long at Stuart. "I'm afraid I'll have to join them," he said. "This isn't the sort of thing I bargained for."

Ballard was already out on the landing when Stuart gave a contemptuous laugh. "I guess I was a fool to listen to my father. I took him seriously when he said that Jeremy Prine and John Ballard were men of honor. Let me remind you, men, that I told you this would be a violent affair from the outset. You were warned, but still you agreed to stick this out to the end. I can see now that my trust in your good faith was misplaced. I understand now that you are out to look after yourself, no matter what you promised me. Go ahead—leave. My father trusted you, and wanted you in on this, and every step you take away from here is like trodding on his memory. I thought more highly of you than this, but I was wrong."

Prine was cut deeply by the words. It was true...they had each given their word of honor to stick this thing out. He recalled his thoughts while he had sat at watch in the night—thoughts of how he was doing this whole thing for Bob Stuart. To back out now would be an insult to the memory of his friend.

"You're one to talk about honor!" Thad burst out. "How much honor has a murderer?"

Stuart looked at him coldly. "I told you he was moving at Prine. I did what I thought necessary to protect Prine's life. If you think me a murderer, then prove it."

Thad was silent, and Stuart continued. "It really doesn't

matter what you think of me, gentlemen. A man's word of honor is binding, no matter what the circumstances. And if you're so concerned about murder, then ask yourself what it is if you leave me here without protection. The Tate gang will have me dead before morning, all because you backed out on your promise and left me to die. That would be murder, gentlemen. Can you live with that?"

When Stuart finished, he knew he had them. He had cut them at their most vulnerable spot. He was not surprised when slowly the men moved back into the room.

Ballard was the first to speak. "All right, Stuart, you've made your point. I'll see you through, just as I promised. But let me make it clear that I fully believe what you did was murder, and if you die before this business is finished it will be no more than what you deserve."

Stuart eyed him with anger. "In days not too long past those would have been fighting words, Ballard," he said. "Maybe when this affair is through, we'll revive those days for a while."

"Nothing could please me more, Stuart," the hefty man said. He looked over at his son. "Thad, don't feel that you have to stay on if you don't want. I'll not force my son to help on a murderer's quest."

"I gave my word, too, Pa. I'll stay."

Prine said, "And I'll stay, too, Stuart. You make me sick to my stomach, but for the memory of your father I'll stay on."

"And I'm sure my father would be pleased," Stuart said. He swept his gaze across the group. "My popularity is totally unimportant here," he said. "But I do need your help, and I'm glad you're staying with me."

He stood and stretched. "We're all tense and angry right now. I'll carry out the body of our friend, and then I suggest we all get some rest. This whole thing won't seem so terrible in the morning."

Prine stood and moved toward the dead body in the corner. "Never mind, Stuart. I'll take care of it. I could use some fresh air before I turn in."

He picked up the dead body. He hefted the corpse over his shoulder and stepped out onto the landing and on down the stairs.

The town's undertaker already was below, and beside him the pale and shaken hotel clerk. The three bodies of Buster's partners were laid out in a row across the floor, and Prine walked over and dumped his burden beside them.

"Here's another one for you, mister," he told the undertaker. The man smiled and tipped his hat in thanks.

He stepped over to the front door and out into the street, breathing the cool night air. He was mildly surprised that the gun battle had not drawn much of a crowd, but in Statler shootings were normal fare.

He stood on the boardwalk and pondered the situation he and his friends found themselves in. He had hoped that the gunfight would end the threat of the Tate gang once and for all, but now things seemed as bad as ever. There were still three of the gang living, besides Tate herself. The Tate gang wasn't gone, only temporarily weakened. They would make no move tonight, he guessed, but tomorrow would bring Prine and his partners to Jericho Mountain. Surely the Tate gang would be there too, perhaps more determined than ever to get their prize.

"Why did you get me into this, Bob?" Prine asked the night. No answer came back.

It was then he noticed her, on the edge of the crowd milling about before the saloon down the street. From the appearance of things, a cockfight had drawn the crowd, for men cheered and cursed alternately in a circle in the street. The blonde girl, however, was looking not at the commotion but at Prine, and when he returned her gaze he saw fear in her eyes. She turned and moved into the throng.

It was Priscilla Tate. Prine moved quickly, darting toward her. He elbowed his way through the mass of yelling, hooting men, and he saw her moving before him, her blonde hair bobbing along as she ran out of the other side of the crowd.

Prine forced his way through the throng and fell into pursuit.

Chapter 14

Prine was slowed by the stragglers and drunks who roamed the Statler streets. He darted through them like a man dodging trees in a forest, but the girl running ahead of him steadily increased her lead. She ran swiftly and cast frequent glances over her shoulder at her pursuer.

Statler's main street was long and well-lit from the numerous saloons, faro parlors, and dance halls that lined it, so it was not hard for Prine to follow the girl. His breath came hard as he ran, and beads of sweat broke out on him. As the girl neared the end of the street, she turned suddenly and darted into a dark building, apparently some sort of deserted structure. There was no front door or shutters, and the unpainted building looked dismal in the darkness.

Prine headed after her. Why was she running? She didn't know who he was, though probably she had guessed he was part of Stuart's group. He realized that none of the Tate gang really knew any of his own party except Stuart himself. The shoot-out in the hotel had been the first face-to-face encounter between the rival groups. So Priscilla Tate was running from a man she didn't know.

Prine headed down the street at a trot and entered the

dark building. He could see nothing at all because of the blackness of the interior. He stopped within a few feet of the door and stood in the midst of the dark room, listening closely for any noise that might betray the girl's hiding place. There was no sound but the faint scurrying of a rat off in some corner. But he knew she was here.

For a long time, he stood still as a statue. He then realized that he was probably silhouetted against the dim light of the street behind him. She was watching him against that background; he could almost feel her gaze. He edged silently to the right and into the thicker blackness of the shaded wall beside him. Still there was no hint of life within the building. Prine wished he could see catlike into the blackness and find her.

A chilling thought came. What if she was armed? The more he thought about it the more certain he became that she was. This was Statler, and few people, women included, dared venture into the streets without some means of protection.

Then there was a sudden flurry of movement from the opposite corner of the dark room. He moved forward. Two rapid shots blasted into the stillness of the room: cracking shots, fired from a derringer.

Prine felt the bullets whistling by him in the darkness and drew in his breath sharply. He ran toward the spot from which the two flashing bursts of gunfire had exploded seconds before, and his hands brushed the softness of long, feminine hair and the slender shoulder of a girl. But she was quick and nimble, and turned out of his grasp. He fell against the rough wall.

She was gone. He saw her faint form as his eyes grew more accustomed to the darkness. She ran toward the back of the building, then a door opened, revealing her for a second against the shining night sky. The door closed and Prine was alone.

He moved toward the door, bumping his shin against something and falling to his face on the floor. The place was covered with filth and trash, and Prine landed face down in the midst of it. He stood quickly, brushed the mess off of him, and continued the chase.

His hands groped the wall, searching for the latch that marked the door. There...he found it. Quickly it gave under his strong hand, and the door opened into the night. He exited swiftly.

Where could she be? Her escape had given her a good lead and a strong advantage. She might well have already disappeared into the throngs in one of the saloons. But he could look for her. It would be worthwhile to have a talk with the girl whose men had done their best to kill him and his friends earlier tonight.

He was in the back streets of Statler now, and the buildings looked remarkably different from their false fronts that faced the main street. They appeared rough and crude when viewed from this angle—shabby buildings. Trash was strewn throughout the overgrown rear areas of the buildings, and Prine winced at the foul odor of the mess. He saw the flashing eyes of a cat as it roamed the area, searching for the rodents that thrived in the trash heaps.

Prine moved into an alley that led back to the main street. He heard a low groan at his feet, and started in surprise, as if he had nearly stepped on a rattler. He looked down and saw a man reclining there, drunk as a sailor, his hand around a half-empty bottle. Prine felt disgust mixed with pity. No doubt this fellow lay drunk in some alley every night. But such was life in Statler.

He walked quickly back onto the main street. There was no sign of a blonde head among the crowds, and Prine was fearful that the girl had escaped him. He turned to glance in the opposite direction.

He saw a sudden flash of yellow at a corner. He ran

toward it, mildly surprised that the figure did not try to run. He grasped the shoulder and wheeled the person around, then stared into the face of a grimy, bearded man who had apparently not had a shave or haircut in months. He looked dull and dissipated. He appeared old, yet the thick blond hair told Prine that this was a young man, aged only by liquor and the opium available in Statler's back-street dives. The man's eyes registered not a trace of surprise at Prine's unexpected jostling.

"Sorry," Prine muttered. He turned away.

She was gone. Vanished into the crowd. He stopped the pursuit and leaned against a post to catch his breath. He looked, bewildered, at the many saloons that lined the street. If she were in one of them it might take all night to find the right one. And he had no proof that she was in any of them.

This had been a wild night, and he was only beginning to realize how tired he was. There had been little real rest for the group since this adventure had started just short of three days before. Three days! Yet it could have been a month. Prine was growing very weary.

He walked slowly down the street. He glanced up randomly and took in the side of a stable back some distance off the street. There was a large window in the side, crisscrossed with rusted metal bars. Through that window he could see the lantern-lit interior of the building, and there he saw her. She was talking rapidly to someone. She seemed disturbed.

This must be the place she and her gang are holed up, he thought. He stopped in his tracks, debating what to do. Should he go back to the hotel and get the others? No...especially not after Stuart's demonstrated penchant for murder. Somehow Prine couldn't let him have a chance at Priscilla Tate. Prine felt that vague and unexplainable tenderness toward her that he had first felt in the forest, hidden with Ballard beside her camp. He would check this out himself.

Besides, there was no point in risking the life of all of them, he rationalized.

He looked for entrance to the stable. There was a front door, but it was closed, and walking through it would be an invitation to quick death, anyway. Perhaps there was a back way. He crept to the side of the building, crouched under the window, and glanced cautiously inside.

She was seated on a crate inside. Three men were with her, and Prine recognized them from the forest camp. One of them was the man who had preached Orville Beecher's unorthodox funeral. The other two he could not attach a name or label to, but their faces were familiar.

Prine looked toward the back of the stable. There was a large rear door, open to the night, and beyond a field overgrown with weeds. A wagon sat halfway inside the doorway, its rear portion outside. Prine quickly formulated a plan.

He trotted quietly around the side of the building toward the rear. He rounded the corner and came up beside the large doorway. Light streamed from the stable, the sound of voices accompanying it.

"...dead, ma'am. Every one of them. I saw the undertaker carrying them out of the hotel just a little while ago. So now it's down to us three and you. Do you think we can handle that group by ourselves?"

Prine recognized the voice of the preacher. His words had a cutting edge, a kind of sarcastic disdain for the lady. Prine crawled beneath the wagon, where he could observe and listen closely.

"I don't know what to do," said Priscilla Tate with despair in her voice. "Somehow this whole thing is so different than I planned it. I never thought it would be like this. I thought the threat alone would stop him, but Tom must be more dedicated than I imagined. I knew he would go far, but I never guessed anything like this!"

Prine was surprised at the familiarity with which she

spoke of Stuart. He had guessed that she would know little about him, but she had talked about him as if she were well acquainted with him, calling him by his first name as if it were a natural thing. Prine was slightly unnerved. He realized that he knew very little about Thomas Stuart, and even less about Priscilla Tate.

"I think we can handle 'em alone," said one of the other men. "It's best that the others are gone—that will be that much weight off of us, so to speak. We can move quicker and easier with just us."

Priscilla burst out angrily, "How can you talk like that? You talk as if they were animals instead of men! That's what I mean when I say this thing has gotten out of hand. I would never have thought it would be like this at all—if I had I would just have let Tom have it all. Maybe that's what I should do now, before anyone else dies because of this."

There was a rather threatening silence. The preacher rose from his seat and looked down at the distraught young girl.

"I'm afraid that's out of the question, ma'am. There's no way any of us will back out of this thing now, not this close." He shook his head. "You came into this thing mighty ignorant, lady, mighty ignorant. All that wealth is hidden out there somewhere, just like grapes ripe for the picking. Maybe you want to let someone else get hold of it, but I got no such notions. Miss Priscilla, I think maybe our use for you is finished. We can follow that bunch without your help." His hand dropped to his gun.

The girl rose from her seat and began backing away. The preacher drew his gun and raised it slowly.

"G'bye, Miss Priscilla." He grinned as he took aim.

Prine's shot blew the gun from his hand and took two fingers with it. The preacher cried out in pain, and Priscilla Tate darted into a stall as the other outlaws rose and drew their weapons. Prine sent a volley toward them that sent them scurrying for cover, though they managed to squeeze off several quick shots that flew harmlessly out the rear door into the night. By the time they realized where those unexpected shots had come from, Prine was gone.

He had no notions of taking on the three gunmen alone. The only thing he could do was to provide the girl with an opportunity for escape. It would be up to her to take advantage of it.

The preacher rose from the straw-covered floor of the stable with a livid face and burning eyes. He gripped his bleeding hand and stared out the back door of the stable.

"Go after him! Kill him!"

The other two gunmen moved out the rear door, guns ready. The preacher pulled a heavy thread from his clothes and tied it tightly around the stumps of his two blown-off fingers, cursing all the while. He tightened the threads and the bleeding stopped. He picked up his gun with his good hand and went out of the stable.

In the instant after the shot had come, he had seen Prine's face. For only an instant, of course, but that was sufficient. The man's features he would not forget.

He had no doubt that the fellow was part of Tom Stuart's bunch. Yet he had not shot to kill, and that mystified the preacher. When his time came, he himself would not be so merciful. He would find that man and make him pay with his life for the fingers he had lost.

He held the gun in his left hand, its weight clumsier there. He moved down the alley and into the main street, searching the street for his opponent, but seeing no one who looked like him.

Then he did see Prine, who was heading into a saloon on the other end of the street. There was no sign of the other two gunmen. The preacher holstered his gun and moved toward the saloon.

His hand throbbed; fury raged in him. He would shoot

the man who maimed him, even if he had to do it right in the midst of the crowd.

Priscilla Tate rose from the stall where she had hidden. She glanced around fearfully to make sure she was alone. She was filled with questions. She too had seen for an instant the face of the man whose shot had saved her life. She recognized him as the very man who had chased her earlier that night.

She knew of the gun battle in the hotel—the same hotel on whose porch she had first noticed the man who had just now saved her. It was from that building that he had come in pursuit of her, and that was the same building that housed Thomas Stuart and his men.

So he must be a member of Stuart's group. Why had he saved her life? It was confusing, but she could not take time to clear up the mystery. She had to leave for her own safety. Her own men had turned against her. She found and saddled her horse, then mounted and moved out the back door and across the overgrown field behind it, heading for the wildland beyond. She breathed a prayer for the safety of the man who had rescued her from death. She wished she could thank him.

Chapter 15

Prine sat in the corner of the crowded saloon, eyes fastened on the door. He didn't think any of his pursuers had seen him enter, but he could not be sure. He didn't regret firing the shot that crippled the preacher's hand. He was glad that he had provided the threatened girl a chance to escape and hoped that she had taken advantage of it.

The saloon was packed, people moving to and fro within it, coming between Prine and the door and cutting off his view. That made Prine uncomfortable, but again he couldn't afford to make himself obvious by craning his neck to see around the man standing in his line of vision.

But the drunk had been blocking his view for so long that Prine couldn't resist looking around him to the doorway. He was glad he did, for standing there in the door was the preacher, who was searching the crowd over the batwing doors. Prine ducked behind the drunk again, but at that moment the fellow decided to move. The preacher's eyes fell on Prine, and a grin came onto his face.

Prine stood and moved quickly toward the back of the

saloon. The preacher didn't even bother to push his way through the swinging doors of the front entrance as he fired three fast shots that punctured the wood of the doors and drew screams from the barmaids as it sent saloon occupants scurrying under the tables and behind the bar. But the shots missed their mark, for Prine was already gone out the back door.

The preacher scowled and hurried through the saloon, ignoring the angry shouts of those all around him. The fat bartender rose from behind the bar with a shotgun in his hands. The preacher fired nonchalantly in his direction with hardly a glance. The glass behind the bar shattered and the bartender ducked again.

The preacher went out the back way after Prine. His gun felt strange in his left hand; his aim was slightly off. Where had that fellow gone? He couldn't have gotten far in the past moment.

The preacher heard running feet in a back alley, and moved toward it. He fired a quick shot that almost nipped Prine's heel as he ran around a dark corner. The preacher quickly darted around the same place, pausing only long enough to reload his gun. He came up on a dark alley that dead-ended into the side of another building. Prine had run himself into a trap.

But the outlaw had no time to take advantage of Prine's plight, for as soon as the preacher showed himself around the corner, a huge cask that had sat empty in the alley came hurtling through the air to knock him in the face and send him sprawling onto his back. Then Prine leaped directly over him and darted around the corner again.

The downed man was up in a second. His gun had been knocked from his grasp, but he recovered it and took off after Prine.

He wondered where his two companions were. They had

obviously lost track of Prine, but perhaps now that Prine was back in the street they would pick up his trail again. He rounded the front corner of the building, and then felt as if a club had pounded him in the face. He fell backward, then looked upward through blurred eyes to see Prine descend like a fighting mountain lion directly upon him.

The preacher cried out involuntarily, and reached up to deflect the man falling toward him. He caught Prine's shoulders, but he could not keep Prine's rock-hard fists from pounding into his gut. His breath burst out from him, and he let go of Prine's shoulders, thus letting him fall directly on top of him.

Prine continued pounding the man's kidneys and stomach. His weight pinned the preacher's shoulders to the earth and made it impossible for the supine man to return the blows. A crowd began to gather around the pair, whooping and laughing and calling words of encouragement to both.

The preacher's teeth clamped down hard on Prine's left ear. The flesh of the ear was crushed between the clenching teeth. Through Prine's mind for an instant came the image of an uncle who had lost an ear in just such a manner. He had no desire to turn such occurrences into a family tradition, so he sent a particularly hard blow into the preacher's stomach and sent the man's breath bursting from his throat with a grunt. The preacher's teeth opened their vise-like grip momentarily.

It was just long enough for Prine to roll away, his chest heaving from exertion and his ear throbbing in pain. He felt for it. Good! The ear was still there, though it felt as if the preacher's teeth had almost bitten clean through it.

The preacher stood, a little slower than Prine, and the two squared off and faced each other. Both were panting, wet with sweat and covered with grime, but neither was about to quit.

The preacher looked with hate at his opponent. He held up his right hand, the stumps from the missing fingers bleeding slightly again, and growled, "You'll pay for this with your life."

The preacher moved quickly, amazingly fleet for a man of his size and state of fatigue, and in an instant the gun he had dropped when Prine jumped him was in his left hand. He leveled the muzzle at Prine's head.

"Now it's time to die, friend!"

The gun roared and Prine dropped suddenly to his knees. The bullet passed a mere fraction of an inch from his ear. His hand dropped to his own holster.

It was empty. In the frantic fight he had lost his weapon; he saw it on the ground several yards away, out of reach. He was left unarmed against a man who was determined to blow his head off. He dropped and rolled as the preacher's second bullet buried itself in the dirt beside him.

He was amazed that neither shot had struck him and realized the reason for the man's poor aim—he was firing the gun with his left hand, and he was no southpaw.

Prine rose and ran straight at his foe, arms grasping toward him, and the barrel came up into his face. This is it, Prine figured. With a loud death yell, he leaped toward the preacher just as the gunman's finger squeezed down on the trigger.

The hammer clicked on a faulty cartridge, and Prine found himself pounding his fists into the face of the man whom he had expected to kill him. He felt a sudden exhilaration and let out a whoop of joy as his fists drove the man backward.

The preacher fell on his back, and Prine's boot caught him hard on the thigh. He yelled and rolled, and Prine moved in on him again. All about the crowd gathered once more, for it had moved back when the shots were fired, and

Prine saw from the corner of his eye that he was surrounded by a circle of grinning faces.

That circle parted suddenly, and it took Prine a moment to figure out just why. Then he heard a shot. A slug ripped right into the wall beside him. He wheeled and looked wildly in the direction of the gunfire, as the preacher fell unconscious at his feet.

It was the other two gunmen who had been in the stable with Priscilla Tate. And they were coming his way, with weapons drawn. The crowd disappeared as quickly as it had formed, like mist beneath the sun, and Prine stood transfixed for an instant in surprise.

But then he moved swiftly, darting back into the alley from which he had come shortly before. He vanished in the darkness, and he heard curses as the gunmen came after him. The roar of gunfire echoed between the walls and spurred him onward. He rounded the corner.

Where to go? Where to run? In his haste to escape, Prine had run into the same dead-end alley as before. Now what could he do?

He could hear the gunmen approaching down the alley behind him. He leapt upon another empty cask and grasped the edge of the flat roof of the shed that blocked the exit of the alley. He heaved himself up onto it as the gunmen rounded the corner. Their weapons belched flames in the darkness.

He ran across the top of the structure as bullets whistled around him. Before him rose the slightly higher wall of a barn, and an alley opened beneath him. In the barn wall facing him was an open window, slightly lower than the wall of the building upon which he stood.

He didn't even think about it as he did the instinctive thing—he dived. Straight from the shed's roof he leapt headlong, and his body arched through the open window to land on something soft.

It was a mound of hay, thick and deep. He rose from it, looking like a straw-stuffed scarecrow, and glanced desperately around. The gunmen would be upon him in a moment, for he could hear them climbing the wall of the low building across the alley. He had no weapon with which to face them, and there seemed no good place to hide.

He heard the voices of the men as they moved across the roof, and ran quickly to the best hiding place he could find—the haystack against the opposite wall, toward the front end of the barn. Straight into it he dived, crawling to the very base of it, and heaped the hay up behind himself as best he could. He heard the scurrying of a rat close by. Apparently, he had disturbed its nest. The short, stiff fur of the rodent brushed against his arm as it exited the haystack. Prine shuddered. He hated rats.

He lay silent, the hay scratching him over every inch of his body. His breath came in short, hard pants, but he tried to avoid inhaling much of the dusty atmosphere inside the haystack. Sneezing would not be advisable with two men so close by ready to kill him. He could hear them entering through the window.

"Where did he go? Did you see him?"

The other responded with a grunt. Prine heard their boots on the straw-covered dirt floor. A horse whinnied slightly in a stall.

"The door's shut. He couldn't have got out. And I swear he didn't run into the alley. He jumped right in here."

"Keep poking around. He's probably hidden somewhere."

All around the barn they moved. Prine could hear them kicking stalls, opening doors, and peering into storage bins. They wouldn't stop, he knew, until they found him. They drew nearer, and it made him quite uncomfortable.

"Check up in the loft, Ben."

Feet hit the crude rungs of the ladder to the loft, and

Prine heard the man moving about above. He heard the noise of hay being scattered and barrels and crates being turned over. The other man loitered below, just next to Prine's haystack. The men said little for a time; then the man below called up:

"Is there any kind of pitchfork or anything up there?"

"Yep, here's one."

"Toss it down. I want to poke through this hay."

Prine felt like a man about to be shot.

Something clattered on the floor, and Prine closed his eyes and bit his lip as, moments later, he heard the thrusting of sharp metal prongs into the hay all around him. The thrusts came again and again, each one at a slightly different place, each one getting closer to where he lay. And he couldn't move, for that would give away his location just as quickly as if he cried out. He bit his lip harder. Better a pitchfork prong than a bullet, he told himself.

Ever closer the thrusts came, steady as a ticking clock, coming almost in rhythm with the beating of his pounding heart. Again...again...

He stifled a cry with all the willpower that was in him, for a prong of the fork had passed through the soft flesh of his calf. It had struck barely beneath the surface of his skin, but still it probed deep enough to send burning pain all through him. He hoped desperately that he had not moved when the thrust struck him. It had been only with extreme, excruciating effort that he had avoided crying out.

"Sam!" the man above cried with a note of warning to the man with the pitchfork.

The fork's thrusts stopped, and the man responded, "What is it?"

"Three men headed this way."

The man with the pitchfork stood silent for a moment, in an atmosphere of indecision. "You're right," he said.

Prine heard the descent of the one above on the ladder;

then both searchers scurried toward the opposite wall and the window that opened in it. They climbed out, and Prine lay still long enough to be reasonably sure that they were indeed gone. Then he pushed his way out of the haystack.

He stood carefully on the wounded leg, testing how well it would bear his weight. The puncture wound was small. It would close and heal rapidly—that is, if he didn't come down with lockjaw or infection. He limped slightly over to the stable door.

He opened it a crack and peered into the street. Not far away he saw Ballard and the others moving down the street, their backs toward him. He knew they sought him, no doubt worried by his long absence since he had taken the body of Buster downstairs to the undertaker.

"Ballard! Over here!" Prine tried not to cry out too loudly, fearing that perhaps the gunmen were still close by.

Ballard wheeled quickly, his fast reaction betraying his nervousness. He looked very relieved when he saw Prine, and the group moved over to the barn door to join their companion.

"Prine! Are you all right? Where have you been?" Ballard sounded like a mother doting over her child, and Prine grinned.

Prine related quickly what had happened since he had carried Buster's body from the hotel room. He omitted, though, any mention of the familiarity with which Priscilla Tate had spoken of Stuart.

Stuart stood silent throughout Prine's story, but his eyes showed deep interest. Prine glanced at him, feeling uncomfortable and suspicious in his presence.

"Prine, let's get you back to that hotel and patch up your leg," said Thad. "Then let's get some sleep."

"Sounds mighty inviting," Prine said. "But first let me go see if my pistol is still where I dropped it."

It wasn't. Prine shrugged. "Well, at least I didn't lose my life. That I couldn't replace."

"Let's get back indoors," Ballard said. "This town makes me edgy."

They walked back to the hotel together.

CHAPTER 16

Prine's eyes were bloodshot and red-rimmed when he rose, but he felt no desire to stay tucked away on the bed's feather mattress. He was ready to get out of Statler. He had taken his fill of the place. All the men stirred when he rose, and moments later, were up and pulling on their boots. Thad was at watch outside the door. Prine buckled on his gun belt, the pistol he had lost last night replaced by a spare Ballard had given him.

The hotel clerk refused to take their money, or even talk to them face to face. "Just leave, quickly!" he shouted from the back office where he kept his bunk. "And the next time you're in Statler, kindly stay somewhere else!"

"And a good day to you, too," muttered Ballard. Then the group headed out into the street and around back to the stable.

They really wouldn't have been too surprised to discover their horses missing, taken by some Statler horse thief. But apparently the clerk's assurances about the night watchman were accurate, for the animals were all there, looking rested and strong. They led them out of the stable and saddled them, then rode out into the street.

"Let's find a general store," said Prine. "We need to pick up a little food and a couple of lanterns. I don't want to have to stop in this town for supplies on the way back."

The store, to their chagrin, was not open, so they sat on the rough bench on the porch and waited until the storekeeper arrived. Prine wondered how the man managed to do much business in a town in which much of the populace slept in the daytime and roared all night.

The man opened his store with only a grunt of greeting to the men waiting for him. Prine and Ballard entered after him and bought some food, lanterns, and a supply of kerosene. They laid the merchandise on the counter and paid the storekeeper.

Outside they loaded the packhorses and mounted up. Then they turned their backs on the streets of Statler and headed west. It would be late evening before they reached the vicinity of Jericho Creek and the pockmarked crag of Jericho Mountain.

They fell into single file along the trail, and Ballard kept his shotgun across the saddle in front of him as he led the group. The trails were rough, and the horses had to step carefully over many roots, stumps, and boulders. The day wore on and their progress seemed slower than they had expected it would be.

Prine caught himself thinking about Priscilla Tate. Where was she now? Would she attempt to assemble a new gang in Statler? Somehow, he doubted it.

Prine also pondered the general situation in which he found himself. He felt increasingly skeptical about Stuart now, full of doubt about the young man's motives. Stuart was a mysterious fellow, and Prine had always been one to want everything in the open, all cards on the table. He was suspicious that the tale Stuart had related about Priscilla Tate was not true. After all, it was only Stuart's word they had to go on that Priscilla Tate was who and what he said she was.

Prine was a man who trusted his instincts, and those said clearly that the young blonde girl was no killer, and no girl who had grown up around killers. Every time he had seen her, even in that momentary glance from the Statler hotel porch, he had sensed fear in her, and worry. And even though she had shot at him in that dark, deserted building the night before, he could not feel harshly toward her. Strange, but that's how it was.

Ballard fell back from his lead position and Stuart rode out in front. Prine knew something was up when the burly rider reined up beside him.

"I think I need to talk to you, Prine."

"Don't tell me—it's about Stuart. Right?"

"On the nose. I don't like this, Prine, not one bit. There's something going on here beneath the surface. Something shady and low. That boy's got an ace that he ain't showing."

Prine glanced at the young man leading the party. "I know what you mean. I've felt it ever since he shot that prisoner yesterday. I can't prove it, of course, but I believe Stuart was lying when he said he was about to jump me. The man would have been a fool to try something like that. Stuart's a liar, and a cunning one at that."

Ballard grunted in assent. Prine could tell that his friend was thinking. "There's something that happened the other night out in the woods that I ain't told nobody," Ballard said at last.

"While Stuart was sitting watch," Ballard continued, "I was awake, but lying real still. Stuart looked us all over real close, like he wanted to make sure we were sleeping, then took off into the woods by himself. Well, I followed him, and he took off straight toward where the Tate gang was camped. I swear, it seemed like he was planning to walk right in on them. I tried to stay quiet, but he found me and got pretty upset. Then he cooled down and told me he had gone to check out a noise he had heard. I went along with the tale, but I knew he was lying. I had been awake, and there hadn't been no noise. Crazy though it may sound, I think he was planning to kill them all while the men were drunk. The girl, too, probably."

Prine said, "Why didn't you tell me about this earlier?"

"I don't rightly know, Prine. Maybe I wanted to give the boy the benefit of the doubt. But I've thought about it ever since it happened, and it's bothered me more all the time. And that's not all that's bothering me, either."

"What else you thinking about?"

Ballard was growing more intense with every word. "Prine, Stuart keeps killing men from the Tate gang who could give us information. It's almost as if he doesn't want us to know anything about the Tates. I don't understand it, and I don't like it."

Prine considered his friend's words. Ballard was right.

Stuart had effectively cut off every line of communication with the Tate gang or anyone previously involved with it.

"There's something else besides what you said, Ballard," said Prine at length. The hefty man looked at him with interest!

Prine related to him the part of the story he had left out the night before—the part about the familiarity with which Priscilla Tate had spoken of Thomas Stuart. "You know, I wasn't surprised that she knew his name, but when she spoke of him it was like she had known him well all her life. It didn't set right with me at all. She knows him far too well. According to his tale I wouldn't expect her to be on a first-name basis with him. But she called him Tom—not even Thomas—but Tom. And what's more, I—"

Prine stopped and felt a little foolish. "Spit it out, Prine," Ballard said. "What is it?"

"It might not seem sensible to you, Ballard, but Priscilla

Tate doesn't strike me as a killer. You saw her yourself the other night, and you know how out of place she seemed. And you should have heard her talking to her gang last night. She was upset by all the killing that's been going on. She wanted to back out of the whole deal! Does that sound like a killer to you? Does that sound like a hardcase daughter of one of Wesley Stoner's gang members?"

Ballard thought about it, then slowly shook his head. "No, Prine, it don't. It surely don't."

The two rode for a while longer without words. Finally, Prine spoke. "What do you think we should do about it?"

"I don't know. We gave our word, and we've come this far. We've drawn blood. If Stuart isn't on the up-and-up, he'll have to tip his hand soon."

"I wish ol' Bob Stuart were here. He'd make things different."

Ballard merely grunted.

Priscilla Tate was weary and bedraggled after her all-night stay out in the wilds beyond Statler, but she couldn't rest now. Stuart's men were not far ahead, and she had to keep up with them. Had to—or this whole quest would be in vain. She slumped in the saddle and longed for a hot bath and clean clothes. But she had to stay awake and keep a sharp lookout, not only for Stuart's bunch, but also for the members of her own former gang.

The betrayal of the night before flashed yet again through her mind, and she shuddered. She had come close to death. Only the unexpected help from the man hidden beneath the wagon in the stable doorway had saved her. And the irony of it was that he was one of Stuart's men. She hadn't even been able to thank him.

His had been a brave move, one that had placed him in

terrible danger, and that was in a way quite irrational. It had saved her life, but it had also put her former band of gunmen on his trail, probably more bloodthirsty than before. She had worried through the night that perhaps they had killed her benefactor, but when Stuart's group had ridden past her this morning as she lay hidden beside the trail, she had been relieved to see him with the riders, looking a little the worse for wear, but very much alive. That was good. She was grateful to him, and she didn't want to see him die.

Too many men had died already in this horrible affair, and she feared that before it was over there would be others. She felt partly responsible. She, after all, had hired the gang that had betrayed her. But what else could she have done? She couldn't let Thomas Stuart get what he sought, even though she had briefly considered that option. He had the directions to the wealth, and that was bad enough; to let him actually get that wealth was unthinkable.

But there was nothing to do but follow him. She had no idea where at Jericho Creek the treasure was hidden, and only Stuart's papers gave directions to its location. So here she was, alone and hungry on the trail, trying to stay close enough to Stuart's gang to follow it and yet also stay out of its sight.

She heard hoofbeats on the trail behind her. Not one horse, but several. Quickly she guided her horse off the trail and into a thicket. She dismounted and grasped her derringer tightly in her slender hand.

It was the three remaining members of her former gang. They rode single file along the trail, hunched down in their saddles. They were on the trail of Stuart, just as she was. But now they were not allies but her enemies. How could she deal with two opposing groups of armed men, both of whom might kill for that treasure? It seemed hopeless.

After they passed, she came out of hiding. The sun was moving toward the west, and as she mounted and moved onto the trail again it shone brilliantly into her eyes. She would have to stop for the night somewhere up ahead. This would be a night spent without even the comfort of food.

Ahead of her on the trail Prine and his group stopped for the night. Above them, illuminated from behind by the setting sun, stood the imposing peak of Jericho Mountain.

CHAPTER 17

When the light of the rising sun shone down on the rugged side of Jericho Mountain it was a magnificent sight. Prine stood and looked at it for a long time. Along the slope, and here and there across its stony surface, Prine saw dark openings: entrances to mines that had not functioned in years, and other natural openings that went into the cave system deep in the heart of the mountain. He couldn't tell which one was the entrance to the mine where the money was hidden. Stuart had been very closemouthed about specifics and had kept the packet close to him at all times.

Prine had heard descriptions of the mountain years before, back when the mines were operating. The mountain had a vast chamber in its center, at the bottom of which was an underground lake. All through the vast chasm were caves, running through the mountain like termite tunnels through old wood.

The mines often merged into these caves unexpectedly, only to return to man-made tunnels again. Many a miner had been lost in the cave system, and a few had actually plunged into the central chasm itself. Now the mountain's wealth was exhausted. Except, of course, for the wealth buried somewhere inside it by Wesley Stoner.

Only Stuart knew the exact location of that particular mine, but today he would reveal it to all of them. Prine glanced back over his shoulder toward the trail they had passed the day before. Today would be a momentous one for certain. Either he and his partners would lay their hands on that treasure, or die trying to do it.

They ate some of the food that they had purchased in Statler, and Prine rolled a cigarette as Ballard bit off a chew of his tobacco. Stuart ate little. His agitation was great, and his eyes flashed with excitement. Doubts about Stuart still bothered Prine, though he too felt excited about what lay before them. But Stuart was not a man to be trusted, Prine had decided, and what would happen in that mountain no one could guess.

It was still early, but in excitement Stuart rushed things along. "Men, there's all that gold sitting up here waiting for us to take it. Let's not wait any longer to do it!"

Ballard rose ponderously, like a lazy bull. "First off you're going to have to tell us just where it is, Stuart," he said. "Just how are we supposed to locate the right entrance to that mine? The face of that mountain looks like Swiss cheese to me."

Stuart pointed off through the morning haze toward the sleepy town of Jericho Creek. "You see that church steeple over there? Well, that's our pointer. It will point right to the entrance we need, if we stand at just the right place."

"And where is that?"

Stuart reached inside his vest and drew out the packet. He carefully untied the strings holding it together and pulled out the piece of paper scrawled over with Wesley Stoner's writing. "There should be a large stone just a little to the southwest of here. If you stand on top of that stone, that church steeple points right at the entrance we need. Stoner carved his initials into the rock."

"Sounds like something out of a storybook," muttered Thad.

"I'll grant you that, but that's what the directions say," said Stuart. He was in a remarkably good humor, even better than when the group had first assembled. His enthusiasm was becoming infectious, even in spite of the disgust that the others felt toward him. Prine stirred about restlessly, anxious to get the quest under way.

"Let's go find that rock," he said.

The group broke camp and mounted, moving, with Stuart in the lead, toward the southwest. The woods were low and scrubby, though relatively thick. Rocks abounded, some rather large, but most of them small. Prine looked dismayed. How could they tell which one Stoner referred to? Surely one of the larger ones, but which?

Stuart didn't appear too disturbed about the problem, moving swiftly and surely, looking about at every sizable boulder he passed. After close to an hour of riding, though, they didn't seem anywhere near finding what they sought. Stuart turned in his saddle and looked back toward the mountain.

"We must be in the wrong place," he said. "I can't even see the tip of that church steeple from here. Let's move to the west and see what we can find."

The group moved off through the woods after Stuart. It was thicker here, and the rocks were less numerous and larger. Prine strained his eyes through the trees toward Jericho Creek. As they moved farther west, the ground sloped up slightly, and after several minutes passed, the steeple became visible again. He was encouraged.

After about thirty minutes, Stuart suddenly stopped. He was gazing at an exceptionally large, tall boulder, a huge shapeless chunk of stone.

"Take a look," Ballard said.

"There—see the letters?" exclaimed Prine. "W.S. Stoner carved his initials. Let's get up there and see where that money is!"

Stuart already had leaped down and was scrambling up the rock, breathless with excitement. Thad went up after him and together they peered over the treetops toward Jericho Creek. Prine and Ballard watched the young men frown in concentration for a moment; then Thad whooped.

"We see it! It's as clear as anything! We can get there with no problem."

Stuart said, "Thad, do you see that clump of brush growing out of the side of the mountain right above the mine entrance? That'll be our landmark."

Thad nodded, and the two young men scurried back down the rock. Both mounted, and Stuart set off in the lead, eagerly heading back toward the road that led past Jericho Creek and on up the mountain. Only the top of Jericho Mountain was visible as they rode into the thicker part of the forest.

As they moved along the road Prine began to realize just how careless they had become in the last few hours. In their excitement they had virtually forgotten the threat of the men who almost certainly were tailing them. They couldn't afford to be that forgetful. Once they reached the treasure, they would be facing perhaps the greatest danger yet, for the outlaw gang would have no reason to keep them alive. Once the gang knew the treasure's whereabouts, they would not need Stuart's packet, nor any kind of further guidance.

They skirted around Jericho Creek. Instead of the usual facing rows of buildings, this town was spread out in a circular pattern, sitting on a sort of plateau at the base of the mountain. It was small, but fairly well inhabited, and most of the buildings were kept in good order. The men would not pass through Jericho Creek, for there was nothing for them there, and the road bypassed the town on the south.

When they reached the base of the mountain and the road began sloping gently upward, Prine became nervous. At parts of the trail, they would be limned against bare rock and in clear view of anyone below. But there was nothing they could do about it.

And once they got inside that mine, they would be in a very vulnerable position. It was likely that their only exit would be through the same passage they entered. And if the outlaws blocked that, there would be nothing to do but try to fight their way out, and that would be close to impossible within the confines of the mine.

The road became steeper as they ascended. The view across the town was magnificent as the sun climbed ever higher and shone down brighter on the countryside. Blue mountains lined the horizon, and the landscape was a panorama of green and purple, mixed occasionally with the gray of massive rocks that rose here and there among the trees below.

Prine couldn't help but admire the beauty of the land, even as his eyes scanned the road for the pursuing riders he knew must be there. But no one showed himself. Prine realized that the outlaws were in good position; all they had to do was sit and wait until the money was brought out of the mine, then move in and take it. Or perhaps they would sneak into the mine while Prine and his partners were still digging it out. Either way, it would be easy for them to get that treasure.

Priscilla Tate crossed Prine's mind again. Where was she? He hoped that somewhere she had found safety. Strange, the tenderness he felt for her, Prine thought. She had actually tried to kill him, but he hadn't the slightest bit of hard feeling toward her.

After about an hour on the trail they reached the

mouth of the mine. It looked much larger than Prine had anticipated, and its black depths were ominous and frightening.

Stuart was in a virtual frenzy—one that had been growing ever since that morning. Prine took note of it and cast a meaningful glance toward Ballard. Thad was dismounting.

"Someone will need to guard this entrance," Thad said. "I'll be glad to do it."

"Could be dangerous, Thad."

"This whole business is dangerous."

The group assented to Thad's request. "Keep a close eye on that road, son," Ballard instructed. "You should be able to see 'em coming, unless they find some sort of back way around the other side of the mountain. If they do that then there'll be no warning."

Prine felt a cold chill. The possibility of a back way was something he hadn't considered.

Stuart was in a tremendous hurry to get on with things. "Where are those lanterns, Prine? Let's get them lit."

Prine went over and removed the lanterns and digging tools from the back of the packhorses. Prine filled the lanterns with fuel and lit them, taking one for himself as Stuart and Ballard took the other two.

Ballard patted his son on the shoulder as he entered the dark mouth of the mine behind the others. "If there's any sign of trouble, don't try to be a hero." Thad nodded, and Ballard entered the dark cavern.

The light from the outside penetrated only a few yards into the mine, then seemed to be absorbed into the dark walls. The lanterns cast a weird glow all around them, and the dark, lonely creatures that made their home amid the crevices of the rocks and on the dank surface of the mine walls scurried away as the beams fell on them.

About a hundred feet back into the mine Prine stopped

suddenly, raising his lantern and pointing to the ceiling. "My Lord, look at that!"

The ceiling of the mine was alive with bats, hanging upside down only a few feet above the heads of the men. Not a trace of rock could be seen through the dense carpet formed by the furry bodies, and their ugly faces were glaring down into the lantern light as they wrapped their leathery wings cloak-like all around them.

Without warning, the bats swarmed down and struck against the men in an effort to get outside. The men dropped to the floor; there was a mighty rush of air against them, stirred by thousands of rapidly beating winds as the multitude of bats escaped the mine.

Thad called back into the mine once the swarm had passed, and Prine assured him they were all right.

Even Stuart was a little shaken by the unexpected encounter. Prine's lantern had gone out when he dropped it to the floor, and he lit it again before the group moved on.

"This shoring looks awful weak, Prine," said Ballard. "It's about rotted out. It wouldn't take much to bring the roof down on our heads."

Prine inspected the shoring. Ballard was right—a well-placed kick could easily knock some of these beams aside.

As they progressed farther into the passage, Prine noted a slight curve in the tunnel. And off to the side opened another passage, then another, leading to dark chambers that had not seen light or life for years. Stuart had to stop several times to check the directions in the packet by the light of the lanterns before proceeding.

The air was close and thick in the cavern, heavy with a musty smell from cavern walls, that seemed to close in more with every succeeding step.

After several more turns and corners the passage widened; there was a sudden feeling of openness in the lantern-lit tunnel. There was also an increasing dampness in the air. Prine could not see what might be causing the dampness, but he felt something lay before them. They proceeded slowly, lanterns held high.

The pathway disappeared, dropping into nothingness. They had reached a central chamber. Prine held out his lantern over the depths. The light faded into blackness only a short way down into the emptiness. He kicked a loose stone over the edge. For a long time, there was no sound; then, faintly, a splash echoed up from the abyss. The drop-off was sheer and maybe hundreds of feet deep.

This was a vast place, ominous and awe-inspiring. Prine felt small here, and insignificant, like an ant in a cathedral. He glanced over at his partners. Ballard's face showed awe at the deathly silence of space out before him, and Stuart's eyes glittered strangely.

The young man knelt at the edge of the abyss, and his lantern revealed a narrow ledge that wound its way along its edge to their left. He smiled and turned to the waiting men.

"This ledge leads to the spot where Wesley Stoner buried his treasure," he said.

CHAPTER 18

Prine grasped his lantern in one hand and hugged the cold stone of the wall with the other as he edged along behind Stuart on the narrow ledge, wondering all the while why he was doing such a fool thing. When he had seen how narrow and dangerous was the ledge along which they must pass, he had felt ready to throw the quest to the wind and head home. But now here he was, inching along, with a deep and dark lake hundreds of feet below, hoping the thin ledge would hold and praying that he would not lose his footing.

"The ledge widens out just ahead," Stuart gasped before him. "It should be right there that the treasure is buried in the wall."

"Just how wide does it get, Stuart?" groaned Ballard. "I hope it's wide enough for me to lie down and kiss it."

After what seemed an eternity, they reached the spot. The ledge widened into a kind of natural balcony over the depths of the abyss. As each man reached it, he let out a sigh of relief. Ballard was pale and panting.

"Stuart, if that money ain't here I'm not staying around to see where it is. I never have been too fond of high places."

Stuart ignored him, intent on exploring the face of the

rock wall beside him. He held up his lantern, letting its beams roam over the stone. Prine looked at the young man's face. Never had he seen such an expression of fierce determination. Beads of sweat shimmered on Stuart's brow as his eyes flashed in the lantern light. And when at last the young man made out a patch on the wall of a slightly different color than the surrounding rock, he looked almost as animalistic as Buster had in the hotel room in Statler moments before Stuart killed him.

Stuart exclaimed: "Here...here it is! Just like the paper said! Stoner buried the money in a hole in the wall and then patched it up."

Prine hefted one of the picks. He swung the metal point into the mortar and the tip dug in, the echo resounding weirdly through the vast and hollow heart of Jericho Mountain.

Again, and again the pick struck. Stuart had an eager, intense expression and seemed deeply impatient. Prine had hardly chipped away a few chunks from the mortar patch before the young man took a second pick in hand. "There's not room for both of us to dig—let me go at it for a while," he said. Stuart all but pushed Prine aside and began chopping furiously at the old mortar. Prine slipped back a little farther on the ledge and joined Ballard, who had his back against the wall. It was obvious the height had Ballard nervous.

Rapidly the patch gave way under the continual impact of Stuart's pick. His pace never slowed. When at last the pick broke through into the empty space beyond the patch, Stuart became even more frenetic, knocking away big pieces of mortar. Some fell to his feet and rolled back off the ledge to splash some seconds later into the unseen waters below.

At last Stuart threw the pick aside and reached into the black opening. He pulled out two heavy black bags wrapped in oilcloth, laughing as he did so. Prine was surprised Stuart was able to so easily heft bags that supposedly were filled with federal gold. He glanced at Ballard and read the same thought.

Stuart, trembling with excitement, knelt and began pulling the oilcloth off the bags, but abruptly he stopped. "No need," he said. "We know this has to be it."

"Mighty lightweight if it is," Ballard said. "And I never knew gold to be kept in bags before. I was expecting a strongbox."

"Forget about it," Stuart said with unexpected harshness. He glared at Ballard, sweat gleaming on his face in the lantern light. "Come on. Let's get these out of here."

Stuart picked up one of the bags. Prine took the other.

He knew at once it wasn't gold. The bag felt as if it were filled with paper.

Prine looked sternly at Stuart. "What is this?" he demanded. "It sure ain't gold, that I know."

"I will explain when we get back into the tunnel where it's safe," Stuart said, not quite as harsh with Prine as he had been with Ballard. "I assure you everything is as it should be."

Ballard started to say something, but Prine lifted his hand. No point in getting Stuart riled in so dangerous a spot as this. Once on safer ground they could explore the question fully.

Ballard, holding his lantern, went first, edging out along the ledge toward the opening to the tunnel. Stuart and Prine followed, each carrying a bag and a lantern, each walking carefully along the way.

Ballard slipped and almost fell; his lantern slid from his hand and fell over the precipice. Prine watched it arc through the blackness. It shattered on some upthrust rock far below, bursting into a flower of yellow fire that for a half second revealed the surface of the underground lake. Then the lantern splashed into the water, and the spilled coal oil burned itself quickly out on the surface of the rock.

"Ballard, you all right?"

"Fine. A horrible place to fall, that would be," Ballard said. His voice quaked a little.

"Move on!" Stuart ordered. Prine shot a hard glance at him; he didn't like Stuart's tone.

For long minutes, they progressed silently. Ballard was slower now that his lantern was gone; he picked his way along carefully because he could not see the ledge ahead so clearly. At last, though, they reached the tunnel entrance and clambered to relative safety. They walked some distance, then Ballard sat heavily on the damp tunnel floor and breathed fast and deeply until he had relaxed. Prine dropped beside him, and Stuart pulled the two bags together and knelt beside them, grinning in the light of the two remaining lanterns.

"So why did you lie to us?" Prine said to Stuart.

"About the gold, you mean?" Stuart said.

"That, and whatever other wild tales you might have spun to us."

"An easy question to answer," Stuart said. He drew his pistol and pointed it between Ballard's eyes. "I lied because I needed your help to obtain two bags of cash and various valuable financial papers stolen years ago from an Omaha bank by Wesley Stoner. Given your penchant for honest dealings, I needed a tale that would allow you to help me while keeping your consciences clear. My story of stolen federal gold and the reward offered for it did the job well. Now, unfortunately for you, the job is done. Remove your pistols, slowly, and toss them away."

Prine and Ballard complied. "I knew you were rotten," Ballard said.

"Knowledge that has come too late to do you any good," Stuart said. "I'm afraid I must now dispose of you."

"How? Shoot us?"

"Oh no. No need for a murder when an accident will suffice." He flicked his glance toward the shored-up mine roof. "These timbers give away and this place would collapse. An unfortunate but predictable accident in an old mine. I'll let you perform the honors of using your pick on the shoring beams, Prine. If you don't, I'll shoot your friend here between the eyes, like the pig he is."

"And what about Thad? How will you dispose of him so neatly?" Prine asked.

"Not your concern," Stuart said. "I'll deal with him after you're gone."

"What about protection? You need it worse now than ever," Prine said. "You can't afford to get rid of us now."

"I can't very well afford to leave you alive, can I? You're right—I do need protection. I'll just have to be careful until I can buy some of it. Certainly I've got enough money to do that now."

"Priscilla Tate's old gang members will be out there, looking for you. They may be coming up the mountain right now."

"I'm aware of my difficulties," Stuart snapped. "My plan may not have been perfect, but so far it's kept me alive and gotten me what I wanted. Now, get up. Ballard, you stand against that wall. Prine, take that pick and knock out the shoring beam."

Prine felt a burst of fury, and as he stood, lunged a bit at Stuart. But he pulled up short, for he knew Stuart truly would kill Ballard.

"The pick, Prine."

A few moments later, Stuart was slowly backing away from the area, the pistol still raised, and Prine was poised at a shoring beam, pick ready. He looked at the beam, at the cracked tunnel ceiling above it, and hoped Stuart was wrong.

Maybe the mine would hold up without the old beams. Yet he doubted it.

"Goodbye, Prine, and thank you," Stuart said. "Knock away the beam."

"We'll survive this, Stuart. We'll find a way out and track you down."

"I doubt it. Now do the job. I have no more time to waste."

Prine closed his eyes, took a breath, and swung the pick. The beam shifted. A terrible groaning, crackling noise filled the tunnel—the sound of loose rock shifting.

"Again!" Stuart commanded, still backing away.

Prine lifted the pick again and swung. This time the beam fell away completely. The crackling noise became far louder. Prine ran back toward Ballard.

Stuart wheeled and began to run as the first small pieces of rock showered down.

Chapter 19

A burst of gunfire echoed down from the entrance of the mine. Stuart stopped and swore as the noise of running feet and blasting guns came ever closer, echoing loudly through the mine.

Stuart had forgotten Prine and Ballard for an instant, and as he turned his back on them, both men recovered their guns. More blasting gunfire reverberated through the tunnel.

It could only mean one thing: Thad had been surprised by the remaining members of the former Tate gang. Prine remembered Ballard's warning about a possible back way up the mountain.

Stuart let fly a long string of oaths as Thad ran into view. Prine heard voices and men running into the tunnel.

Thad took no notice of Stuart, ignorant of his treachery, and there was certainly no time for him to be told with both the threat of a cave-in and death by outlaw gunfire hanging over them all. The only thing they could do right now was to try to move back far enough to escape the tons of rock that would come crashing down within seconds.

"Tate gang...came at me from behind..."

The flickering lantern light illuminated three gunmen

moving at a run straight back toward them. Prine recognized the face of the preacher by the glow of the kerosene flame.

Stuart came out of his daze, grabbing one of the lanterns as he moved back farther in the passage. Prine grabbed the other, then sent two quick shots at the intruders and scrambled after Stuart as bullets kicked up chips of stone at his feet.

The three gunmen came on, their shots more carefully placed now, and the preacher obviously making for Prine. Prine's foot struck a small boulder that lay in the passage, and his body pitched to the side just as the remaining strained shoring at last gave up its burden and collapsed.

Stone and dust, choking, stinging, pounding into flesh like a horrible hammer blow, filling the eyes, nose, blinding, hurting. The ominous rumbling had become a roar that sounded as if the very mountain itself were groaning in pain as a portion of its matter broke away. Prine didn't realize until it was over that mixed in with the noise of the crumbling stone was his own cry. Then suddenly it was done, and he was aware of nothing but being in a small chamber of stone, breathing a dust-filled atmosphere, and seeing a strange, flickering glow.

He raised himself, painfully, and looked about. He had been thrown aside by the falling rock, pushed into this side chamber like a feather before the wind. And the dim light came from the lantern he had held, now half-buried in dirt and rubble, its flame growing steadily lower.

His gun—where was his gun? He felt for it, straining his dust-filled eyes to see it, but could not find it. He half-rose again, failed, then tried once more, this time making it all the way to his feet. And he stared groggily ahead, somehow not even surprised to see a man standing before him with a .44 leveled at his gut.

The preacher. Prine stared at him almost stupidly. The outlaw was disheveled, coated with dust, and blood trickled down from a wound in his scalp, but there was a grin on his face. He let loose a sort of low laugh before he spoke.

"Well, friend, it looks like it's me and you again, doesn't it? This time I'm going to kill you...you won't escape me now." He raised the gun and leveled it at Prine's forehead. Prine rather groggily recognized the weapon as his own.

He dropped and rolled as the preacher fired, the blast intensely loud in the small chamber. Prine's entire body was stung by tiny pieces of something that blasted into the rock all around him, and the preacher let out a cry of anguish almost at the same time he fired the shot.

Prine rose to see the man grasping at a bleeding hand. The shattered handgun lay on the ground before him. Its barrel was shredded, splintered, and as Prine's mind began to clear, he realized what had happened.

The gun's barrel had apparently been choked with grit and rubble during the cave-in. The preacher's shot had turned the weapon into a miniature bomb that had maimed his good hand and sent forth the shower of grit that had stung Prine a second before.

The lantern died away into a dull red. Prine feared it would go out. Without a moment's hesitation he attacked.

His hands closed around a throat as thick and stout as a young oak. Immediately the preacher's hand struck his jaw, and he was knocked away, the salty taste of blood in his mouth. Whether it was his own blood or that of the preacher he could not tell. He fell back, his gripping hands shredding his opponent's shirt and dragging him down on top of him.

A bloody hand pounded Prine's face, but he ignored the pain and shoved the heavy man off him with strength he didn't know he possessed. A primitive feeling flowed through him, as if this weird battle by lantern light had turned him from a man to a beast. He struck his opponent with a viciousness he had never known before, and the blows that were returned were every bit as fierce. This would be a battle to the death, he knew deep inside, and he almost welcomed it. He rained down more blows with ever-increasing force.

Then the preacher was gone. Prine wheeled, his arms out and his fists clenched, and listened. Where was he? He heard gasping breaths, but he couldn't tell where they came from. Then something hard struck his head with a grazing blow, and he fell.

He was dazed again, his head throbbing and his senses reeling. He realized what had happened: The preacher had thrown a large stone, striking him cruelly. Had the blow been a little more direct, it probably would have killed him. Instead, it had only grazed his head, but that was bad enough, for he was stunned now, and down, ready for the Preacher to finish him off. He writhed on the rough stone floor, and heavy kicks began pounding him. Prine's mind raced toward senselessness.

With the last effort he could muster, he reached out blindly in the darkness, and his hand closed by sheer chance on the preacher's ankle. Suddenly the man was falling, landing atop him, then sliding away over him into a void directly beside Prine. A hand closed on Prine's shirt, pulling him after the falling outlaw, drawing him too toward a pit that the preacher had fallen into, a pit that neither had known was there, and which opened for hundreds of feet straight down. Prine heard the preacher's pitiful cries as he dangled for a moment over the black hole, then his scream as he plunged far, far into the blackness, deep into the very roots of the mountain. Prine almost went senseless, his body dangling half into the hole, teetering on the very edge as if undecided whether or not to fall. Unconsciousness threatened to engulf him.

He awoke in a soft but brighter glow, a hazy light from an origin he could not ascertain. A soft hand stroked his brow. His eyes focused slowly, and he realized that he was lying on his back in the same chamber as before, and the hand was that of a young lady. He squinted and looked into the face above him. Confusion swept over him.

"Pri—Priscilla..." His voice failed him before he could say the whole name.

"You know me? How?" Her pretty face showed her surprise. Then it returned to its former expression: one of concern, tenderness. "I guess Tom must have told you. But now isn't the time to worry about that. You were almost gone, you know—almost into that pit. I got the lantern up again and pulled you away from the edge. You saved my life once. Now I've returned the favor." Her voice was soft, and her hand stroked his brow almost lovingly. "I'm glad I had the chance. It was a way of thanking you."

Prine's rationality began to return slowly, and the scattered pieces of the jigsaw puzzle of the last moments began to put themselves together. He realized what had happened; how the preacher had knocked him to the ground beside the natural well farther back in the chamber, how his own hand had unbalanced the preacher and sent him hurtling into the dark hole to his death at the bottom far below. Priscilla Tate had obviously managed to sneak past Thad and follow them into the mine. And it had been she who had pulled him from the brink of the pit. Priscilla Tate had saved his life. Even in his still-groggy state the irony of it was not lost upon him.

He sat up, looking into her face. "But we're supposed to be enemies...why?" Prine asked.

"I don't know who is my enemy, and who is not. All I know is that we're trapped together here and if we don't stick together, we'll never get out. You saved my life and I've saved yours. You don t seem like an enemy to me."

Prine paused in thought. "And you don't seem like an enemy to me." Then into his mind came something he had forgotten in the confusion of the last moments: Ballard, Thad, the cave-in.

Prine leapt up. "Ballard! He was out there when the roof caved in! And Thad!"

Priscilla stood. "The others? I don't know what happened to them."

"Hush!" Prine said, a little more sharply than he intended. "Listen!"

They stood quietly, trying not to breathe.

It was faint and muffled, but it was an unmistakable noise: gunfire, coming from the other side of the rubble heap. Someone was alive out there after all, apparently several people, for that was a sizable gun battle they were listening to. So even if they got out of this chamber, which itself seemed impossible, the danger would not be over.

Prine said, "Give me that lantern."

She handed him the lantern, and he began a close and hurried inspection of the pile of boulders. She looked on too, and her heart sank. It seemed like an impenetrable mass, a hopelessly thick barrier to escape. It began to dawn on her what being trapped here would mean. Slow death, thirst, hunger—she tried to block out the thoughts.

Prine scrambled up onto the heap, his lantern held aloft and his free hand probing into the crevices of the rocks, trying to move them aside and make some sort of passage that would accommodate them. But he was having no luck, for in spite of his efforts the huge boulders remained immobile. He continued for long minutes, moving all over the face of the rock mass, trying to move every small boulder. It looked hopeless.

In a sort of desperate gesture Prine heaved hard on one last boulder and was surprised when the rock gave way. It exposed an opening blocked with small stones. Prine smiled.

"Here, hold the lantern. I think I can dig our way through here." He began moving the stones, making a sort of tunnel through the rubble, burrowing like a human mole. And as he knocked more and more rock aside, the sound of the gunfire grew louder from the other side of the stone.

With a groan and heave Prine broke through the barrier. And at the same moment he realized that but for his knife he was unarmed.

CHAPTER 20

Prine looked out of the narrow opening he had made into a scene out of hell. There was a dim light in the main passage of the mine, the same flickering lantern light as before. The atmosphere was dusty, and it was difficult to see. Occasional flares of light exploded sporadically from various places around the mine, accompanied by loud, echoing blasts and the sound of ricocheting bullets. How many people in the mine had survived the cave-in, Prine couldn't tell.

Prine stayed far enough back in his little tunnel to remain safe from flying bullets and studied the tons of earth and stone that blocked the main entrance to the mine. He could see no opening at all. Apparently, the collapse had completely blocked the way out of the mine. Whether friend or enemy, all in the mine had one thing in common: They were most definitely trapped.

Prine longed for a gun.

He prayed fervently that Ballard was still alive. He couldn't bear to think that he had died beneath the crushing stones.

Priscilla's voice reached him from behind. "What can you see out there?"

Prine inched along backward until he stood beside her in the small chamber again. "I can't see much, and I'm not sure who's out there. But it must be some of my friends and your old friends, or else they wouldn't be shooting at each other." He suddenly recalled the treachery of Stuart and realized that the statement he had just made might not necessarily be true. Even if the former Tate gang members had been killed, it was possible that Ballard and Thad were still alive out there, fighting it out with Stuart. Or Stuart might be fighting the outlaws.

"Priscilla, you stay here until it's over. There's no point in you risking your life." He paused, unsure of what he wanted to say. "I'm glad I met you, ma'am, and I'm grateful for what you did for me. I'm sorry we had to be on opposite sides in all this. The name's Jeremy Prine, ma'am. I'll be going."

He climbed up on the rocks again, scrambling up into his escape tunnel, an unarmed man going out to try to help friends even though he didn't know where they were or what he could do for them.

Priscilla noticed that the gleaming lantern light flashed on something in the corner. It was the derringer she had lost when the mine collapsed, almost hidden in the dust. She ran toward it, picking it up and inspecting it for damage. Everything appeared in working order. She brushed the dust from it.

Here was a weapon for Jeremy Prine—not a good one, certainly, but better than nothing. She ran to the small crawlway he had entered a moment before and looked into it just in time to see him slip out on the other side. She thought of calling to him, but the fear that her cry might draw dangerous attention to the unarmed man stopped her. He was out there, right in the thick of battle, with no weapon but a knife to aid him.

Prine felt like a shooting-gallery target as soon as he

dropped from the passage onto the rubble heap and down to the floor of the mine. The lantern light was dim, hardly sufficient illumination for a chamber of this size, and the only other source of light were the flashes of gunfire that burst from various portions of the passage. He noticed that the crack of a particular gun would come from first one spot, then another. These men were moving about as they fought, and that made things pretty confusing.

So far no one had taken a shot at him, and he was surprised at that. He could see the areas where the opposing sides were holed up, but who was a friend and who was an enemy he could not tell.

There was also no way to remain standing where he was, a clear target for whoever might first decide to take a shot at him. He had to move somewhere. He glanced around to his left.

Two quick bursts of gunfire came from behind a pile of dirt, rocks, and old shoring wood. The flash of the blasts illuminated the face behind the gun for only an instant, but that was sufficient. It was Ballard.

Prine ran toward the spot, hoping he wouldn't spook Ballard by his sudden appearance and maybe risk taking a bullet from his friend. He made a headlong dive over the rock pile, landing in a heap beside his hefty partner.

"Prine—where have you been? I thought you died under the rocks!"

"No, sir, Ballard. I wouldn't think of doing a thing like that. But I did manage to lose that gun you loaned me. You got another?"

Ballard's answer was a grunt and a gesture to their left. Prine gasped when he saw the body of Thad lying there very still, hardly breathing, it seemed. His face was pale, and dark blood stained his features.

"What was it, Ballard—a bullet?"

Ballard squeezed off another shot as he nodded. "It just

grazed his head, I think, but it put him out colder than a light. You can use his gun."

Prine took the young man's weapon, a Colt, and spun the chamber. It was fully loaded. He started to rise to fire, then realized that he didn't know where the enemy was—and based on the ambiguous standing of Stuart right now, even who the enemy was.

"Who are we fighting, Ballard? Is Stuart with us or against us?"

"He sure ain't with us, Prine. Only one of them outlaws survived that cave-in, and he's holed up to the left, back toward the tail end of the mine. Stuart's over there about straight in front of us, and he's taking on the whole lot of the rest of us. This is a three-way fight."

"What about the money?"

"Stuart's got it."

Prine glanced up over the pile long enough to see Stuart duck back down behind a boulder that apparently had been tossed to its resting place by the force of the cave-in. He readied his gun for Stuart's next appearance, and when the young man again thrust his head up, Prine let loose with a shot that almost scalped him. Stuart ducked again.

"I'm back, Stuart! You're fighting me and Ballard together now!" The words were a warning, a challenge. It felt good to say them.

Stuart gave no answer, save for two well-placed shots that actually clipped off some of Prine's hair when next he showed himself. Then came another burst of fire from the back of the mine, smacking all around him and Ballard. The gunman apparently sent a slug Stuart's way, too. But the bullets struck harmlessly on all sides. Prine realized this was a battle that could go on for quite some time. The thing that would end this fight would be when one side ran out of ammunition.

Quickly he assessed their situation. He had a handful of

cartridges in his pocket, and Thad's gun belt was circled with others. With Ballard's supply they should be able to fight for some time yet.

The outlaw moved at the back portion of the passage, and they concentrated attention on that area. The lantern light was dim, but still they could make out the shadowy form of the man as he ran from his hiding place toward the other side of the tunnel. What prompted the man to move Prine could not guess; maybe he was running low on ammunition and wanted to find a better vantage point. But it was a fatal move, for Stuart's gun spoke out three times, loudly, and the man fell to the floor of the mine, a corpse before his last breath was out of his lungs.

For a long time, there was silence. The smell of spent gunpowder hung in the air, and the dimly lit chamber was choked with dust and smoke. Stuart spoke first: "Well, gentlemen, it looks like it's down to you and me again. I was certainly sorry to have to kill your son, Ballard."

"You didn't kill him."

Stuart laughed. "Well! I'm not quite the shot I thought! But no matter—I'll take care of him later. Now, throw your weapons over the rock pile and onto the floor where I can see them."

Prine laughed. "You seem to forget that there's two of us and one of you. It seems to me that you're the one who should toss over your gun, boy. You got nothing to back up your bluff!"

"Tom!"

The feminine voice echoed in the mine. Prine frowned. The girl had done the very thing he had told her not to do.

Ballard looked confused, but Prine had no time to explain. Stuart laughed derisively on the other side of the passage. Prine looked over the rock pile. Priscilla was standing there, her back toward him, and in her hand was a derringer. Her trembling fingers betrayed her fear.

"Well, Priscilla! What a surprise!" Stuart said. "What do you want of me?"

"I want you to give up, Tom."

"Priscilla—don't be a fool! He'll kill you!" Prine shouted.

"I'm sorry, Mr. Prine. This is something I have to do. This man was the death of my father, and I intend to see him pay."

Prine knew the girl was in danger, and he had to intervene. But before he had made it halfway over the rock pile, the roar of Stuart's .44 filled the mine, and Priscilla screamed. Prine went over the pile and toward her just as Stuart came out of his hiding place to grasp her around the neck and place the barrel of his gun to her head. Then he wheeled so that he stood behind her. His gun was firmly pressed against her temple.

Prine stopped in his tracks. He saw the girl's derringer on the floor of the mine far out of reach, its barrel shattered by Stuart's last shot.

"Don't move another step, Prine. If you do, I'll kill her. You know I'm not bluffing."

"Yes, Stuart, I know."

"Prine, what's going on here?" Ballard asked with exasperation.

"I'll explain later, Ballard," said Prine. "Right now, let's just take it real easy, real easy."

"That's right, Prine. You're smarter than I gave you credit for," said Stuart. "Now you just step back and get rid of your gun—you too, Ballard—and I'm going to take this young lady toward the back of this mine again. I think I may have seen a way out of here. If you make the slightest move, I swear I'll kill her, and you, too. C'mon! Drop those guns!"

Prine's weapon clattered to the floor. With more hesitation, Ballard too yielded up his gun, then stood with hands raised. "That satisfy you, Stuart?"

"Very much so. Now, you gentlemen stand aside while I collect my money." He kept the gun on Priscilla's temple as he picked up the bags and hefted them under his arm. Then he shoved her along as he moved over to where the lantern sat. He picked it up and held it before him, not caring that the hot metal occasionally swung into his lovely prisoner, burning her.

Then he was off, moving toward the rear of the mine, the lantern light fading, leaving Prine and Ballard in darkness. Neither moved for a time, then Ballard said, "Well, what are we going to do?"

"Help her," Prine said. "It appears to me that we've been helping out the wrong one so far." He struck a match and held it aloft for light.

"That's for certain. But what can we do? If he sees us, he'll kill her, and us too. I'm surprised he didn't shoot us just now." Suddenly he paused, then said, "C'mon—there's not a second to lose. Our friend Stuart isn't the threat we think he is. Let's go!"

"What...but..." Prine's protests were no use. Ballard was already heading down the passage, feeling along like a blind man. Prine shrugged and followed him, hoping that whatever he had in mind would work. He certainly couldn't guess what it might be.

After a few moments of blind scrambling, they saw the light of Stuart's lantern moving along before them. They were almost to the end of the mine, where the passage opened into the massive central chamber. Unless Stuart was planning on moving out on the ledges again, he would be forced to stop.

Chapter 21

As the two approached Stuart, they slowed, trying to remain silent as they drew steadily nearer. Stuart still held Priscilla, the gun pressed against her head. He was moving fast, obviously trying to reach the central chamber as quickly as possible. But why? He had mentioned an escape route, but what route could possibly open from that vast chasm filled with cold water?

The light from the lantern Stuart clutched cast a weird glow all about him.

Prine wondered what Ballard's plan was. How could he hope to stand up unarmed against a desperate man with a hostage and a .44 in his hand?

Stuart had reached the very end of the mine now, standing on the brink of the chasm, and he had an expression of uncertainty on his face. Priscilla looked frightened, but there was dignity in her bearing, and a defiance that would not be masked by her fear. It was obvious that she would face death bravely if it came to that. Prine admired her in the midst of his apprehensions. He still knew next to nothing about her; what information Stuart had given them probably had been fabricated. But nevertheless, he felt she should be defended. His mind flashed back to the night he had first seen her in her camp, gun in hand and that same expression of fear on her face.

Ballard had stopped now, and Prine halted beside him. Prine had a sense of helplessness to which he was very unaccustomed. The next few minutes were to be crucial ones, and he wondered what his role in them was going to be.

Stuart still loitered nervously at the brink of the chasm, the image of insecurity. It was a singular way for him to act, Prine mused, for it seemed that if anyone had the upper hand in this situation it was he. What could he be afraid of?

"Stuart!"

The young man jumped, a low cry coming from his throat. His eyes were open wide, fearful. From his reaction to Ballard's voice, one would have suspected he had been stabbed with a needle. Prine glanced over at Ballard, who strode slowly yet confidently toward the young man and his hostage.

"What's the matter, boy? Didn't you expect to see us again? Did you think we'd cower back there in the dark while you walked out of here with that money and the young lady? Surely you didn't think that, now did you, Stuart?"

"You stay back! I swear I'll kill you—and her first! I swear to God I will!"

My Lord, Prine thought, the fellow's panicked! What had happened to the confident fellow of moments before? There was no logical reason for it, as long as he held that gun in his hand—unless that gun was not as threatening as it seemed.

As Ballard laughed at the frightened young man, Prine realized what his friend had thought of moments before back in the blackness of the mine. Before the cave-in Stuart had been ready to kill them, and the only reason he had not shot at them was so Thad would not grow suspicious outside the mouth of the mine. But that consideration was meaningless now; Thad was back in the darkness, unconscious.

Yet Stuart had not shot them back there when he took Priscilla as his prisoner. Why? Why hadn't he just finished them off then and there and been through with it?

There could only be one answer—his gun was empty. His threat on the life of the girl, and their lives as well, was a bluff. Ballard was calling that bluff, and apparently thoroughly enjoying doing it. Prine smiled as the big man moved forward.

"Well, c'mon, Stuart—kill me! Why are you waiting? You said you would kill me, but I don't see you doing anything about it."

Stuart retreated steadily backward until he stood close to the edge of the precipice. He stopped then, the bags of money dropping to the earth, and with a final threat tried to stop Ballard's approach.

"Stop right there, fat man. One more step and I'll throw her over."

But Priscilla lunged forward and away. She tripped, though, and fell against Ballard, knocking them both to the ground.

Stuart cursed loudly and came forward. Priscilla rolled off to the left, but before Ballard was half-risen, Stuart planted a firm kick right in his side, sending him sprawling again.

Prine's knife came out of his belt, and with a shout he approached Ballard's antagonist. But before Prine could reach him, Stuart's boot came up again, striking Prine's wrist forcefully, and the knife flew from his grasp to clatter onto the floor, spin across, and drop into the chasm.

Stuart picked up a large rock, and as his left fist pounded hard into Prine's gut, the stone bashed the side of his head. Prine went down, stunned once more, out of the fight for good. As Priscilla rushed to Prine's side, Stuart turned to take on Ballard again, who had by now risen haltingly to his feet.

Stuart rushed straight into his arms. The big man managed to land one blow before Stuart tore into him like a Kansas tornado, bloodying his face, bruising his gut, sending his head spinning with blow after blow. Ballard had not anticipated such strength, and with Prine out of the battle, he felt a moment of doubt as to whether he would make it through this alive. But he growled like a grizzly and shoved his weight forward, pushing Stuart backward into the wall.

Ballard then spun away, breathless and dizzy, trying to buy time for himself before the young and energetic fighter was on him again. But it was no use, for Stuart bounded back from the wall and again pounded Ballard's jaw.

Priscilla watched the eerie, lantern-lit battle in desperation. She felt helpless, alone, now that Prine lay stunned with his head in her lap. Everything depended on Ballard's ability to overcome Stuart. Should Stuart come out victorious, it would mean death for all of them.

Prine stirred, moaned, and she looked down into his face. He wasn't unconscious, at least not totally, but could he recover in time to save Ballard's life? She prayed he would yet growing in her mind was the frightening conviction that if anyone was to save them, she would have to be the one.

Stuart had the money bags in his hand, and swung them hard at Ballard, catching him in the side, sending him reeling away to teeter perilously on the brink of the black abyss, his hands waving wildly about as if to grasp a handhold in the air.

Then, in tandem with Priscilla's scream, he fell.

Stuart laughed as the bulky man dropped into the darkness. Ballard groped and his hands clutched the side of the precipice, holding on until his knuckles were white. He swung out over two hundred feet of emptiness, only his straining fingers keeping him from certain death.

Stuart walked casually over to where the big man clung to the stone, looking over at him with a smile on his face.

"Hey, fat man—where's your smart mouth now? You can't imagine how much pleasure this is going to give me." He hefted up the money bags for Ballard to see. "Thanks for your help in getting this, old man. I'll build a monument in your memory."

Slowly Stuart's boot came up, his movements cool and deliberate so that his victim could see exactly what was coming. Then slowly his foot began its descent. Ballard closed his eyes.

Prine stirred alone in the darkness, rose, and looked about with foggy eyes. His mind was blank, but he felt distressful, as if he had just had a nightmare he couldn't quite remember. He shook his head violently, trying to clear away the cobwebs from his mind and the blur from his vision.

He remembered it all in a horrible rush. He jerked upright, noticing several things at once.

Stuart stood at the edge of the precipice, his boot pressing down hard on something, again and again. Ballard was nowhere to be seen, but Priscilla was up, moving rapidly toward the young man, who stood with the money bags still slung over his shoulder and laughing like a playing child as he continued pressing with his boot. Just as Priscilla rushed at him, Prine saw out of the corner of his eye a figure staggering in from the dark mine passage, with bloody head and stumbling feet.

Prine saw what Priscilla was trying to do, but also that she would fail, for even as she drew near, Stuart saw her. He wheeled, stepping off Ballard's hands for a moment, and stiff-armed Priscilla in the face. She fell, knocked down by the force of her own run. Stuart laughed, but the laugh choked away as Ballard's right hand came up and closed around his ankle. Stuart, frozen with horror, looked down at Ballard with wide eyes.

"Goodbye, boy," Ballard said as he pulled out and down.

Stuart jerked forward and almost caught himself before the weight of the money bags shifted forward, throwing him out headlong over the precipice, sending his body arching over Ballard to fall screaming for long seconds into the emptiness, his hands never losing their grip on the bags of money.

Even after the noise of the splash had reached the ears of those on the brink of the chasm, the scream echoed for many moments.

Prine was up now. Quickly he moved over beside Priscilla Tate, who stood weeping, and pulled her back from the brink of the abyss. Then the figure he had seen moving out of the darkness came up beside him. It was Thad, weak and pale.

Without a word Prine and Thad went to where Ballard clung with weakening fingers to the rock. They grasped his wrists, his massive weight threatening to drag them after him to the dark water below. With straining muscles, the two men heaved, their task made all the harder by their weakened condition. But slowly Ballard moved upward, his face pale but his eyes reflecting determination to reach safety. Straining, Thad and Prine managed to pull his hefty form up onto the rocks, and he moved at a crouch back as far as he could from the chasm to collapse on the mine floor in a silent, gasping heap.

Prine and Thad moved slowly away from the opening, but not before Prine looked down into the depths that had swallowed Stuart. For several moments, he looked, then spoke: "Rest in peace, Thomas Stuart. You have your treasure now."

It was all so ironic Prine couldn't hold back a shudder.

He moved away from the brink and sat down beside Priscilla. It was a long time before anyone broke the silence.

Ballard finally spoke. "Prine, if he had only let go of that money, he might not have fallen. But he wouldn't let go, not even for his life."

Prine shook his head. "I think that money *was* his life, Ballard. I think it's the only thing he lived for. In a way I'm glad it's gone. All that money has brought is death."

Thad spoke groggily. "Would someone fill me in on what has happened? It's all pretty hazy."

Prine told of the fight between him and the preacher in the side passage right after the cave-in and of the role of Priscilla in the whole affair. Ballard eyed the girl closely, impressed by her bravery, and Thad looked at her with a different sort of expression. For several minutes, Prine told his side of the story, though he too wanted information from the others to fill in the gaps he couldn't.

So after he was finished, Ballard took over, giving all the information he had, further piecing together the story. Then the men in the lantern-lit passage looked toward the girl.

"Ma'am, it looks like you're the only one we don't know much about. Stuart told us that you were the daughter of one of Wesley Stoner's gang members, a man named Tate. I don't hardly believe that anymore," Prine said. "Would you care to fill us in? I'm a bit curious to know."

The girl nodded. "Mr. Prine, I think you'll be surprised at what I have to say. But before I tell you about me, let me set you straight on Thomas Stuart. I'm sure he didn't tell you what he really is."

"He said he was the son of Bob Stuart, an old partner of ours from the war," Prine said. Then briefly he told her the story Stuart had related of how Bob Stuart had come by the packet. Priscilla appeared sometimes disturbed, sometimes infuriated by what she heard.

"There's more truth in his tale than I would expect," she

said. "But not nearly enough for you to really understand what Tom was. It was true that he was the son of Bob Stuart, but he was illegitimate, the son of a prostitute, the accidental offspring of an unfortunate set of circumstances that haunted his father for years afterward. Bob Stuart supported his son, for he was not a man to shirk responsibility, and in a way, I think he really loved the boy. But he never told his wife of him, in spite of the fact that he was conceived before he married her, and he hired a woman in a town not too far away to raise him. He would visit Tom a lot, telling him stories of his past, his days in the war—that's why Tom knew of you—but still the boy never returned his love. Maybe he resented not being allowed in the family, and the fact that he was not mentioned in the will. Bob Stuart had made provisions for his son other than the official will, but that didn't seem to matter. As the boy grew, he came to hate his father, and to plague him constantly."

Prine interrupted. "Begging your pardon, ma'am, but just how do you know all of this? Who are you?"

"Because my name is not Tate. My name is Priscilla Stuart, and Bob Stuart was my father."

Chapter 22

Priscilla's pronouncement brought a stunned silence to the men. Yet even as he sat dumbfounded, Prine could see a bit of family resemblance in her face, and suddenly he realized why he had felt such a strange tenderness for her. She reminded him of his old friend.

"But that isn't the whole story, gentlemen," Priscilla continued after her words had sunk in. "Let me give you the background of that packet that Tom carried, as well as a little history about his relationship to my family.

"While my mother never knew of Tom's existence at all, Father told me at a very young age, as soon as he thought I was grown enough to understand what he was saying, as well as the need to keep it all a secret from Mother. I'm not sure just why he told me; maybe he needed to let out the secret to someone just to clear his mind. The guilt of having an illegitimate child really bore on him, aging him more quickly than he would have otherwise. But that's not what's important here.

"I actually grew quite close to Tom during my younger years, for my father would often let us play together while we were still children. Tom had not yet become the kind of individual he finally became, though in retrospect I can see that the roots of his bitterness toward my father were growing even then. We were very close playmates, though our time together was greatly limited, since we could only see each other when my mother wasn't around. But my father showered us both with love...well, I'm not sure he exactly loved Tom, but he certainly cared for him. We were happy.

"But as Tom grew older his bitterness increased, as did his wildness. He grew to be a source of grief to my father, and Father's inability to share that grief with my mother only compounded his troubles. When Tom had grown to be a young man, he realized the hold he had over my father, and threatened to expose the truth to my mother if he didn't receive a sizable bit of money. My father gave in to his demands, over my objections, and Tom was satisfied...for a time.

"I was infuriated at the way in which he used my father, especially after the way he had been given so many privileges while growing up. I begged Father to go ahead and confess the whole affair to Mother, telling him that she was strong enough to take it, but he wouldn't hear of it. So things went on pretty much the same.

"Then Tom began gambling, running up huge debts, and his demands on my father increased steadily. It was growing almost impossible to satisfy those demands without making Mother grow suspicious, but somehow Father managed to do it. He made a lot of sacrifices just to keep Tom's mouth shut.

"All the while I grew to resent Tom more and more. I longed to do something to stop him; I even dreamed of killing him, but it was all just a fantasy. But when I saw what he was doing to my father, it really hurt me. And things just got worse and worse.

"Then came Father's encounter with Wesley Stoner out in the woods near our farm. Stoner was dying and told

Father of the hidden money—a way of clearing a black conscience, I believe. Father had no plan to do anything but report the incident, but before he could, Tom came around again, demanding far more money than ever before. And for once my father stood up to him, refusing him. I think his rage had built to the point that he could stand no more. Tom grew violent—it's not something I like to talk, or even think, about—and killed my father, murdered him in cold blood right in front of my eyes. I don't think he really intended to do it, for it was like cutting off his money supply, but his fury got the best of him. Later he seemed to have no real remorse about it at all, except to say that he was sorry he couldn't get more money out of the old fellow.

"Then he began talking about Mother, saying that if I didn't provide him with some cash, he would reveal himself to her, even dump Father's body down in front of her. I knew that something like that would be far too much for her to take, so I gave him Stoner's packet, and told him how my father had come by it.

"I fabricated a story about a robber to explain the murder of my father. My mother was heartbroken; it was much harder on her even than you might imagine. She lived for Father—he was her very life.

"After Father was buried, Mother became ill. She died within two weeks of his murder, and we buried her beside him.

"Then I grew very obsessed with stopping Tom, and I'm afraid I did some pretty rash things. I came west and began frequenting saloons and similar places in order to pick up a gang of men hardy enough to stop Tom. He learned of what I was doing and gathered you men for protection.

"Members of my gang began betraying me soon after I was on Tom's trail and going off on their own after Tom. My last three gang members turned against me in Statler. If you hadn't fired that shot, Mr. Prine—I hate to think what would have happened.

"After that, I still couldn't give up on my plans, so I came after you alone. I followed from a distance, knowing all the while that my former gang members were following too, and I managed to slip into this mine while your sentry was tending your horses. I hid in that side passage, planning to follow you out and try to get that money somehow.

"Now it looks like my quest is over. Tom is dead, and that money is gone forever. In a way that's best, I guess."

Ballard shook his head slowly as the narrative drew to a close. "That boy sure made fools of us! We were mighty gullible."

"We all swallowed his bait," Prine said. "We're lucky we're still alive. Y'know, this story makes a lot of things hang together. Like why Stuart was so quick to silence anyone who had come into contact with Priscilla's gang. He was afraid that they would tell the truth about him, and that would be the end of his scheme."

Thad was standing on the brink of the chasm, and he peered intently upward, his eyes squinted. The others walked up beside him. "What do you see, Thad?" asked Ballard.

Thad shook his head. "I'm not really sure. Take a look up there. Is that a light I see, some sort of opening?"

They all looked closely, eyes straining in the darkness. Suddenly Priscilla burst out in an excited voice: "He's right! There is an opening up there! Look!"

Then Prine saw it, along with the rest. A faint spot of light, circular, minuscule across the expanse, but definitely opening to the outside. It was so small that Prine could not even tell if it would accommodate a human form, and what was more, there was no way to know if any of the ledges that spiraled the vast chamber reached the opening. But still it was hope, no matter how remote.

"Prine, do you think—?"

"What else can we do, Ballard?"

Thad already had the lantern in his hand. "I'll go first. We'll have to move slow."

"Ballard, do you think you can stand the height?" Prine asked. "You say it gets to you after a while."

"So do hunger and thirst, Prine. I'd rather risk falling than starve to death in here."

Prine nodded. "Let's climb."

Chapter 23

It seemed that years had passed since they had first moved out on the narrow ledge again to begin inching around toward the left, creeping snail-like toward the small opening high above. Thad was the leader. He first searched out the ledges ahead by the light of the lantern, then decided which way to go. Travel was more difficult for him than for the others, for he was encumbered by the lantern, and when he stepped, he didn't have the advantage of having seen someone do it before him. But he moved along as quickly as could be expected.

Every muscle in every body ached. The rocks were dark and covered with slime, making them extremely hazardous, and what was more, no one could be sure that they would even reach the opening. They were still too far away for the lantern light to strike around it and show whether or not there was any sort of access to the exit. But the hole was growing ever-nearer.

Still, how long would it take for them to get there? And what if the hole was just out of reach? It could be merely a tantalizing opening to the outside just above them while they died a slow death, clinging to the rocks until they were so weakened that they slipped off into the dark lake far below.

Ballard's brow was coated with dank, nervous sweat, in spite of the coolness of the cavern. His hands trembled, and his legs seemed to be made of jelly. High places had never been comfortable for him, and as the group members progressed, they were getting ever higher. His horrifying experience of dangling over the chasm while Stuart crushed his hands had not given him any more of a favorable feeling about this place.

Time crept on slowly. Ballard looked at the young girl before him. Her face was hardly visible, for the lantern light hardly reached back to them in spite of Thad's efforts to direct the beams, but from what he could see she was flushed, weary, bone tired. He felt the same way. For a moment, despair filled him; death seemed to whisper in his ear. Ballard forced the feeling aside. He planned to live, not die.

Thad stopped ahead of them, the lantern held before him.

"What is it, Thad?" asked Prine. "There some sort of problem?"

Thad nodded his head slowly. "We got a gap up here, a big one. At least four feet with no ledge at all. I can see enough ledge on the other side of the gap to get us right below that opening. But this gap is a problem."

"Can we jump it, Thad?" Ballard called from the rear.

"I don't know...it looks like we'll have to try. I wish we had a rope—maybe I could tie some sort of safety line on the other side."

Prine frowned thoughtfully. "Maybe we can improvise something, Thad. Men, take off your gun belts. We can hook them together and make a line. Then Thad, you hold one end and jump across while I hold the other. If you should slip, maybe I can catch you."

"Then when I get to the other side, I can do the same for you, then together we can help the others," Thad said, completing the picture. "I can't say I relish the idea of playing mountain goat, but I can't see any other way."

"Here's my belt, Prine," said Ballard, handing his gun belt forward.

Prine removed his own gun belt; Thad did the same with his. When Prine linked them, he had a strong leather strap several yards in length. He handed one end to Thad.

"Strap that around your waist, Thad," Prine directed. "Make sure it's tight. I'll brace myself against this rock here —good, I think I'm set. Now you go ahead and jump when you feel like it." He paused. "And try to make it on the first try. Good luck."

Thad braced himself, quietly offering up a prayer. His leg muscles tensed, he crouched, waited, then leaped. The brief second he was in the air sent his stomach leaping inside of him; then his feet rested on solid rock and his hands grasped the cold and slimy stone on the other side of the gap.

"You made it, Thad!" exulted Prine. "You made it!" But his smile soon faded, for now it was his turn. Prine unsuccessfully tried to ignore the impulse to take one last glance down into the dark below him. As soon as he did it, he wished he hadn't.

"Leap away, Prine!" Thad shouted.

Prine flashed a deathly grin and jumped with all that was in him. He was surprised a moment later to find himself safely beside Thad on the other side. He looked at the young man and broke into a grin.

"I gave you a little help there, Prine," said Thad. "I yanked as you jumped. You almost landed on top of me!"

Prine laughed and slapped the young man on the shoulder. He examined the ledge on which they crouched. It was wider by far than that which they had previously passed over, and relative to the perils they had just faced, Prine felt as safe as an old maid sipping tea in her parlor.

But there were still Priscilla and Ballard to be brought over the opening. The girl, Prine thought, would be no problem, as light as she was. But Ballard might face difficulties.

They repeated the same procedure as before, this time with Priscilla. And almost before they had begun, she was across, falling safely into Prine's arms, kissing him out of sheer joy to be alive. Thad wished jealously that he had been the one to whom she had leapt.

Thump!

Prine was shocked by the sudden tremor that shook the ledge. He turned and looked into the beaming face of John Ballard. The man had leaped unexpectedly, without help. And he had made it.

Prine was upset at the risk Ballard had taken.

"Why did you do a fool thing like that? Don't you know you could have fallen? Why didn't you wait until we were ready?"

"Shut up, Prine. Do you think for a minute that the three of you could have held me if I had slipped and fell? My weight would have pulled you right in after me."

Prine gave Ballard back his gun belt, then grinned. "Glad you made it. If you had fell into that lake the splash would have wet us all the way up here." Ballard didn't seem to appreciate the humor.

An hour later, they had inched their way around to the side of the mountain where the opening was. From the flickering lantern light Prine could see the ledge that passed under the hole. It looked thin and weak, and far too low for them to reach the opening. But they would have to risk it, for there was nothing else they could do.

Within five minutes, they stood almost directly below the opening, eyeing the thin ledge with doubt. Prine felt a vague despair.

"There's only one thing to do, the way I see it," said Thad. "Me and Mr. Prine will go out on that ledge—we'll just have to hope it holds up—and he can boost me up to get into that hole. Then we can link the belts like we did before, and maybe I can pull everyone up."

Prine looked carefully at the ledge and the opening. "You're right, Thad. It's the only way I can see."

"No," said Priscilla. "That ledge might break with both of you. I'm lighter than either of you. I think I can climb up that wall to the opening. It doesn't look too steep. I'll crawl up in there, then Thad. Between us we can get the rest of you, using the belts like before. Don't argue with me about it—if you two go out on that ledge you'd likely wind up down in that water."

There was no arguing with a command like that, and before many more moments had passed the pretty blonde was out on the thin ledge, linked belts strapped around her waist, Prine and Thad holding them at the other end. She looked carefully at the face of the rock leading up to the hole. Thad held the almost-empty lantern so she could see where her feet would rest, and then she began to climb.

Slowly upward she went, breathing hard, concentrating. It was excruciating work, but she made progress. She squelched her impulse to look down, and after several minutes of slow climbing, her hands at last grasped the rim of the opening, and she pulled herself upward and into it.

She felt a burst of joy at the mere sight of the sky out the other side of the opening. For a time, she could not take her eyes, and only with reluctance did she at last turn about in the narrow passage and call out to the others.

They returned her call. Within moments, Thad was scaling the wall, Priscilla pulling with all her strength, looking down at him, and also past him into the vast blackness below him. Inch by inch he drew nearer, then he was up beside her, swinging the belts down to Prine.

"There won't be room for all of us up here in this little hole," said Thad. "I'll pull up Prine—you crawl on back toward the outside."

She heard the scuffling of Prine's feet against the rock wall as she moved on back in the tunnel, again drinking in the beauty of the sky. She could hear Thad groan as he fought with the straining belts. Prine pulled himself up into the tunnel beside Thad.

Ballard was alone in the chamber below, the lantern in his hand. He saw the chain of linked belts descend and swallowed hard. He sat the lantern down as he did the best he could to secure himself. He began his climb.

Thad and Prine strained hard at the burden as Ballard's feet struggled to find a hold on the rough wall. Far slower than the others, he rose, his eyes nervously studying the taut belts that held his weight. He prayed they would hold.

His foot came down on an unseen patch of slime and he slipped. He stared up into the horrified faces of his partner and his son as suddenly he dropped, his weight making it impossible for them to support him completely. He struck the thin ledge, and it broke beneath him, sending a shower of rock falling to the black lake below, the lantern making a magnificent arc of yellow light in the heart of the cavern before it was extinguished by the waters below.

Ballard was swinging out over the chasm once more, his life depending on the strength of the chain of belts and on the men who held it.

"Try to get a toehold!" cried Prine. "Start pulling yourself up!"

Straining, sweating, hurting, Ballard struggled up the wall, sliding, slipping, occasionally finding a hold that would let him move up a few more inches. His hands clasped the belts that held him until his fingers were bleeding, and yet often it seemed he was losing the fight, sliding...

"Hang on, Ballard! Hang on!" Prine encouraged the

hefty man, whose boots now found a firmer hold. They struck the tiny outcrop left by the falling ledge, and he pulled himself up several inches. Hope overcame panic.

Up—higher—he continued his climb, never taking his eyes away from those that looked down from above him. Higher...just a little more...

His hand clasped Prine's, then Thad's, and then he was up, safe, secure, and weeping like a baby. He threw his arms around the neck of his son, then his friend. Together they joined Priscilla at the end of the passage, then on through onto the grassy slope outside, beneath the sky, smelling the open air, the scent of rain coming from the west.

Down the slope they walked without a word, around toward the south, circling the mountain until they reached their horses, still tied near the main entrance of the mine. They mounted, Priscilla taking one of the packhorses, and began their descent, heading back down the mountain road, approaching the sleeping town of Jericho Creek.

"Prine?"

"Yes, Ballard?"

"Ain't it good to be alive!"

Prine grinned. "Amen to that, brother."

Chapter 24

Prine sat beside Ballard on the boardwalk outside the only doctor's office in Jericho Creek. Prine's leg was in a bandage, making his pants leg buck out like that of an overstuffed scarecrow, and his ears were still ringing with the harsh scolding he had just received from the doctor for ignoring his pitchfork wound for as long as he had.

Thad walked out of the office, Priscilla beside him. Thad removed his hat long enough to show where the doctor had shaved his head along the scalp wound.

"You look like the Injuns got to you, boy!" said Ballard.

"Fool doctor," muttered Prine. "I never met a sawbones yet fit for anything 'cept patching up horses." Ballard grinned on the sly to the two young folks behind him and Prine and winked. Prine was sullen as a dejected child.

"I'm starving. Let's go find some food," said Thad. "I know we ain't got much money, but we got to eat sometime. "

"I can tell you where you can find a lot of money, Thad," said Prine. "Course, you might have a bit of trouble getting to it. But if you're willing to try—"

"No, thanks. I'll pass on that. I'll stick to farming from now on, if you don't mind."

The group moved down the dusty street toward the nearest cafe. It was a surprisingly nice place, and they ordered a hearty meal, every bit of which they devoured. Ballard had three huge mugs of strong coffee, then patted his middle and smiled.

"Now, folks, that's eating!" he said. "I don't plan to touch another bite of jerky for a year or more. I think I'd rather starve."

Prine was still in a foul mood. "Looking at the size of your gut, it wouldn't hurt you to starve a little," he muttered.

It was two days before they left the little town at last, after their various wounds and bruises had healed a little. During that time, they avoided any mention of their plans, for it was painful to think of being apart. Prine especially felt the pain, for he knew that he had nothing to return to but a life of riding and roaming, picking up work where he could find it.

So when at last the four of them sat mounted on the road, their smiles were few and forced. Ballard settled his chew of tobacco into his jaw and looked at Prine. Thad and Priscilla were off to the side, out of earshot, talking intently to each other.

"Prine, you know you're welcome to come with me back to the farm. There's more than enough work for all of us. Even Priscilla's going to ride back that way, maybe even stay a while."

Prine snorted. "From the looks of how she and Thad are getting along, I'd say she might stay permanent. She started out as Priscilla Tate, then we found out she was really Priscilla Stuart, and now it looks like she might wind up Priscilla Ballard. I'd say you'll lose your boy, Ballard."

"Just gaining a daughter-in-law," he said. "But you didn't answer my question. Are you coming with us?"

Prine looked down into the dust. "Ballard, there's no life for me but the one I'm living. And anyway, I couldn't abide having to stomp through manure on some farm."

Ballard looked at him sadly. "Suit yourself, Prine—but make sure you know that you're welcome anytime. I expect to see you again, real soon. All right?"

"You got a deal." Prine extended his hand, and the other took it. "Ol' Bob would have had a lot of tales to tell if he'd been around, wouldn't he!" Then Prine felt an overwhelming sadness and turned away.

Priscilla and Thad came up to him, and their parting with Prine was difficult, especially for the girl. She hugged him, kissed him, and before she was through, tears were in the eyes of both of them. Then they were on their way, Ballard and his group heading east, Prine sitting alone and watching them for a long time before he turned his horse west. He rode for several yards, then stopped. His eyes lifted to the massive peak of Jericho Mountain; then a smile played across his lips.

"Y'know," he said to himself, "maybe stomping through manure for a while wouldn't be bad at all."

He wheeled and headed at a gallop toward the band of riders, calling out to Ballard.

He saw the smile on the big man's face even before he was within a hundred yards of the waiting group.

A Look at: Flee The Devil and Sawyer's Quest
Two Full Length Western Novels

Writing as Will Cade, Spur Award Finalist Cameron Judd pens captivating tales of adventure in America's western frontier. Together in a single volume for the first time are two of the best Cade novels published.

In *Flee The Devil*, it was a thief's dream come true. Dex Otie couldn't believe his luck when he saw the railroad trestle collapse, hurtling the Bluefield Golden Special into the gorge below. It got even better when one of the bodies he was robbing turned out to be Wade Murchison, carrying the loot from a bank job. So what if Wade wasn't quite dead yet? Dex could take care of that.

Only problem was, Wade didn't die that easily. He lived just long enough to tell his brother, Devil Jack Murchison, who it was who took the money and left him there to die. Now, they didn't call him Devil Jack for nothing, and he wasn't the forgiving type. Dex was in for the fight of his life...

In *Sawyer's Quest*, it appears to be just a simple metal box. But what it contains might very well be worth its weight in gold—or blood. Inside the box is the latest manuscript by famous author Charles Oliver Farnsworth, and there are scads of people who would do just about anything to get their hands on it.

But the man who finds the box is Billy Sawyer, and all he wants to do is return it to its rightful owner. So Billy sets off for Dodge City, where Farnsworth is scheduled to appear. All along the way, though, Billy is trailed by shady characters, threatened by mysterious strangers, and set upon by ruthless hardcases. How can Billy complete his quest when it looks like every con man and killer in the West is dead set on relieving him of the responsibility of that box?

"Judd is a fine action writer." — *Publisher's Weekly*

AVAILABLE NOW

About the Author

Cameron Judd is the author of more than fifty published novels of the American frontier, two of his works having been national finalists in the Spur Awards competition of the Western Writers of America. He has written under his own names and pen names including Judson Grey, Tobias Cole and Will Cade. A native and lifelong Tennessean, he has three adult children. He and his wife, Rhonda, share their Northeast Tennessee home with a cornbread-loving dog named Lola. He is a former award-winning newspaper journalist and editor.

CPSIA information can be obtained
at www.ICGtesting.com
Printed in the USA
BVHW072052230922
647842BV00009B/516